doggone

a novel

Tamas Dobozy

Gutter Press

The publisher gratefully acknowledges the assistance of The Ontario Arts Council and The Canada Council for the Arts.

Canadian Cataloguing in Publication Data
Dobozy, Tamas, 1969-
Doggone
An N.J. Dodic Book.
ISBN 1-896356-14-1
I. Title.
PS8557.O2223D63 1998 C813'.54 C98-930769-7
PR9199.3.D62D63 1998

Published by Gutter Press, P.O. Box 600, Station Q,
Toronto, Ontario, Canada M4T 2N4
voice: 416.822.8708, fax: 416.822.8709
www.gutterpress.com, email: gutter@gutterpress.com

Distributed in the U.S. and abroad by D.A.P.
Distributed Art Publishers, Inc.
155 Sixth Avenue, 2nd Floor,
New York, NY 10013-1507
To order, call 1.800.338.BOOK
Represented in Canada by the Literary Press Group.
Distributed in Canada by General Publishing,
30 Lesmill Rd, Don Mills, Ontario

Portions of this novel have appeared in *Sub-Terrain* and *Dalhousie Review.*

Special thanks to Marcy Levy, N. J. Dodic,
Suzanne Buffam and Craig Burnett

Design: 4dt
Printed in Canada

To my father, who told me what to read; and to my mother, who read what I wrote

The cowboy drew a deep breath, as if his mind was passing into the last stages of dissolution. "Well, I'm doggoned," he whispered to himself.

Stephen Crane

Someday soon I hope to snap; until then, number me among the crazies in training. My soulmates (being the soulful guy I am) include the postman driven to the post office, the student to the classroom, the war vet to the water tower. Now if only I had the guts for their great acts of cowardice. But my fears produce nothing that newsworthy.

If you must call me something, call me the potential suicide. But no, that's yet another apprenticeship position. Geez, there's so little money where my mouth is.

Okay. Here's the real state of affairs. Honest to gosh. At twenty-nine I weigh in at a hundred and ninety-five pounds, measure six feet two inches. To date, the missions I've chosen to accept run as follows: searching for a dead girlfriend called Lala, scrounging up a father-figure and nationality, and, most importantly, deciding on how to murder my parents' dog. I'll tell you about these.

Much gratuitous detail following....

Let's start with that December night, when I wouldn't scrap for any kind of money, when I swallowed every insult smiling. Night of my death, twenty-four years of age, gracelessly fattening in the mid section, a tire roll round my belly. I remember dancing in the old ballroom. The wooden floor, built to certain specifications, with critical stress points, acted as a spring under your feet. Gravity had less pull there. Lala and I had been drinking, nearing the close of our relationship's maiden voyage. Nothing flowed in my mind but a boozy river of faces, T-shirts and plastic cups. Dancers flashed between sparklers and strobe lights. A seedy glamour modified the oak and chandelier and belated soul of the ballroom. The loggers and rednecks soaked themselves with liquor. In a hybrid of old and new music, Rolling Stones, Led Zeppelin and tiresome, mid-eighties bands like Motley Crüe played back to back. In the corner the local underground, the so-called "punkers," picked lint from their Salvation Army suits and gathered like angst mannequins around a small table with their dyed hair and makeup, drinking vodka. I remember lots of gin; that's what I recall. A man knocked another one down onto his back and stood double-fisted above him before the public citizens intervened to draw them apart. A girl with nice, fat, juicy lips sat in a chair with her arms folded, face up and proud, but letting the tears flow in such volume it surprised me not to see her bent with the weight of them; her boyfriend sat beside her, kissing his other girlfriend – polygamy all over the place like an unwritten code. The women had more than one partner at a time as well, hence the endless pugilistics in the ballroom's corners. The occasion was like the flip side to Christmas. But some of them palsied with laughter. Some of them bought each other drinks. Some went arm in arm with bantering camaraderie.

On the way out, the crowd lingered in the entrance, seethed through doorways, collected items from coat-check. I searched for Lala, finally catching sight of her over by the door, two men – one squat, one long, former blond, latter dark – speaking to her. The blond one gripped her arm. I went over. Someone shoved me and I bumped into him by accident. "Let's go," I said to Lala.

The blond turned to me: "You hit me."

"Oh sorry."

"I don't like your haircut."

It always began this way, with non-sequiturs. Drunk beyond mortal comprehension I turned to him, put my hand on his shoulder. "Well, I'll change it just for you," I quipped, as condescendingly as possible.

"Don't touch me," he said. This was the point. I could feel it coming. "You're such a beautiful chick," he went on, addressing Lala. "Why do you hang out with a guy like this? If I dropped my pants he'd probably kneel down and suck me off right now."

I scanned the floor. Shocked so she couldn't swallow, Lala just stared at the blond guy's mustache. A million uncertainties whittled my backbone. My spine peeled off me by itself, like a hangnail.

His friend wanted to take him away. The blond guy tightened his hold on Lala's arm. She was still too much in shock to shake him. He pulled her roughly along.

"She's coming with us," he said to me.

And I let them go. I let them take her with them. Just staring at the floor.

The archetypal argument between my parents went as follows: my age at the time was eight or nine. I chiseled their words, upside down, into my chest with a screwdriver and, despite the obvious drawbacks to this form of note-taking, the calligraphy came out totally fine, the blood negligible. Just kidding.

They hoed beans in the garden. I hid behind a pile of chopped wood, my face the one between the creeping vines. Father held the hoe, occasionally piking it in the air like a proclamation man.

"I don't want my kitchen to look like some peasant place in the old country! Take those jugs off the wall! Throw them out. This is our country now. Our kitchen should look like America, Canada I mean."

"This will never be my country!" She pounded the dirt with her foot. "Not my home country."

"Well, go home then, if that's what you want."

"You brought me here and I won't leave my children. I don't hate Canada either. I just like my kitchen."

"Change the *kibaszott* kitchen!" he yelled, shaking the hoe in front of her face. With her amazing reflexes, my mother grabbed the hoe out of his hand and swung it back at him, but my father caught the iron head of the implement just before it hit his cheek. Mother relinquished the hoe and stormed into the kitchen.

"A man needs two lives," I heard him mumble, running a fingertip like tap water over the bruised palm of his hand. "One for where he comes from and one for where he wants to go."

He packed all the gardening paraphernalia away right then and got on the phone, dialed and started a conversation with these words: "About that transfer? I have a proposal...."

His work began to call him away, three or four days a week, to another town. And so, with one decisive step, my father went from bitterness to bigamy.

Never during either period of our relationship did Lala speak her dreams. She called the retelling of dreams an excuse for being stupid. Nor did she condescend to the banality of farewells. Nobody had told her about good-byes except the women who'd left her father. She knew desertion well, though, and the drifting off.

The death notice mailed to me had the imprint of a lipstick kiss on it. Far as I know, my notice was pairless, a collector's item, a personalized copy – Pauline's notification stamped only with black writing and border, on blank card stock. Lala was the innocent vamp, the woman whose eyes showed not only her scars but yours, too. The kiss seemed prepared in haste.

I don't believe Lala really committed suicide. I have my reasons.

"Robbing old men is a waste of time," announces pale, skinny Pauline, and shakes when she says it. I'd never have guessed she bothered with break and entry but here we stand, among unmown grasses, clutching at vinyl siding in the dark, finishing a joint she predicts will, "Get me through 'til later." Out loud, I wonder, "'Til later what?" but she leaves the business unfinished. Pauline stretches her lithe figure breathlessly up on tiptoe, flats of her palms pushing upward against the dirty glass window, leaving two perfect hand prints from the oil and sweat byproducts of her altered metabolism. "Old men don't own nothing, don't care about nothing. Old men carry their tombstones around just in case. Whereas old ladies.... Well, now, old ladies don't give a shit about nothing either but they're always the ones stuck with the goodies. The older and lonelier they are" – she gasps as the window slides up a foot – "the more they've got stored. Now's your last chance to run away," she says fiercely. "Otherwise help me up."

I weave the fingers of my two hands together. She puts her foot into the impromptu jack, the look on her face almost one of disappointment. The evening has all the fixings for fiasco. I do not need stolen goods or pawn-shop creditors. Oxbow's pulp mill pay office watches splendidly over me, and – or so she says – a job as night watchman provides for every one of Pauline's needs.

Walls over-decorated with photos of men, or a man, immediately identify the home as widow's space. I find it tough to make distinctions in the twilight. As we creep past sheaves of curtain I become a blind calf, stumbling into so much furniture. Sofas stand end to end, three easy chairs to a corner, a side-table for every seat. Plants rustle in the breeze from the open window. I bump into lamps, smash my shins against a plaster dwarf. "Pauline, I think maybe we should go," I advise.

"You wanted to come!" She whispers harshly through the darkness. "There's no fuck of a way we're leaving now!"

I hear a light movement and a hand closes tightly on the back of my neck. The heat and fumes of Pauline waft against my face and I smell poor chemical combinations, choices made in entirely wrong frames of mind. "You just come with me." I wrench my neck free and follow her almost indiscernible silhouette into another room, bang my head into a low door-frame and curse. Pauline fishes me a flashlight out of her knapsack and I dance the beam over waterstains on the ceiling. "Get down to it," she orders.

Pauline scrounges through a jewelry box, dropping trinkets into her leather bag. "Check all the vases," she says. "I hear old ladies love keeping money in vases." We begin to forage like mad thieves, traipsing through the rooms, the closets, eyes grown accustomed – permanently, I feel – to the dark. I find nothing in the vases, but an unmarked envelope in the roll-top desk disgorges over four hundred dollars. Pauline liberates drugs from the medicine cabinet, crushing any useless medication underfoot. I find a sealed plastic bag holding the pricier jewelry in the toilet's pump box. Larceny intoxicates us. We follow the logic of theft to where loot might hide the way we would follow the direction of a drug, going for the maximum benefits, the uppermost high.

A latch in an as yet unchecked closet snickers and I turn to face the widow. My ray of flashlight bounces right off her face – an old complexion with a lot of powder to it, crows' feet, deep wrinkles, a cyst and hairy mole or two. The earlobes droop like hot mozzarella (maybe from the combined weight of sixty years worth of earrings). She wears track pants and a windbreaker, with hightop running shoes. The old lady turns her face from the small circle of light and reaches into her pocket. The bullet she fires from the handgun whizzes past my head. Within world-record time both Pauline's and my flashlights go out and we're prone on the floor.

The old woman panics, obviously never having done this before. She fires blind, her finger only too happy with the trigger. The handgun spits a flame that burns its color and size into my retina; even under closed lids I see the frozen shape of fire. She yells at our invisibility, words with a Russian coating: "I hear you leetle bastards outside. So I hide. I vait." Vases pop all over the room. Bullets ricochet off the floor. Glass shatters. I wonder how I'll possibly make friends with her now.

Pauline crawls up beside me just as an exploding flowerpot showers us with shrapnel. "We've got to stop her somehow," she says. "The cops are going to show up." She starts to howl with laughter. I grab her face while tears form in her eyes and dribble down. She can't catch her breath, stomach heaving painfully. Pauline laughs like an aviary in an earthquake. The bullets gouge into plaster. "I hope she doesn't remember to turn on the light," squeals Pauline, eyes rolled back in her head, right up to the whites. "If she remembers to turn on the light we're finished," she roars. During a pause in the fusillade the old lady reloads.

"Do you have any last wishes?" Pauline asks, laughter giving her the strength to break my grip on her face and roll back and forth, banging into me on one side and a massive ceramic flowerpot on the other. She begins to hyperventilate, her legs kicking the dark. I pound her back.

At least fifteen minutes go by before we're collected enough to act. I circle in one direction and Pauline the other – a two-pronged assault. When we come close enough to the biddy I turn on my flashlight and Pauline turns on hers. "The sudden flash should blind her," I tell Pauline. We sprint towards the widow, with the singular miscalculation that she's used to firing blind and doesn't drop the firearm. She pokes the end of the barrel up against my chest and, eyes squeezed shut, says, "I vodn't put it past me. I rilly vodn't." I drop my flashlight. With much honking and horn-blowing, a flock of geese flies overhead in what I can only assume to be a v-formation. Their noise reminds me of travel agencies. The trigger gives a mouse-like squeak. The smell of bluing touches me cool and impersonally as drugstore cologne, combined with the scent of denture cement wafting off the old lady's gums.

"You drop your flashlight too, leetle girlee." Pauline's face peers over the widow's shoulder as she pushes the tip of the handgun farther into my sternum. Their faces appear like the faces of partners in some midnight crime, one face – Pauline's – gapped-out, uncertain, while the other's looks dishearteningly determined. "You tell your girlfriend sonee," the old woman raises her vodka-throated voice, "dat I never like peeple reeding over my shoulder."

The old woman stands us up against a wall, hands flat on our heads, and troops up and down, shifting the gun from nervous hand to nervous hand to dry her sweaty palms along the seams of her track pants. I look over at Pauline, needing that confident smile always present in the corner of her eyes, but her face hangs like old drapes. In the faint light of a side-table the old lady switched on I watch beads of sweat, fat as tadpoles, drop into Pauline's collar; the fingers of the hands she's placed on top of her head tap obscure drumbeats into her skull.

"Peeple say I haf no senz off humor," the old woman barks into our faces, nosing the gun from one face to another. "But I can understand good joke, yes?" The lamp casts a vague light over the spilled and trampled artifacts of her home: old jewelry boxes upturned, cushions taken off the couch, a burst down pillow, a shattered vase, drawers from desks and dressers yanked out of their tracks and turned upside down (their letters, elephant-underwear, old daguerreotypes, peacock feathers and cigarettes strewn everywhere). The old woman nestles the barrel of the revolver between Pauline's fidgeting eyes. "I tink I veel not call da police. You veel help me instead, yes? You veel help me punish yourselfes. You do as I say and you no get shut." Pauline nods, docile as a puppy, the barrel moving with her face like an appendage. The widow commands her to unfold two deck chairs, to go into the utility closet and haul forth a roll of duct tape. Pauline stops every two minutes or so to control involuntary muscle spasms flickering the length of her body. "Notink veel happen if you do ekzaktly vhat I tell you," the old lady informs Pauline, though a hint of grandmotherly concern creeps along underneath the harsh tone, undoubtedly due to Pauline's obvious ailment. Shakes overtake her body and subside, only to build again. The widow has Pauline bind my ankles and wrists to one of the chairs. The barrel of the handgun reinforces certain passive tendencies I've battled all my life. Pauline begins wringing her hands for no good reason. Her upper lip glistens in the mood lighting. Her feet nudge the scattered trinkets in some unconscious soft-shoe. "Now you seet too," the widow orders, and while Pauline can't exactly stare the old woman in the face, she nevertheless stands firm, refusing to bend. Pauline's nose needs new washers or a refitting because snot streams slowly but surely from both nostrils. The old woman parts half of Pauline's bangs with the tip of the revolver, catching the face in both hands when the body crumples forward. The revolver goes off as Pauline slumps completely into the arms of the Russian émigrée.

With an agility that belies her years, the old woman takes a short step forward and reverses the weight distribution of Pauline's body so that it falls back, fully seated, into the chair. "Be careful, you fucking Nazi," I say. "She's sick." The widow turns and delivers me a face-benumbing slap with the side of the handgun. "I know vhut she is, you edeeot! And I'm Soviet, not Nazi." She laughs at her correction of my faulty history, then indicates Pauline, gun flashing back and forth: "Drug addict?"

And I honestly can't say – fifteen years of near-sibling love and hardly a clue as to how much Pauline really shoots, snorts or otherwise imbibes, though I now suspect it's considerable. The old woman hauls out more rope and lashes Pauline in for the entire ride, then grabs a bucket from the closet and disappears down the hallway. I hear gasps of dismay (inspired no doubt by the wreckage), running water, a fridge door open and shut, shell casings removed, the chamber reloaded and spun like some miniature wheel of fortune. I swivel my head to watch Pauline's eyes move erratically under their lids. Her face winces unconsciously while the rest of her strains against the bindings. "Pauline," I hiss. "Hey Pauline!" I don't know why I should wake her, except maybe to free a friend from one nightmare into the next.

Our lady of geriatrics returns in a housecoat, stooping from the bucket of water in her left hand, the revolver in the other. She places the pail between Pauline and I, winks at me coyly, sits on the backrest of her chesterfield and pulls a can of beer out of her pocket; she cracks the tab and tilts her head back, forcing down a big gulp, neck straining with vertical lines of taut sinew. Afterwards, she taps the side of her neck with a finger. "Troat operation," she admits. "Beer not cold enuff." The widow sighs. "Smoking. Removal of tizue," she rolls the R while repeating the diagnosis of the specialist, who braved fogbanks and hailstorms in a little twin-engine just to get from Vancouver to Oxbow. She motions with the beer to Pauline but directs the question at me: "You drug addict also?"

"None of your business," I reply.

"Okee-dokee." She shrugs, sets down the beer, picks up the bucket of water and sends a cold wave crashing over Pauline, who bolts back to life like someone receiving the first jolt from an electric chair. Pauline – blinded by the hair in her face – screams at the old lady, "You fucking bitch, let me out of here!" and thrashes against her fastenings so furiously she tips the chair and spills onto her side. Her long black hair spreads out and sticks to the floor. The clunk of head against hardwood makes both the widow and I exchange winces, but doesn't knock Pauline unconscious. Instead, she begins to cry – long, bowel-loosening sobs. She shudders severely, speaks in tongues like a Pentecostal on Sunday. The widow walks over, pulls her pathetic captive's hair off the floor and, with a guttural grunt, heaves the chair upright. The old woman smoothes Pauline's face with the back of her hand until she quiets. "Vy you haf to do dis to yourself?" Pauline delivers up a cockeyed stare. "If you ver my datter, I leave you tie to dis chair until you get better."

I take our captor's side. "Yeah, Pauline, you have to stop playing these games."

Pauline turns on me – her face a mess of tears, snot and sweat – enraged at the possibility that I've forgotten who's the unjustly imprisoned and who the warden. "It's a game for you! You don't have a drug habit to support! You know I can't make it without. You know it!" The widow returns to her perch on the back of the sofa to observe our crossfire.

"What do you mean you're an addict? Since when?" Down the hall a clock chimes midnight. Pauline's eyes go dark and retract into their sockets, her body rigid from toenail to eyelash. Pauline's teeth jut from her mouth when she speaks.

"Not everyone's a Sunday druggy like you. Not everyone has your control, your disinterestedness." Her voice runs like velvet before the big shout: "You're so lost in yourself you could never be hooked! You don't have time to think about how much you'd like drugs!"

"Okay, okay, enuf's enuf," the widow referees. "I tink I vold like to clean up my house now." She picks up her purse, pulls out her chequebook and pen, pauses wickedly, ballpoint poised above paper, and looks at Pauline a lot harder than previously. "I tink you learn lesson?" A movement in the hasp of Pauline's jaw warns me to speak before she does; so I do.

"Yes, yes. We've learned a lot, thanks!" The old woman scowls and fills out the cheque, which she rips off and puts in Pauline's breast pocket. She pats the younger woman on the face, "Remember you come back venever you like; I tie you to chair for free. It's better than jail, no?" The widow dodges the flying goober from the back of Pauline's throat and tsks-tsks to herself while slashing me free with a steak knife. Gun inches from my head, I rip my nails undoing the tape around Pauline's wrists and ankles.

We slip out the window while the old lady aims (but does not fire off) a hundred mortal injuries our way. We leave under hedges, down lanes and over fences, across streets, up the hill. Nightlights glow vaguely through the windows of happy living rooms. I grab Pauline's hand to help her along. We come huffing to a stop beside the rock wall of an orchard children steal apples and cherries from, an orchard with a creaky golden gate we'll trespass through on the way to respective homes.

Pauline pulls the cheque from her pocket and rips it up under the streetlamp. "I wouldn't take a cent from that old cunt," she whimpers, throwing her hands down and looking hopelessly up, her face assuming that painful shape preceding tears.

"What about your job?"

"Oh Gabe," she gulps, "they fired me weeks ago."

And I pull Pauline to me, smoothing my hand along her spine to take the wrinkles out of her hysterics – her body wiry, all sinew and aerodynamics. One day she might kick alone in a holding cell. One day she might kick in my arms like this. One day she might inject an air bubble that proves nearly fatal. Meanwhile, I'll think words, words, words – something to the effect of "help."

The Oxbow pulp mill, my employer, regards theft as worse than murder. When one employee walked into a lunchroom with a sawed-off shotgun and wounded three, then drove to the west mill area and blew his brains through his scalp the company said: "Well, all's well." The wounded went to the hospital to convalesce, the suicide note (intimating job harassment and megalomania) was published in the paper, and the funeral had record attendance.

Theft is their real pet peeve. Every meeting covers thievery. Discouraging posters appear in such quantity people sneak them home to use for lighting fires, making notepads, wrapping paper. Company bulletins urge us to honesty. They've implemented a pass system, making it easier to borrow from the mill. But the security posse is on to you if the wrenches, power tools, hose attachments aren't returned by date due. Everyone is a petty thief.

I met the most notorious of these thieves – an old-timer who'd lifted everything from dryer felts to wrenches to sheets of glass to paper to knives – the night he shot himself in the foot with a forty-four magnum while taking a shower. He'd just moved into the apartment next to mine that afternoon. I heard a scream, rushed over, and found Bill completely hosed on rye, sitting under the drizzling showerhead and watching his blood pour into the drain. I drove him to emergency.

A few days following the incident, he calls me on the telephone to explain, speaking with a voice like a down-and-out bounty hunter's. It turns out that, just after they'd decided to split, his ex-wife had phoned the company office and told them to send two watchdogs from security, as well as a cop, over to their place. She invited them into the garage and they discovered over ten thousand dollars worth of goods ripped off from the mill. Bill was fired at age fifty-four (after twenty-one years of accumulated seniority), arrested, arraigned; not to mention lovelorn. The wife vanished.

Half a week later he phones me again from an undisclosed place off the road.

"Gabe?"

"Huh? Who is this?"

"It's Bill. Forty-Four Magnum Bill."

"Ah yes, Bill. How are you Bill?"

"I'm phoning to say good-bye."

"You've said good-bye already, Bill."

"I've got a gun and some money and some attitude. I'm gonna hit that road and find my wife."

"Good-bye Bill. And good luck. You keep in touch now, you hear?"

"Thanks Gabe. I will. Take it easy."

"Maybe I'll do that, Bill."

"Yeah, you take it easy, Gabe."

The phone was so inert in my hand after his voice disappeared that I thought the monster under my bed had cut the line.

I stumbled through the post-dance carnage the night those two took Lala with them, a mask of anger on my face, but no wolf inside. Canvassing the gin and tonic cartel of belligerent rednecks. I'm usually pissed out of my brain at the turning points. I slipped between the crowd, not looking for Lala, no; I didn't need to meet her abductors again. I talked to myself, the phrases terse, part nagging and part harangue.

Idiot. You should have hit him. How could you let him say that? I didn't mean to let them take her away. You're a fucking goof now.

Some people in the mob heard me mumbling, turned to their friends, spun their fingers centrifugally beside their heads, laughed. I went outside onto the curb where the fights would soon commence. Taillights will 'o wisped along. The nearby mill hummed a monotone with possibilities for melody. The grass behind me was thatched with wet mud. I couldn't sit; I couldn't stand; I couldn't take my hands away from my head except to wag a finger occasionally. I got up and browsed the crowd again, trying to remember parking my car.

I was shaking my head like a dog with water in its ear when I bumped into Pauline; though high on acid, she recognized me. "Hey Gabe. Where's Lala?"

"They took her." *All I could say*. "They took her."

"Who?"

"Some blond guy with a mustache."

"What do you mean? Who?"

"They took her." Depleted of speech. My adam's apple the most prominent feature on me.

"Gabe, what's wrong?"

I flared my hands, palms upward, out from each shoulder like an Egyptian figure. My face felt impossible to wear. "They took her."

Pauline came off the LSD. She could do that, experienced enough to temporarily block it. "Gabe, you have to tell me. Did you see them? Where did they go?"

"A blond guy with a mustache. A dark-haired friend." I shook my head, swallowing balls of saliva. I looked up at her, crossed my arms, glanced away straight downwind. Weathervanes spun on the old turn-of-the-century houses above us.

"Let's go," she said. She grabbed her drunken boyfriend. Pauline drove because, luckily, the police have no way of checking for LSD.

The three of us bumbled along in the truck. There was no pleasing the itches on the bottom of my feet. Pauline's boyfriend's teeth showed under his mustache like a rat's. "You're a chickenshit little fuck," he told me, turning his face against mine, a scrutiny that put nine stitches in my lips.

The whole way he tore me. I was grateful for it. It was less work than coming up with self-deprecations all by my lonesome. Rusty screws held the moon to the sky. Pauline's hair hung in front of her face like long stalks of violet grasses. Her glassy stare stripped every bush like exfoliant, casing the landscape, looking for the telltale foot out of the ditch. "What kind of pussy are you?" *I don't know, what kind do you want me to be?*

We found Lala behind a bush of broom, naked, shivering. A tail of vapor wagged from her mouth. Ants scrimmaged over each other, all over her feet, and Lala was too fazed to brush them off. The ground beneath her broken and furrowed by rain. Her right hand, covered in blood, gripped a pairless high-heeled shoe, likewise bloodied. Her face cocked towards where streetlamps glowed. Beefsteak bruises stood out all over her neck and arms. Her intricate head was silent as we approached, like someone with an ear to the train track. Only her eyes slashing towards us betrayed the person within. Pauline knelt down beside her: "Lala?"

And then, like off a film screen, Lala rose, head still cocked, and came forward; she put her arms around my neck, eyes still averted to the light, and kissed me.

In the hospital I swerved to and from Pauline's boyfriend. His eyes went completely merciless after the doctor came and spoke to us. I would look at him and then look away. He stared at me for twenty minutes. I squinted up at him, my eyebrows scared, and then away, away. He shoved knives in me the whole while. It was a feeling I needed. He kept stabbing at me – may one of the gods repay him – until I looked up to find him gone.

There was only Pauline, still hidden behind her limp greasy hair. She hadn't said a word the whole way in the truck. She'd spoken only to say Lala's name and wouldn't speak again, not tonight. Pauline remained.

Then she finally turned as well, and that left nobody.

I went up to Lala's room. She was bandaged, asleep. The police not yet arrived. And what would I tell them? I'd been drunk. Distinguishing marks of assailant? Every man between the ages of twenty and thirty in Oxbow capable of rape averaged a mustache – all of them.

I picked up Lala's hand and put it to my cheek, hard, then ran her knuckles over the place she'd kissed, feeling the pattern of nerves under the skin as if in relief. It was a new structure. I felt my guts twist up. I wanted them to. I wanted to step outside of my body so that I could attack myself, put myself down on the floor and strike until there was nothing under my fist but pulp. I wanted to kill the coward, but given a chance I'd probably wimp out. My brutality never got past incentives. So I didn't cut the teeth out of my gums with broken glass, didn't slap my head up against the wall or take pliers to fingernails, didn't chew through my cheeks or peel the skin off my face, didn't cut off my ears with scissors, drive nails into my head. I did none of the things that a real go-getter would have done.

Instead, I procrastinated. Sat by Lala's bed and let it gnaw me from the guts upward. Let it eat me alive. Nothing better to do.

The worst was knowing that I felt only a fraction of what Lala had gone through, an inconsequential smidgen of her horror.

I put my arms across my stomach and bent over in the chair, waiting for the police.

It's hot enough to blister paint, to fry eggs on a bald man's head. Heat turns the ocean into a tin roof. Logging trucks zoom along, weird and fast in the haze, leaving flurries of dust behind Pauline's dilapidated mobile home. We sit on the porch of her trailer and look out over the empty lot, over a vacancy made of sand and standard weeds like dandelion, briar, horsetail. No other mobile homes clutter the newly developed trailer court. The nearby pine and cypress trees leak liters of hot sap. Pauline found her furniture abandoned in the bush. A lot of things get tossed into the wilds here. Every acre of forest has its abandoned car, relics of failed communes and trappers' cabins. Pauline discovered an old couch and two lay-z-boys, none of which match, none of which complement one another.

We drag her couch onto the porch and crack a few beers, sit there with squints in our eyes, tilting cans to and fro. Until now the climate had been humid, but the heat ripped that weather up by the roots. The metal siding on the mobile home rusts but still manages enough silver to glint. Occasionally a cloud of dust takes us by the throat like negative oxygen and we almost swallow our tongues.

With my mom and her second husband, Benny, vacationing in the Okanagan – sleeping in a tent, buying fresh fruit from roadside vendors, and swerving away from rattlers on the highway – I've taken the liberty of transporting their Hibachi up to Pauline's for a little barbecue. I've also brought up the wiener dog for Pauline's viewing pleasure.

I grill a slab of steak for myself but Pauline prefers her tofu dogs cold. "Tofu's a funny thing," I say.

"Why's that?" she asks

"They usually try to make it look like meat, like in tofu loaf or tofu dogs or tofu burgers. Those vegetarians are so concerned with getting away from meat and then they make recipes for it that disguises the tofu like flesh. You think they'd have enough imagination to come up with a new form for tofu."

She squints at me. "You mean like an abstract structure, something to complement the philosophy behind tofu?"

"Yeah, I guess so. I just think that if it's such an alternative to meat why make it look so much like animal parts?"

"Because," says Pauline, "somewhere out there – and most tofu eaters are afraid to admit this – live tofu cows and tofu chickens and tofu pigs. These animals are slaughtered for their tofu."

"Really?"

"Of course," she says. "Personally, I eat tofu for health – not political – reasons." She takes a big bite out of her tofu dog and smiles the big smile at me, lank hair waving slightly in the Indian Summer, a gap between her front teeth that on no one else but her sticks out sexually.

Pauline looks down at the family dog every once in a while and gives a toothpick grin, as if the animal perplexes her – all gray hair and wither, half lame and wholly ignorant, mild as a still-life, with an eau de cesspool stink. Pauline drinks from a can while staring into the weepy eyes of our fourteen year old wiener dog. Her eyes crawl the length off its body. Either the beer or an epiphany about the cracked scars on the dog's back cause her to hack with coughing.

"You," she spoke, eyes bulging, trying to work the gorge back down. "You've put cigarettes out on the back of your dog!"

"It wasn't me," I said, red-faced. "My father used to do it!"

Pauline looks down at the runt and then up at me and gives her head a shake: "Such an ugly dog. It probably deserved it."

"It did. When I pet him I have to be careful not to think about what I'm touching. I think I'd like to kill that thing."

"I had a feeling you were going to say something like that."

"I decided a few days ago. It's just a question of method now. How about a stiletto? I could turn my dog over onto its back and stiletto it right to the floor boards."

"You going Hollywood on me?"

"I just don't think I can live with the knowledge of its continued existence."

"You have no choice. Your dog would survive any assassination attempt. Even if you really wanted to kill it, and tried, you never could. That dog's the Roadrunner, man. Have another beer instead."

"Thanks."

I'm not the one to come to for reference points. It took me years to learn the telling of time. I failed mathematics with a geometric consistency. And as for telling stories, well, I remember moments, like cities on a map, but not the linkages between, no byways or thoroughfares.

Under a certain amount of force I suppose I might relate the details that helped me discover my father's renegade life: incriminating letters or a new watch with strange initials scratched into the back or a sudden taste for a new sauce to go with steak or finding him down the aisle of a drugstore sniffing away at an unknown perfume – the suspicious signals of one life crossing over with another. Believe me, he did all these things, but it never made me think.

I followed him to the other town just for kicks. Yep. Must have been twenty or so and bored out of my nitwits.

The "other" town, River City, was a link of muddy white houses divided by potholed streets. The papers had no want ads but ran a healthy obituary. In the summer, I'm sure children ate fruit while riding their bicycles in bathing suits, but the fall left them indoors, watching the rain through picture windows. The bar manager had long ago put up plywood in place of glass where the windows had been. None of the neighborhood dogs had tags, vaccinations or a steady meal-ticket. Every once in a while you came to a lot without a house on it. You could circumvent the town by keeping the white cross on top of the church at an even distance from yourself.

I went to the bar to find out where my father stayed. The bar ran a hotel out of its second storey. The girl at the front desk looked at the photograph of my father and smiled. "Christ no!" she said. "He doesn't stay here. Not Joe. Why would he want to stay here when he can stay at home?"

I double-checked the photograph to make sure of the face it showed. My father's name wasn't Joe. "You know this Joe guy's address?" I asked. She reached for the telephone directory.

Outside, the rusty autumn sounded a car horn.

I tried knocking on the door but no one answered.

Leaning against a pear tree was a red, woman's bicycle, with a basket and a bell, a rusty chain and a bent frame. With the bike's help, I climbed the tree outside the house's window. Through it I saw the bedroom. On the night-stand, in a silver picture-frame, was a shot of my father, his arms around a woman, a small child on his shoulder. The three of them smiled, but my father's eyes were apprehensive of the photographer.

My father argued with the woman in the bedroom using untamed gestures. The woman sat on the bed fascinated. Sometimes she folded her arms or reached down to pull up her socks.

I crawled out on the prickly branch. When I pressed my ear to the window I heard splintering and the limb dropped two feet – not necessarily in that order. The end of the branch went through the middle of the window. Plates of glass fell past me onto the ground. "What the fuck?" shouted my father. The branch broke right off. I ran.

I was headlong down the main street in seconds, pumping my legs, knees grazing my chin. Five minutes into the run I heard a rattling coming closer. Turning I saw Dad on that red, woman's bicycle with nearly flat tires, tires so flaccid the wheels had no traction on the turns, rims sparking when they hit stones. The chain squealed like a hundred songbirds riding a chainsaw. He must have panicked and grabbed the first form of locomotion.

Wheezing, fists punching the air in front of me, I rounded the top of a hill and came, committed, to the descent in front of me, a fifteen percent gradient. I only made it halfway down before my legs spun out. I skidded to a rest on my chest, and my father, close behind, ran over my thigh, the two edges of the rims ripping through my pants and skin. My father tried to brake the bicycle but it bucked him off against a telephone pole. Both of us took a spot of rest.

He jumped up first, grabbed me by the scruff of the neck, brought me to my feet and looked into my eyes. "Do you know what they're going to say about me?" he screamed, eye sockets so wide I thought the eyeballs would roll out. "They're going to call me that 'Fucking Hungarian' again! Now go home and don't ever come back!"

My father yanked up the bike and walked it away.

Lala cheated with other guys just to show she loved me.

The night I waited for Lala to return from one of her "Sunday fucks" I was soused as a kerosene wick. I'd put her fish bowl on the stove to boil. An alcoholic's sweat wetted my hair and made it stick out of my skull like terminal electro-shock.

I knew she'd cheated once before, during a trip to Vancouver, at a party. While I tossed beer bottles out a fourth storey window at Mercedes in the parking lot below, she ravaged some punk in the bedroom. She'd tried to talk me out of the fusillade, but my mind centered on the score. The home team's champion stood in a mac jacket beside me. I was the visitor.

I knew she cheated then because they left the door open for all to see. She spoke of the added shame she felt, etcetera. I turned white and went back to Oxbow.

Tonight. Tonight I knew because she'd told me about it over the phone. By the time I rushed over to her place she'd vanished. I waited in darkness like char, the remains of a dead heat. I watched the glass of the fish bowl shatter. Fish fried in their self-contaminated water on the element's surface.

"It hurts me so much to cheat on you that all I can think of is you. When I fuck him it's like you and me are making love, but a billion times more intense."

"Don't give me that bullshit, Lala! You fuck them because you like them."

"Yes, I do. But that's not the point!"

I grabbed her shoulders and pushed her against the wall. "That is the point," I whispered hoarsely, surprised that the words could come out so gritty, sand between the letters.

"It doesn't matter to me who they are."

"Bullshit!"

"Tell me who to fuck. Anyone. It doesn't matter."

"The boy next door."

"But he's retarded!"

"No, Lala, he's 'mentally challenged.' Fuck him."

Lala placed a hand over each eye. "Okay," she said.

Killing the dog would be like killing myself, or eradicating a characteristic of me. It's that special, that unique. The tears, well maybe not tears, but various liquids that flow from its eyes and dry darkly on its cheeks, matting little patches of hair there, might as well be mine. The dog is turning gray now, whereas I go bald. Nothing looks uglier than a hairless dog, an albino dog, slavering at the eyes. The growths and scars sticking out of its back ... well, I've had warts too, and psoriasis on my arms. I carried a wart around on my penis for years, getting so used to it that even now when I piss my index finger goes down the shaft of my cock to press upon a friend no longer present. Thankfully, though, my warts never leaked any fluid the way the wiener dog's do.

Never one of those children to enjoy picking scabs or anything like that, I was impressed, as always, by unusual fetishes. When a childhood friend told me that after his mother cut his nails he would take a sickle of clipping and run it along the inside of his nose, I fell in supplication. He said the snot would coil around the fingernail clipping. No other method so satisfied him. I did many things. I never picked my nose. Certain activities sicken me, believe it. There are few grislier sights in my world than having to watch a wiener dog, its back arched in a painful convex, tremulous tail straight up, its stomach swelling and contracting painfully, as it shits. It's so gruesome as to fascinate. I've seen people, certain ones, so ugly I couldn't take my eyes off them. There's something tremendous about monsters, grotesques and sheer vulgarity. Sometimes the pursuit of disgust becomes a passion. No, I didn't pick my nose, nor did I ever masturbate. I fantasized a lot but soon as it came time to actually manipulate my organ – to be a kind of organ-grinder – I lost all arousal. The only time the dog ever growls is when boys – boy dogs, that is – try to fuck him.

My dog and I have a few things in common.

But what we don't both have is an extraordinary sexual potency. No matter how I tear the condom during sex (back in the days when I engaged in intercourse, that is), the woman always fails to get pregnant; this makes me proud, as I don't have to worry about unwanted progeny, like most guys. The dog, on the other hand, walks within fifteen feet of a bitch in heat and she drops a litter of puppies almost instantly. In the alleys and forests of Oxbow live tens of such mongrels sired by the wiener dog, most of them abandoned by disgusted owners (we have yet to determine how it manages to breed with German Shepherds, Huskies, and other dogs ten times its height).

Mrs. Roriarity leaves a set of puppies on our doorstep once or twice a year. She's done everything short of plugging Mou-mou's sexual orifices to try and keep her pedigree poodle "undefiled" by the wiener dog's seed, but even the custom-made chastity belts fail to work. For her part, Mou-mou shows little interest in the purebreds Roriarity introduces her to, preferring the craven lump of two foot long dog waddling from fire hydrant to fire hydrant.

The puppies that appear at our door bother my sister incredibly. I can't remember how many times she's booted them brutally off the top steps. Of course, she thinks nobody sees her do this. "That piece of shit makes more babies than I'll ever see," she spits, pointing at the dog, and then begs my mother to get it fixed. But my mother, who doesn't like Mrs. Roriarity because she once called her a "bohunk" in front of a garden party, refuses to give up her one source of revenge, leaving my sister the lesser satisfaction of delivering each and every puppy to a death by gas at the local pound.

Crank calls keep me up all night, coffee in my cup, and pissed off. My telephone has engineered this harassment to deprive me of priceless unconsciousness. "Hi," the sprightly callers say, "is Connie Lingus there? No? How about her sister, Annie Lingus? No? What about her boyfriend, Phil Atio?"

"I do not know these people," I tell them, but the phone never stops shuddering on the hook, every half hour, give or take. The reading lamp in my bedroom shows me up like a stumblebum in flat light. My coffee, cold as a milk carton, tastes of foreign soil.

The phone jangles. I lean forward and my elastic-less boxer shorts straggle down my pelvis.

Forty-Four Magnum Bill reaches out and touches me. A long time gone between calls. He sounds grouchy, dispirited with the flight towards marital retribution, his voice like a prodigal echo I made coming back for more. One day I'll be a lawyer or factory boss and then I'll tell a success story, but for now, Forty-Four Magnum Bill is the only exaggeration I've got.

He calls me.

"Hello?" he asks.

"You've reached my residence. State your business. I'm standing by."

"Jesus Christ, Gabe, what kind of shit games are you playing?"

"Who is this?"

"Bill. Forty-Four Magnum Bill."

"Oh! It's you, Bill. For Pete's sake, I was about to tell you to eat my fuck. Do you realize what time it is?"

"I'm broke, Gabe." He sobs in desperation. "And I don't know how to swim and I lost her. Now my car's going. . . ."

"Tell me your story, Bill. Update at leisure. Reverse the charges. I can't sleep with this phone dangling off my wall anyways."

Bill turns out and up in Washington State. Seattle in fact. I hear the sound of rain leaking into his dialogue. The bristles from Bill's cheek scrape against the receiver.

Bill found his wife on the freeway by chance. He'd been driving for days, watchful for the license plates of passing cars, knowing she'd transferred their old plates to a new vehicle. Many numbers and letters came and went for Bill, but he never forgot the incriminating designation. Almost unerringly, Bill discovered his wife in the zone they call thirty kilometers above the speed limit. Speeding scared Bill, though, and she eluded him. But he caught up to her again because some cops ambushed his wife from a radar trap. Bill waited while she signed for the ticket. Then she outdistanced him anew: just too much of a hot-rodder to follow.

Sometimes she used her new cellular phone to call the hotels he stayed in, hanging up the minute the front desk connected them. Bill tried calling back – never got an answer. She'd bought the phone to keep track of him, not to communicate.

He kept on, trucking along, eating in diners. His vehicle became a bivouac. Sometimes he got homesick and sometimes he had low blood pressure and sometimes musty body odor. He took matches to the lavatory because he couldn't love a pungent fart anymore. Bill slowly became strange to himself. He bought newspapers and read the business columns. He examined his personal politics. Bill basically rediscovered himself on roadsides of little renown. He kept running up against intersections, thinking hard about the choices until his brain turned to sludge.

He found his wife, by luck again, in a Tacoma bar. A gay bar as it turned out, but Bill wasn't a clever guy, not enough to associate the bar's name, BUDDIES, with sexuality anyways. But sure as stepping through the door, he was the deviant now, social mores – he figured – being relative.

In the foreground a pool table. The street-side window had a heavy painting of hairy-forearmed lumberjacks drinking martinis out of glasses shaped like flamingoes. Light didn't fall amply on the pool playing area. A pile of guys, some large, some small, some young, some old, scoffed at each other's strategy, shooting stick with an old-boy network's chumminess. These guys stared bemusedly at Forty-Four Magnum Bill's entrance and pocketed their hands. He took his eyes off theirs and went to the bar, where a man much younger, still in his late twenties, removed a beer cap, exposing clumps of hair growing in patches on his dome like archipelagoes. Bill cleared his throat and ordered a beer. He got one. "Do you have a menu?" he asked.

"No. Sorry hon," said the bartender, with a smile from Venus.

Bill grinned back and then consternated for a second, shaking his head. He opened the beer but sipped like a teetotaler, looking darkly at the two pensioners in old, rumpled, finely-tailored suits at the far end of the L-shaped bar. The pool balls clacked behind. The rain sloshed down from the sky, filling streets with the sound of rising water. Bill shook droplets off his jacket, turned around to hang it on the coat-rack and came face to face with a furrowed brow. "You aren't a fag are you?" the man leered.

"No," said Bill, returning the stare, snubbing the guy like someone who gets beat up a lot but fails to be dissuaded.

"Well," he said, "everyone else in here is, 'cept me." He rose up from the confidential position. "Hey fairies," he yelled, half laughing, "there's two of us dudes now." He slapped Bill on the back. The boys at the pool table wrinkled up their faces tartly and ignored him. Both of the guy's legs bounced at the knees. Bill noticed how he rocked on his feet. "Have you ever had a homosexual experience?" the man asked.

"Fuck off," Bill said quietly.

"Want to do some coke?" he wondered.

"Yeah," Bill said, "that would be right." The bouncer pulled out a small bag and railed up a few they snorted off the counter. The bartender beamed before them. Bill ordered beer for the pair, and the man sat down. Bill drummed his fingertips on the counter-top, trying to make his fingers hit the arborite hard.

"I'm the bouncer downstairs," his new friend said. Bill hadn't noticed a lower bar on the way in, but he still had some capacity for faith, and believed.

"Downstairs?"

"Yeah, a straight place," he replied, raising his voice. "No fag boys there." He smiled at the bartender.

"Shut up," the bartender said, like someone voicing a platitude or laying brick.

"I got shot before," the bouncer commented, setting his jaws squarely. He raised his shirt and showed Bill a torso smooth and hairless – as if from electrolysis – in the glimmering lights: eight random puckers on the skin, each ribbed like a little wheel. "Somewhere, sometime, in New York, someone did not approve of my affiliations," he explained. "And they shot me eight times. Not flesh wounds either, meat wounds! And now I'm fine." He laughed and jumped up off the chair, pogoing on the balls of his feet, legs slightly spread. The bartender leaned over the bar, the smell of cologne musky to Bill.

"You are not allowed to break glasses tonight," the bartender yelled at the coke-head. "I'm not paying for more of your broken glasses! You hear?" Bill ordered a bourbon. The bouncer jumped up onto one of the lounge chairs, gripped his crotch in one hand, kept the other on top of his baseball hat, and jiggled up and down.

"In the army I knew a Colonel Sweeney, who taught me how to fist-fuck homos ..." the bouncer sang. Bill stared at his bourbon. The pool game continued at his back. Everyone lent him plenty of privacy, except for the bouncing bouncer in back of him. "Come around guys," the coke-head shouted, "and hear my tale!"

"Oh fuck!" the bartender commented dryly to Bill. "If he freaks out we're going to be in such shit. He's so wired." Then the bartender spoke harshly again: "Get down from there, now!" The bouncer laughed with the congested sound of someone turning the key on a car already ignited. Bill stopped mollycoddling his bourbon and hammered it home. The bouncer walked over to where the men were playing pool and shoved one of their heads.

"I said get over here and listen to my Goddamn tale," he shouted, with a look like a lobbyist for some neo-nazi organization. "I'm going to tell my straight friend here why I'm not a homosexual and I want you boys to listen!" They walked around to Bill, hands in pockets like schoolboys. Bill ordered another shot and tried to ignore the bouncer, but it was impossible. "You know why I'm not a fag?" he shouted. The bartender pouring the drink for Bill was so nervous and distracted he missed Bill's glass. "Because I promised my mother," the bouncer admitted. "I promised my mother I'd never have gay sex." The bouncer looked at the tips of his shoes, which had curled upward from travel.

For a minute there was silence. The bartender was the first to laugh, slowly but gradually bowling over. Soon the whole place floundered. Even Bill had a bit of a chuckle, and Bill hadn't even felt like so much as a smile in a long time.

The bouncer reared up. "Why are you all laughing?! It's true," he shouted, gripping the shoulders of people too far into laughter's extremes to respond. "I promised my Mom," he yelled into their faces. "That's the only reason. Otherwise, I'd cornhole you all."

The bartender collapsed on the floor. Bill reached over the bar for the bourbon.

"Stop laughing!" The bouncer grabbed one of the smaller men and got him into a headlock. He lifted his arm slightly so the guy had to walk on tiptoe, trying to pull the bouncer's arm away from around his neck. The laughter petered out. "I'll show you what the good Colonel showed me about fist fucking fags in the lavatory." The little man squeaked. The other patrons looked unimpressed.

"Leave him alone," Bill said. The bouncer stopped dragging the guy towards the back. "I said leave him alone," Bill repeated. The bouncer looked down at his subject. He let the man go, came over to Bill and intruded on his face.

"Just having fun." He laughed without meaning, then adjusted his cap and ran downstairs.

Bill turned around to see his wife, alone in the corner, mouth flickering.

Cold nights of driving; flesh tones on the boss's face firing him; empty-headed in the apartment; old hole in his shoe; blaring discrepancies between his previous and new lifestyle. Bill didn't believe even in enigmas, or else he would have blamed God, the gods, Goddess, goddesses. Instead, he targeted the wife as the cause of all ills.

He got up from the bar and sauntered over. "You coming with me or what?"

"Didn't know you frequented such establishments, Bill. You big hero."

"You coming home with me?"

"Do I have any choice, Bill?"

"Not for long," he said, feeling a great and raw deal of hunger in his mouth.

"Still fighting in other people's wars?"

"Seems like someone had to say something."

She laughed. "You turd."

Bill went up beside her and clamped onto her elbow. "We're going now," he said, like somebody stoned. He pulled her up and tried to get her to heel. The shotgun nestled in the back seat of his car; Bill wondered about the best place to plug her. Take her out, I guess, down to the river. "What you doing here anyhow?" he asked while walking forthright, tugging his stiff wife along.

"I was on my way south. Fuck. Let me go, asshole. I'm not going to run." He pushed her out the door, releasing the elbow. She rubbed the place he'd held, straightened her skirt. "Just thought I'd stop for a drink. I liked the sign."

Bill nearly retorted but a sound distracted them both. Fifty feet down, the small guy from upstairs, one shirt-sleeve torn off, had the bouncer in a headlock and was screaming obscenely. The bouncer, for his part, had the little guy in a headlock too. Both of them moved like shamans getting it wrong.

"See?" his wife said. "I told you." Meanwhile it rained. "Your car or mine?" she asked.

"What's an old lady acting so girlie for?" he said. She shrugged one shoulder.

They took his car.

Bill tried to keep glancing into the back seat during the ride to check on the firearm. Fortunately a jacket covered the shotgun but the slugs rolled from the seat to the floor with padded thuds. He didn't know if she heard over the splattering rain. The idea that she'd uncover the instrument of her undoing made Bill queasy. He couldn't stay off the mirror. She prattled during the ride and conspicuous things went supposedly unnoticed.

"I didn't divorce you out of spite or anything, Bill."

"What about turning me into the mill about the stuff I borrowed?"

"The stuff you stole!"

"They fired me Goddamnit! After twenty-one years!"

"Yup. Okay. Calm down. I'll admit that was out of spite. But only because you made it tough for me to get out. You never gave me a penny. It's hard to get out of a house and a marriage when you haven't got anywhere to go or anyone to go there with or a job to provide you with the means ..." she put three fingers together and held them up like an Italian chef, "and a husband guarding you day and night who won't even keep a joint bank account in your name."

"What marriage were you in?" asked Bill, confounded. What was she talking about? She'd always had access to their money. And he hated bosses – a union man by nature.

She ignored him. "So I sold the furniture and the cars and your hunting guns and most of the jewelry and china, the machines, everything. The call to the mill was just payback for the trouble I went through to find buyers. You should have some more trouble in your life, Bill. You're complacent."

Well, I've got plenty of trouble now and plenty more to come, he thought, passing gas stations in the torrential downpour.

He missed the bridge because he was busy with the rearview mirror and back seat. He saw the railing for one second and tried to persuade the steering otherwise. If the river hadn't overflowed nothing would have happened but scrapes on the autobody. That's just a thought, though, and thoughts don't count. Down they went. Sticks floated past like rafts for convicts. Bill especially didn't understand himself at that moment, and dug into the empty box of his body, once filled with treats, but every inner helper for times like this seemed used up by the kid he grew out of being. His wife thought of her life-guarding badges. "Well, now you've done a lot more than eat us out of house and home," she said. "Now. Yes, now, I think," she repeated.

Bill stared at the wet leaves plastered to the windshield, thinking of chlorophyll for humans, something to turn the dark into vitamins. He couldn't even think of the shotgun anymore, only the puddle forming around his feet. After looking down at his soaked shoes Bill looked up of course, to realize his wife's words had been a leader to some pretty quick thinking. Her window was open, water rising. He saw her out in the flood. She'd caught a wave.

"Bill, what happened?" I ask. Phones know no end to the evil they communicate.

"You know damn well what's happening," he screams. "She left all her shit in the car – purse, jacket, shoes, everything. That's howcum I got her cellular phone. And I gotta tell you this, Gabe ..." his voice is boisterous with despair, "this I gotta tell you...."

I know, I know. The water's rising.

Lala and I would goad fun out of each other. For example, the time I walked away, contrary to her will, from the bar and its after-hours menu of fisticuffs, vomit, car wrecks, irreconcilable differences. Lala grumbled through the pole-line's slanting rain. We came to the reservoir. Salamanders darted from water-logged stumps as we took off our clothes and jumped into water the rain only made warmer, water clean enough to drink. Frogs sprang from the purity-testing piers, making heavy splashes. The night held endless hands out to us. I kept looking at my watch, only to realize it wasn't waterproof. Lala pulled me to her in the water and commissioned nostalgia of me, nostalgia in the present tense. Waves broke in musical phrases.

Pauline's boyfriend found me piteous and vile from the night of the rape onwards. The fact that his and Pauline's relationship was approaching foreclosure didn't help. He always had an edge of scorn to his voice when addressing me. But previous to my unmasking I think he reveled in my weirdness. Maybe he thought I kept reasonable depths like other human beings, but a thimble tops up the coward. Afterwards, he never said hello to me when I came to visit Pauline, preferring other rooms. But sometimes he lent me a moral tale, a backwater parable on bravery, a list of alternatives to being chickenshit.

We sat on the porch, in the shade, snorting dust and licking it from our lips. He stared away from me, at the distant sea.

"When I mined up north I met this guy," he began, "this little guy. Not big but tough as shit. We bugged him about not being big enough to be tough as nails but only tough as a thumb tack. One of the happiest people I'd ever met. Always laughing. Even when he scrapped he always laughed. You know how that infuriates the guy you're fighting with? No," he smirked at Pauline, who telegraphed a warning back, "I guess you wouldn't. Anyhow, for some reason he and this one guy, this big fucker, took to disliking each other. Only two bars in town, so the chances of them meeting stood fifty-fifty. And this guy would kick the living shit out of Thumb Tack. I mean, he would mess him up so bad that Medical considered revoking Thumb Tack's credit. But Thumb Tack never took the guy to court. He'd rather keep fighting him, he said. It got so bad that soon as they saw each other Thumb Tack would take a swing. I think he tried not to fight once, but the guy poked at him and called him down in front of friends. Thumb Tack refused to stop living, to stay at home out of fear. After a while they didn't even talk to each other anymore. Until the guy showed up Thumb Tack would holler and joke, with the biggest laugh ever. Thumb Tack had principles, you see. He carried on like the weekly shitkicking never happened. The same optimistic attitude even when it started getting really bad, even after the guy took to breaking his arms after punching Thumb out. Thumb Tack hated our interference. Once, in a parking lot the guy took a big rock and dropped it on Thumb Tack's ankle before we could stop him. Ever heard an ankle shatter?"

"No," I said.

"Thumb Tack just kept on...."

"And when there was trouble he stepped into a phone booth to get his costume on," I interrupted, only to be ignored.

"... until one night the big guy twisted Thumb Tack's head three hundred and sixty degrees. He got manslaughter. I lost touch with everyone up there. I'm sure they're all doing the same things as always. If Thumb Tack could come back, reincarnated as himself, he'd live it up, fight it out all over again. I'm sure of that."

He spat a long stream of beer into the dust, wiped sweat off his forehead and entered the trailer. Pauline went after him.

As he had intended, the story reminded me of my days of failure. If they could market the nostalgia I suffer from, every interrogator would want some, the line of masochists measuring in miles.

When she pushed the boy's erection back and positioned herself above it, I broke. It might have been his Down's syndrome grin that looped me. It might have been Lala's seeming indifference. But truth came down on Lala's side. In the end I was the one unwilling to run with the wager.

She had enticed the boy next door up into her bedroom by flashing the beauty spot on her left breast, a bait irresistible to me as well. I hid in the loft as Lala proceeded with victory, making credible the intentions behind her past infidelities. A few more minutes of this discipline and she'd be free to sleep with whoever she wanted without my voiced disapproval. His pork sausage poised to enter her, a misshapen cock, a fat man's penis. Lala closed her eyes, either out of agony or ecstasy. I still don't know. His eyes opened and his hands squeezed her breasts, face alternating between sloppy smile and something weighty, lips inches from the nipples. When Lala began lowering herself onto his cock, I screamed down from the loft and yanked at her. Gripping her underneath the armpits I ripped Lala off him. He took her hands out of reflex, but on seeing me let go to simper in the corner of the bed. He pulled the blankets up over himself and stared at me, horrified. I dropped Lala, who sobbed, hands brought up to her eyes. Then I pounced on top of the boy, smooching him on the mouth (my way of saying thank-you). I tried to get past that ping-pong paddle tongue, saliva thick as condensed milk. Lala began beating my back with her fists, snarling: "Leave him alone! Get off him!" The boy jumped up, threw me against the wall beside the bed, and stacked a few blows of the fist on top of my head. The bed moved out from the wall and I was jammed between the crack. Lala picked up the confused boy's clothes and led him out of the room by the hand. By the time she came back in I was wriggling, unable to get out from the pinch, stomach muscles heaving drastically, though my sobs had quieted. "Okay," I said, contorted and neutralized, "you win." I passed a wrist under each eye, loyal now to her wishes.

O chronicle of fathers.... Ahem. Forget it.

I had two dads: one biological and one surrogate. And when I speak of the surrogate, I'm not talking about Benny, my mother's second husband, who counts for so little I can barely say his name. No, my second father was called Giovanni Carter, a farmer and fuck-up originally from somewhere south of the border.

To avoid too much clarity, I will first recount his death and funeral arrangements, leaving for later all details essential for following the context.

I discover that my second father has died while reading the obituaries. I come to a "Mr. G. Carter, deceased," cause of death unlisted, not lamented, not dearly beloved, survived by neither friend nor foe, not a body except me. "Outlived by Gabe," it says, in a breach of obituary syntax. I know what the old curmudgeon wanted.

"Pauline," I ask, "how would you like to do me a favor?"

"How about that," she replies. "Hey?"

"Run a distraction."

The trees on the farm go truant of grooming, free of the pruner's shears, and amok, from a distance, in thick hairs. The place has regressed to wild grasses and the animals either gone to market or local pantries. The farm has become one of those maps the old man used to draft: a sketch in need of extrapolation.

Pauline, her hair up in a bun like a villager, shifts the gears many times more than normal. Someone has shot the mailbox. One side contains a neat entry hole, the back splashed open in a metal exit wound. The flag stands.

Cruising along the driveway Pauline wonders what ails me.

"I made the old man a promise to bury him. If I don't he'll find a way to collect."

"You don't believe in ghosts do you?" she asks.

"Not extraterrestrial or intangible ones."

"Gabe, phone home," she smiles.

"Fuck, I don't even know if he's here," I grunt. "Remember, if there is a body, I've got to go out the front way, so get whoever the hell away from the front door. And don't forget, my name's Eddie."

The car skids in the dirt and halts. We let the dust clear before opening the doors. The front steps are missing, so for the sake of nostalgia I try climbing across the banister and groin myself. A different old man, but strangely similar to Mr. Carter, squints at me from behind the screen while I lift my crotch off the railing. I blush. Pauline puts on her sunglasses and stares at the null and void where the steps had been.

"Had to come in that way myself," the old guy says, letting the screen shut behind him. Obviously that part in the obituary about nobody surviving Mr. Carter except me was just another of the old duffer's piss-poor ruses.

"Sorry." I uncup hand from crotch and hold it out to him. "Eddie."

"I'm Giovanni's cousin, twice removed. Name's Ebenezer."

"Giovanni?" I stutter.

"Sure, that's his name, ain't it?"

"I always thought it was Gabe."

"Nah," the old man spits.

My father must have slipped his tongue that day when I last saw the old man. I grab the railing, flabbergasted.

"You alright?"

"Yeah.... Just my balls hurting. Sorry about coming here like this." I turn and give Pauline a helping hand onto the porch. "This is Pauline." She extends her hand. The old man wipes his on his pants before offering it.

"Pleased to meet you."

"So what's the story?" Pauline blurts.

"Well, I'm all that's here. There ain't nobody else."

"What about the missus?" she apes.

"Gone. Years back now. You coming in to see him? I got him upstairs on the bed. Thought someone might come to look him over."

"Shit," Pauline trembles. "I don't want that. This is, uh, Eddie's errand. I'd just as soon stay out here. Does it smell?"

"A bit," the old guy chuckles. "I've been cooped up with it for a day now. I'd just as soon stay out myself."

"I'll go in," I say, pushing off from the porch.

The body reminds me of the way my father's looked, but not arrayed so sumptuously. This second father in my set of two has a worn Persian carpet thrown across him, spacious enough for a partner. Most furniture has been taken from the house, leaving behind only discolored imprints on the floor. Someone put scotch tape on his eyelids to keep them down. I sit prissily on the edge of the bed and take stock of the movements in my wristwatch. Pauline needs ten minutes at least.

We are two, not one. Hadn't he been a Giovanni and not a Gabe, in contradiction of what my father had me believe? Who cares anyhow. With a rapture I realize this dead old man set up this farewell party for our twosome, if only to debunk my father's plot. He knew that hearing the name Giovanni would smash at least one curse I grapple with.

After enough time passes, and without nit-picking much, I grab a handful of the old man's abundant hair, lift him up by it and show him how basic flight feels. He would have loved it, I'm sure. The carpet slips off from around him like a load. Only he's so heavy I can hardly keep him airborne. Naturally, within seconds of me straining to hold him up by one hand his scalp disintegrates, leaving a hunk of hair and skin in my hand while the body slumps down on the floor. His claptrap request won't be fulfilled today. What to do? What to do?

I guess dragging him by the ears will suffice.

Walking backwards and slouched over, I pull Mr. Carter's mortal remains down the stairs. His heels drop from one step to the next. We progress, in a series of soft clunks, down to the landing, and I push the front door open with the heel of my foot, taking one long backward stride out of the house, my hands to either side of his head, firmly gripping each ear, both of which have stretched a little out of shape.

And there, big for his age, stands Ebenezer, hands crossed over his heart. Behind him, Pauline leans against the railing smoking a cigarette.

I hurl Giovanni's body head first into the kitchen, flipping it ass over heels, jump in after him and close the door, locking it with the chain. What's going on? Pauline promised to waylay the old man's custodian. She's usually quite reliable.

Ebenezer tries the door but the chain stops him; meanwhile I lift Giovanni's body onto my shoulders in a fireman's carry, the type of which I've only seen on all-star wrestling.

"Hold on there," hollers Ebenezer, but I'm moving up the stairs. I get to the top flight when I hear the door ripped from its hinges. Sweating, and feeling my jugular pumping huge globs of blood, I look for a way into the attic. Dropping Giovanni's body onto the bed, I close the door to his bedroom and prop a chair under the doorknob.

"I've got words for you, Gabe! Hold on!" shouts Ebenezer, tugging and rattling the doorknob. The square trap-door to the attic is situated above the bed. I grab Giovanni's body under the buttocks and, holding it to me with his chest against my face, begin bouncing off the box-spring mattress, higher and higher, until the corpse's head butts the trapdoor in the ceiling that leads to the attic. I hit it a few times to knock it to the side. Giovanni's raw scalp leaves a blotch on the cover. Rigor mortis makes it easy to use him as a ram, however. I have yet to consider the fact that I have no shovel or horse manure to bury him with and in.

Ebenezer has stopped wrenching the knob, probably gone to get a crowbar or an ax.

With one high bounce, I propel Giovanni's body straight up like a missile into the attic. I've got that much muscle-tone at least. He flies through the square hole and falls partially back out, legs dangling akimbo. So much for seeing the last request off his way. I leap up from the mattress now sprouting coils of springs and grab the edge of the attic entrance, hoist myself up. A very loud crack splits the door. I heave Giovanni's cadaver up and replace the trapdoor, flustered with anxiety. There's no escape except through the window, belly-flopping two storeys. Another muffled crack rises through the attic's grimy floor. What the hell: I use Giovanni's head, again, to shatter the pane of glass covering the attic's only window. A large poplar stretches its branches right to the edge of the roof. Unfortunately, Giovanni's in no condition to make the leap to the tree, never mind scaling down from branch to branch. I grab the old man by the scruff of the neck and pajama bottoms and lob him out the window, hoping he'll snag in the sticks like a kite. I can extract him from there and carry him to the ground. And if I miss? Well, he won't have to worry about walking away from the damage.

Giovanni's stiff body connects with a branch that bends away and dumps his body onto the planet. About to follow Giovanni's example, with better results hopefully, I grab the edges of the window frame and put one foot up when Pauline wails: "Gabe, for fuck's sake. Come down here."

Long-faced and shaking, I slide away the cover and poke my head out of it. Beneath me Ebenezer and Pauline hoot with laughter. I let myself drop from the hole, landing on my back in the mattress and springs. Some wires slice through my shirt.

Ebenezer shows me the note left behind: *Dear Ebenezer, how are you? I am fine. I'll be dead shortly. You're my next of kin so here's what you got to do: put my dead name in the paper,* G. Carter. *Also put in something about nobody else being around to salvage my corpse. That'll get Gabe to come. Then fix up things over by the bog: get some manure and a shovel, dig a hole, lay the bones of the goat in there nice and gentle. The bones are in the bed, under the rug, with me. Don't worry, Gabe'll show. He crossed his heart. Put his name in the paper too. He'll probably think you don't know about this and freak out, probably give a fake name or something, probably call himself* Eddie. *Make sure you're ready for this.* Signed: Giovanni.

Ebenezer turns to me: "You must be the kid. Now do as you were told."

Giovanni made little impression on the earth. The earth, however, revolutionized Giovanni's outlook. The slammed flatness of his face compliments the planar top of his head. Walking backwards and dragging Giovanni by the ears I shrink my neck into my collar, feeling goofy for my panicky reaction, and I keep gawking over my shoulder. Dust touches down everywhere on my eyelids and sore tendons, between my toes and thighs.

A black ribbon on a tree marks a fresh swath cut in the foliage. The old man drags his heels and, like a couple of outlaw louts, we lumber to his personal boot-hill. As I guessed, there's a shallow square hole on the edge of the marsh, a mound of ripe manure beside it impaled by a shovel. Everything in readiness, even a small cross of twigs held together by a rubber band sits next to the dung-pile. I walk over to the square. Dusk gathers. Both my arms pointing in the same direction as, and level with, my nipples, I dangle the old man by each ear above the hole, inside which lay spit-polished bones, a skull with two sharp horns.

The old man's ears begin to tear and I reel him to me from over the pit, rest him on the ground and unnerve myself with a ground-swell of affection. I don't normally feel like getting in touch with my emotions: too far to go, not worth the trip. The top of his head has a corrosive, textile look. Don't get me wrong, systems of brotherly love, love of the father, even the mother for child, function in us self-styled hermaphrodites and eunuchs, but subsumed in hate, like an alternative scripture between the lines of a bible. And the hate ain't no unilateral undertaking; it cuts inward and outward. I pull an uncalled-for move: open a jackknife and saw away at my hair, mainly the bangs and top. What locks of hair rip free I sprinkle onto Giovanni's sticky head until the wound vanishes underneath. I take the old man in my arms and like a sugary bride and groom from a wedding cake we step into the rectangle of earth. After his body and the goat's bones are fitted up against each other like spoons, one behind the other, I come clean with Giovanni. "I'm taking you off the map," I say, standing above him.

I pull the shovel out of the manure and stick it into the soft ground to clean it. "I'm going to put peat and humus on you, Giovanni, not the crap you want." But before I drop the first shovelful I notice the bones again. Dropping the tool I jump down into the grave and jerk the skeleton out. White batons, fragments shower all around. I pick the bones up and toss them underhand, one by one, high into the darkness over the forest.

Pauline steps up beside me. "We came to watch," she says expertly. "Weren't sure if you wanted mourners. Need help?"

I nod. In silence we fling the lengths of the goat up towards orbit. Ebenezer stands at the edge of the forest with a flashlight in hand.

After that, I pick up the shovel and bury Giovanni in the earth. I stick the cross in. Turning to "fuck off," a flashlight beam suffuses my face in light. Pauline holds a bottle of booze, both her and Ebenezer a little unsteady but in buoyant spirits, Pauline panting from hurling bones. "What the hell happened to your hair?" Pauline asks.

We listen to philarmonics on the radio all night drinking and then leave Ebenezer at the crack of dawn. Pauline lets me in on another of her appraisals: "Gabe, you gotta stop trying to make amends all the time."

With a dozen flowers wilting from my grip, I'd come to see Lala every day in the hospital. Our long silences made rhapsodies out of the air conditioner's hum. I sat by the bed and she stared out the window over the mill's belches of smoke. Sometimes I came straight from the machine room to the bedside vigil. I smelt like stove oil and tears. She did touch me at times, my face or my hand, with the ball of her thumb. She touched me the way the needy pick cigarette butts off the sidewalk.

They caught the blond, now one-eyed, rapist wannabe and put him in a penitentiary. He looked so much like everyone else in Oxbow we'd never recognize him again. Once the intensive care of doctors, psychologists, policemen and lawyers finished, Lala left the hospital for home.

What drastic neuroses or devil misguided me enough to buy the bottle of Southern Comfort when I came over for the end of phase one I'll never know. She had killer words planned for that day.

Lala greeted me at her father's door like a hitchhiker with a hatchet behind her back. They lived out in the boonies and we drove the car down a logging road and parked. It was a lower mainland spring, and most of the trees refused to believe it, staying leafless. We walked along the road. Clouds massed according to satellite photographs. No words passed until the bottle was nearly done for and thunderheads had bottomed out. The two of us sat on the car's hood regardless of the rain.

"You remember the boy next door?"

I didn't want to. I didn't want to remember her victory. "Yeah, I remember."

"I was going to make it like that when that blond guy got on top of me." She reached down. Rain fell into the neck of the bottle. Lala took it up. "I thought about you and how much I loved having sex with you. I compared him to you."

I felt my face in the place she had kissed that night. "Don't say that," I said. "Don't compare me to him."

"I couldn't," Lala responded. She shifted on the car's hood as I swigged from the lips of the bottle. And when she put her hand on me … when she put her hand on me I began to mentally hammer out the wording to my last wishes. "I couldn't do it. He wasn't you. That's when I speared the heel of my shoe into his eye. You know, he never even got his cock into me. You should have seen him scream. I ran away … then was safe … then found."

"I love you," she said: those three words just to top it all, to outfinesse me. I couldn't have produced this kind of five-star torment for myself even after advanced classes. She was meeting my needs – the Red Cross of the conscience – knowing I required intense guilt to survive. And Lala knew the result – that I'd leave her – and yet she performed, realizing I would later come to understand what she'd done.

I turned on her. "Don't say that!" I shouted, almost drowned out by the splash of heavy rain. "I won't let you!" Pounding my fists on the hood. "You know I can't understand it. You know I can only understand you by fucking you down to my level." It was true. Her love eluded my intelligence, my knowing. I told myself the only way she could love me was if she was like me, because someone as pure as her loving someone like me was too heartbreaking a reality. I had to synchronize us and since I could never ascend to her, she had to be brought down to me.

I don't rationalize often, no guile for it.

Jumping off the hood, I got into the car, turned the engine over and drove off before Lala had a chance to get in beside me. She ran after the car, a death grip on the door handle like the captain's gone down with the ship. I turned on the headlights through the rain so she could survey the obstacles in the road, the holes and stones that would take her off her toes. Her feet couldn't keep up and when she began to drag I knew I had her. One sharp turn and the torque peeled back her fingers, spun her head over tail into an irrigation ditch. My radials were at a complete loss on the road's washboard. The car tripped sideways over potholes and took the telephone pole on the port side, wrapping around that dead tree. Lala kneeled by the broken windshield until I regained consciousness. Nursing my broken nose and favoring her good leg we came to the nearest telephone. We tried small talk on the way, but nothing came of it. After the visit to emergency it would be a full year before we'd welcome each other again.

"The four of us were on a rooftop," Pauline's boyfriend said one night. He blathered on: "I fell in love with my cousin. I stayed up at night in the hotel bed just listening to her breathe in her sleep. And I couldn't do anything. She was my cousin. The breeze came through the windows but I sweated like a hog. Anyways, that night, on the rooftop, she argued with a guy about politics. He was losing the argument and decided to slap her. The minute his hand left her face my fist connected with his teeth. Both his feet left the ground. He got up, terrified, and scrambled down the ladder from the rooftop. His girlfriend told me he wasn't the kind of man you could do that to. I told her facts proved otherwise, told her I wouldn't hold back a shot from anyone who physically hurt a woman. No one."

"What about psychologically hurt a woman? Emotionally?" I took the next logical step.

"That depends on the woman. And the man. It's unavoidable doing that to someone, I guess."

"That's strange."

"I know. I can't figure out what to do sometimes."

I never told my father he treated me like a turkey-baster baby. I should have. I probably wasn't the only one who left words unsaid but nobody else in the family mentioned regrets. When the lawyer parceled out the will for the Oxbow "estate" my mother announced her engagement. She'd started an affair with one of the mourners at my father's memorial service. My father, that little rascal, was even in absentia at his own final rite. He'd died in a mining accident in River City; I made the family believe his body had gone unrecovered from under the miles of collapsed rock.

Beside the sausage rolls after the service I met this white-haired girl, a friend of a friend of a friend of my father's (which made her, at least initially, no friend of mine). "My name is Lala," she said, "I know your father from my job at the airport. He used to take a lot of flights didn't he?"

"Yes ... he did. He had another wife in River City, you see."

"Very funny. You should have more respect for the dead."

"Tell me about it.... Sorry, I didn't catch your name...."

"It's Lala."

"Lala? What kind of weird-ass name is that...?" Eventually we got around to exchanging phone numbers; I guess my mixture of irreverence and melancholy attracted her.

My mother re-married shortly after Father's interment. Not one person stood at the service to object. Even the priest clasped his hands a lot but failed to wring any worry out of them.

My stepfather is one of those normal joes. There's nothing else about him worth noting. He wears a polka-dotted silk handkerchief in his blazer pocket. It flounces around like a dandy's flower. But he had the dignity at least not to wear it at the wedding. Okay, his normalcy is conditional, more than conditional; his name is Benny and he has dimples and cellulite on his face. Now you know why I have so little to say about him.

Benny came with a boy included. I refer to this boy affectionately as my stepbrother. Along with my biological sister, he seems unable to move permanently away from home. Of course, being a single parent employed part-time, he has sound financial reasons for sponging off our parents. When pressed about not moving out, my sister, for her part, uses the Hungarian background as an excuse; there, it's customary for children to linger at home long as possible. When she says she'll move out with the onset of pregnancy, I realize the years in close-quarters with Benny and my mother have stunted her psychological development. We got to know our stepbrother over the champagne and hors d'oeuvres served at Benny's and Mother's wedding.

The service turned out Roman Catholic. My mother took a holiday from faith just after her first marriage because my father said Canada wasn't a Catholic country. But sometimes, when he'd jaunt off, she'd spread the rosary on a white tablecloth and graze the beads with her fingers, like stirring a pot of feathers. All the technicolors of nostalgia must have arisen like perfume from those brittle glass beads. Then she'd put them away.

My mother tried religion on me once, shortly after her re-marriage, tried to get me to go to church. And I just replied with a "No." She said she always wanted to take us to church but my father stopped her. I pointed out a spider crawling up her back, and left.

"You're so uptight sometimes," Pauline says. We'll give abstinence a chance this evening, allow our systems a break, lay on the tin roof of her home, and watch stars shoot across these warm nights the dog days give way to.

"Maybe because I'm twenty nine years old and looking forward to retirement."

"It's more than that," she says. "Take your dog for instance. Sometimes you get these fixations, like assassinating your dog. What makes you think of something like that?"

"'Assassinating' is too kind. Please stop using it. My dog isn't JFK. In any case, I prefer 'eradicating.' My dog," I say, as something flashes across the sky in front of us with a snipped tail, "disgusts me."

"Every month you get this," Pauline ponders, pulling her dark hair back behind one ear. "On schedule. Like PMS." She leans up on one elbow and looks at me, her ratty T-shirt slipping down one waxy shoulder. "Maybe you get some kind of anal period or something. Maybe that's it. Maybe you should get some tampons for your bum."

"Pauline," I say. "You're one great piece of ass."

"In that case," she smiles, "would you do me a little favor?"

"Anything. Anything at all."

"Would you go get a sperm test and not ask why."

"But Pauline," I say. "'Why' is one of those questions I can't help asking."

"Well, now's as good a time as any to stop."

I nod, shake my head, nod. "Ahhh, fuck it. Okay."

She rocks onto her back, knees pulled to her chest, laughing. Not a breath of innuendo between us, not a sexual chemical in play now or ever before. The sarcasm is pure as light, as the comets zipping in our quadrant of sky, our six feet of sky.

I can never tell when she's on a natural high.

I should come to dinner with a chopper in my hand, but arrive instead the deceitful way – my pocket hiding poison. Mother welcomes me at the door and Stepfather's in the wine cellar reaping beers. Sister bolts the bathroom and Stepbrother minds his baby. The dog's nose hovers a centimeter above the kitchen floor. The back of its body moves independently of the front, contorting a long torso like two boys with varying agility inside a grade-school horse costume. The long tongue slaps down and sucks the floor. You're some kind of gimped soul but you sure ain't a dog, I think.

"Why won't you come in?" The question breaks my trance and I smile at my mother, step through the entranceway. I have been invited into the home. Here we go. I stumble like a castrato. The thing between my legs never helps.

Our kitchen succumbed not at all to Canada: no Murphy's Law posters, microwaves, placemats of famous British landmarks, cushions on seats and, finally, not a rubber dishwashing glove on the premises. My mother's and Benny's hands are coarse-grained and scaly as driftwood. Benny has conformed to my mother's cultural norms, forced to adopt a Hungarian lifestyle the way my father forced what he thought Canada meant on us. The interior decorating represents 1500 years of brutality, pain and exactitude: the ingredients for tradition. Neatly braided tails of garlic hang in a dried garden from the ceiling, not so much spice as weapon. Shriveled red peppers on a string click together in a breeze, also on high. Onions with braided stalks add to the collaboration. Sometimes flakes of these dried vegetables sift through the air into the food we eat. Along the upper part of the walls rests a shelf, bolted down by the original man of the house. On these shelves sit ceramic jugs – *korsós* – each displaying marks of regional ethnicity. The jug that whistles is the most devious of all. The hollow handle contains an aperture to which you put your lips and blow. When filled with water a high pitched whistle said to be unloved by field mice comes from the jug. In this way, one peasant would purse his lips and tune out the field mice while the rest ate. I find the whole thing ludicrous, including the special thin neck of the jug to prevent mice from falling down into it. This frill blocked mice from sabotaging the instrument of their undoing – agrarian paranoia at its finest.

Dinner is the grease glut of Hungarian cookery: ribs deep-fried, heavily salted, laid out over fried potatoes, a side order of *tepertő* (little pieces of fat done to a crisp) and chicken soup, also some pickled beats in a canning jar. I know what to expect. After dinner I will run to the bathroom and my asshole will squirt with the p.s.i. of a firehose.

I go over to the dog's dish while Mother rummages in the larder. The dog eats dinner with us, that is, in the same room; nothing else stops it from begging. I pull out the old arsenic and heavily dose its meal. The dog eats human food, in this case the leftovers of fried liver and onions that the family relished last night.

We settle down for dinner. I watch the dog with unadulterated malice. Nobody notices the way I survey the beast gorging itself, except for my sister, who watches as intensely as I. The dinner progresses while the dog eats, eats. Long after it should have gone rigid it's still swallowing. I put down my fork and stare at the animal. It keeps eating. When finished with the leftovers the dog wags its tail, completely unharmed. I used to feed it in the days of affection and now it comes begging to me out of habit, or perhaps gloating.

Before anyone reacts I jump on top of it. My hands encircle the dog's neck and squeeze. It opens a sharp triangular grin above my grasp, sticks out a tongue, the family in uproar behind me. I drown their sounds out in the stream of fertile hate that firecracks in my head. I let myself enjoy strangling the dog.

My stepfather and mother unlace and remove their shoes to smack me on the head with them. My stepbrother tries to pry my hands from around the dog's neck, then stabs my knuckles with a fork. My sister excuses herself. Benny uses his fists before I relent.

My dog remains motionless for a moment on its back, heaves, twists a bit and gets to its feet, trots out of the kitchen. I wring my hands, look wildly around for allies. Benny asks what the hell is wrong. "I want to kill that dog," I feverishly reply. My mother swacks me on the head with her shoe again, trying to break my stasis. It works: "For the life of the dog," I say, "bar me from the house."

Lala went on a fast the first time we parted. For a while she subsisted. Lala became a rope trick. Then something killed the music and they found her collapsed along a forsaken hallway in some apartment building. She transferred herself to an institute in Vancouver, then bought a flight to France. Europe reversed only her physical dwindling.

I tried to fix my demolished car, but neither spanners nor wrenches nor big hammers and then even bigger hammers helped. The serviceable parts sold out. The rest went to the wreckers.

I prepared myself for the financial burden of first year university by trying to save the paycheques earned at a local fishfarm over the summer, coming home from the bloody harvest with another creature's scabs under my fingernails. Lala never sent me a single note from France, which gave me license to suppress the memory of her, placing all that shame into my subconscious, where it could do the most harm.

With my father nice and dead, and Benny off playing golf, Mother wandered through bright mornings in the house, looking out windows at the sunny, blue and frothing sea. Mother always had dinner waiting on the table: so I was eating beans. I asked the question in Hungarian and she answered in the same. "Mom, didn't you ever miss Dad when he went away all the time?"

"Are you kidding?" she said, stacking dirty dishes beside the sink. "That new mining job was the best thing that ever happened to us."

"But weren't you even a little curious about what he did in his free time up there?" My mother shrugged. He could have run the River City whorehouse for all she cared. I pushed further: "If I could have gotten him to come back full-time, would that have been good?"

My mother strolled over and cupped my face between her hands: "Gabe, why would you want to curse me like that?" She'd have preferred he left her alone even more. "I don't want to hear anything more about River City, or your father."

"Okay," I acquiesced. She smiled motherly and released my face. While she stacked another five dishes I swallowed two forkfuls of chicken and managed to scoop a mouthful of corn halfway to my lips. Changing the subject, she asked: "Gabe, if I can convince Benny to pay, how would you like to go to Hungary for your last month before university?"

"Oh, I don't know," I hemmed and hawed, remembering childhood trips to the old country when my father still lived, the ledges in the toilets and all the cabbage dishes that proved so inedible.

"It'll help you understand yourself better," my mother said, eyes oval with worry for me and what Lala and I had just finished going through. "It's your culture," she said, "more your culture than America, anyway."

"Canada, Mom. We live in Canada," I pointed out.

"There's no difference," she snorted.

"Yes there is." I then went on to regurgitate some grade twelve social studies. "We have welfare programs and medicare. That's a big cultural difference."

"Well, if that's what you call culture, you'll never experience it."

"Why?"

"Because I'd die before letting you go on welfare. It's disgraceful. Wait until you see what that kind of thinking did to Hungary."

"Everything is Hungary to you," I shook my head. "You're still so wrapped up in Hungary you don't know you've moved to another country. And it's been almost thirty years!"

"A country? You call this a country? Show me where the country is. Show me one true Canadian person."

"That's not the point, mother. Canada isn't its people. This country lets you be whatever you like – Hungarian or Chinese or Italian. And that's the great thing about it; Canada doesn't oblige you to be anything in particular, not even Canadian! Not like in Hungary, where every hill and tree and river and grain of sand reflects some incident that made the Magyars. Here, the landscape doesn't have to become a mirror. And we're better off that way! Better off calling a valley a valley and a prairie a prairie, instead of labeling them so we can identify with it all; we're better off not knowing where we live! It makes me so happy just thinking about all these lakes and mountains I can't name."

"Stupid. Try asking for directions to Toronto without saying Toronto."

"Come on. You know what I mean."

"Yes. And when you go to Hungary you will know what I mean."

And so, after a quick, amicable discussion, Benny and she reserved a return ticket, handed me a suitcase and waved bye-bye from the other side of customs. A month after Lala went to France I left also, for Hungary, all prepared to stumble through a new city, to forget the breakup, the night of the dance and her venomous kiss; but Europe provided no miracle cure for either of us. Luckily, I never ran into her over there, which seems in keeping with my favorite narrative device: anti-climax.

I walked off the Jumbo in Amsterdam and dozed fretfully on the Dutch airport's reclining chairs before braving the terminal's corridors to my boarding gate. Departure to Budapest on Malév, Hungarian airlines flight number #471. The plane shook like an experimental rocket module from take-off to landing, the temperature inside approximating a Swedish sauna. I kept asking the stewardess for birch branches to whip my back with. Instead, she gave me vodka and tomato juice through the entire flight.

I got off at Budapest, Ferihegy Airport number two. Some cousin of mine waited in his rattletrap Trabant to drive me to my great-aunt's. The old lady greeted me with sausages that erupted grease at the touch of a knife. The city had centuries on anything Canadian, architecture crowding my eyes with ornaments, the skulls of angels and kings, trams spitting blue sparks off their overhead cables into the poorly-lit night, the streets full of entrepreneurs in Mercedes and misfit workmen in knitted toques. If not for the jet lag I wouldn't have felt like myself.

Budapest bewildered the bejeebers out of me, therefore allowing some respite from Lala. The alleys of the sixth, seventh and eight districts were impenetrable to the foreign mind. I was foolish enough to get smashed in the local *sörözős* and *borozós* and then try to navigate the streets. Chimney smoke moved from one place to another, enveloping people and not letting go easy. Clocks ticked from somewhere inside open windows protected by masterfully crafted but rusting bars. For the first time I saw iron roses on high gates leading to the courtyards of crumbling mansions converted years ago into general housing. Budapest had a statue on every street. Maidens and Gargoyles, heroes and poets, staunch communist statues of proletariat men and women you could only tell apart by the tits. Garbage cans jumped in my path, stumbled against me in side-streets no more than five feet wide. Art Deco buildings peppered with bullet holes from recently as 1956 or far back as World War Two. Balconies sheared off the sides of walls from bomb blasts. I wondered if some of these holes didn't date back further, to World War One or that other glorious failure of a revolution: 1848. Every armed conflict the Hungarians ever took part in since the temporary routing of the Turkish forces at Nándorfehérvár in 1456 ended in their total defeat and subjugation. Many of the city's statues were of people who'd failed to free the country: monuments to defeat. My kind of place.

The Saint Stephen's basilica extended a bigger welcome to bats than humans. Pigeons flapped under the cupola in the wan sunbeams falling through the stained glass. Chipped paint, darkened frescoes, mouldy air, a crucifixion in every nook and cranny.

In the back chapel of the basilica I put a twenty forint piece into a machine that lit up Saint Stephen's incorrupt hand, for ten seconds. The old lady stationed there told me to drop another twenty forint piece in for more viewing pleasure, but I told her looking at a piece of wood carved into a fist was fine the first time; you can't tell the same joke twice. She crossed herself; I snickered.

The brown Danube looked thick and chunky, a soup you could eat with a fork.

Up at the castle the flowers and leaves were budding. A rain shower sent most tourists into cafés to eat marzipan and drink espresso. The palace was huge: pillars, porticos and ornamented windows. Copper statues oxidized green showed nobles partaking in royal hunts, taming horses, brandishing swords, all of them decked out in flowing robes, billowing dresses for the bare-breasted women. The copper clothing on the statues frozen in another wind, one that manipulates metal after its own fashion, a wind with no allegiance to real meteorological conditions.

The most conspicuous statue of all was that of King Mátyás, the most famous Hungarian sovereign. Hungary's golden age lasted about five hundred years – your historical equivalent of fifteen Warholian minutes – and after that it was under Ottoman, Austrian or Russian overlordship.

The city was also full of dogs, big beasts – Dobermans, German Shepherds, Rotweillers and Afghans. Nobody cleaned up after them. Budapest was a minefield of shit. Stop walking when you look up at buildings. Pause when you speak to someone beside you. Don't hail taxis in mid-stroll. Keep your eyes to the ground, ignore the monuments, ignore the churches, ignore the city, unless you want to be up to your shins in crap.

My father's disdainful relationship with our dog meant I never saw him pet it for a good nine years out of its fourteen, if not more. Though time was when my father still had some hope for the household pet, that it might become a 'real canine,' like the kind he'd hunted with in younger, predatory days, when he was more uncomfortable in the hide wrapped around him and took on the snow and sleet with a rifle strapped to the back, when he fired on big game. Later he pretended the arthritis hurt so bad that only a shoehorn got him into an overcoat. But while we slept he'd roam the house like a panicked security guard. You should have seen the calisthenics he performed with my mother unawares.

"Don't tell her I'm off to the bar," he said. "Tell her I'm sleeping in my bedroom. Tell her anything except the truth."

My mother knew. She just started smoking more.

Our dog was unbecoming as far as Dad – may Satan rest his soul – ruled. And since he refused to admit to abnormality or defects within the family, the dog didn't exist for him. Its existence was validated only when it ingratiated itself: when it shat on his slippers, chewed the neck of his guitar, ate his tobacco.

Christmas time. The stars wore pajamas, the moon a nightcap, fresh snow sprawling the ground, the sky filled to the brim with ink.

We gorged on winter dinner, all quiet over the place, except for the smacking, chomping and crunching from our mouths. Conversation broke to nil.

We'd left the dog outside so we wouldn't have to endure its begging. It began to howl, which, for our dog, means a prolonged yelp. In the summer, a whining dog is something easy to tune out without a twinge of remorse, but in the winter that's an impossible thing. In the winter it bothers your conscience. The dog's cry gets right under your fillings. And so it happened with us, because after fifteen minutes of high-pitched wailing my father told one of us to let the dog in. My sister opened up the door to a whirl of snowflakes and the wiener dog trundled in like a dignitary, swinging that ass.

We went back to the food like farm animals.

My dog, still young at the time, saw handouts weren't forthcoming so it began to play with our feet – nipping gently at our socks with those baby teeth it had. Nobody paid much attention until my father's face went up like he'd been smacked with a wooden spoon. He let out a shout of pain and punched his foot full throttle into the dog. The dog shot, with loud yapping and tail between legs, straight out from under the table. It's pointy teeth had punctured some blood vessel in my father's foot and blood pumped all over the floor. My father in disbelief. My mother running for first-aid.

Only after dinner did we discover that my father's reflex kick had broken one of the dog's back legs. It lay in a corner with a snivel and a cower.

We took the dog to the vet. He expressed surprise that the dog let us pick it up. "Most dogs with a broken leg will snap at you, rip you up, if you try touching them. It's an instinctive response for protection."

It cost eight hundred dollars to have the dog repaired. Medical covered father.

Whoops! Ready for another chronology shift? Torn between rambling and ordering a narrative, I'll always opt for the former, as it involves less work. Besides, relating Lala's and my final meeting before I've even begun to speak of her return from France, the second phase of our relationship in Victoria, the slam-bang breakup that followed, and the year between then and the scene below, proves conclusively that one remembers a past romance by theme rather than timeline. (My favorite kind of logic, as you might have noticed, is the circular kind.)

The last night I'd ever see Lala alive I got drunk at the party and walked like a three-legged dog around the house I rented in Victoria with two fellow students. It seemed that all around were horrible grins interspersed with teeth: a hazy labyrinth of white dental work, jokester lips and laughter. Everywhere laughter. You could almost see letters spelling ha-ha and tee-hee swarming in the air. I was always underneath tittering faces for some reason, always looking up at the funnies. Winter spooked around outside, frosting on its jurisdiction like dog-piss on fire hydrants. That's all I knew about it: a rogue winter, unfriendly, unapproachable and territorial. A winter I never got to know personally. We held the party to celebrate my forced departure from university.

I chased a cat around the house, trying to get it out. My mother taught me to hate cats in company, in front of others. Of course, she hated them in private, too. Not me. I remember the cat was white and I tripped over legs trying to get at it. Nobody else cared. They told me to stop but every time I saw the cat I gave chase and the sure-footed beast eluded me in the crowd.

Boys poured olive oil onto the floor in front of the fridge so they could watch people slip off their feet when they went for beers. By the end of the night everyone's clothes were smeared, the kitchen a slick.

The year since that second try at togetherness had effected a chrysalis for the worse. We turned up emotionally obsolete. Lala reintroduced herself to me and the cat's tail slipped from my grasp, the shape and quality of her lips, eyes, nose and hair catching me in the nick of memory.

"Gabe, Trixy tells you to leave the cat alone," she said.

"I was told by someone once – I don't remember who but I think it was at a party – that if you twist a cat's head counter-clockwise exactly three times it pops efficiently off. I couldn't believe that guy," I mumbled as if the words had gone to egg-yolk in my mouth. She had a waif's way of turning up her lip, the way only a true ex-anorexic/present suicide-in-the-making could do. She formed a gun with one of her hands and pointed it at me, let the thumb fall down once, raised it. The thumb fell again. She turned and left.

I stood alone in the kitchen, leaned against the counter, let a solution of beer dribble into my mouth, smoked absently as if only my mouth needed the cigarette while the rest of my body had long ago walked away from it, like a smile left on the x-ray machine after the skeleton's stepped down.

Lala had the white cat in her arms. I'd almost given up the chase.

"Here," she said, dropping it onto me. The cat stuck its claws through my shirt into my chest and hung there staring up into my eyes. "That guy over there said that if you didn't stop chasing the cat that he was going to shit-kick you." She flashed a low-stakes sneer.

"Who's that?" I slurred, sounding concerned, though I was too drunk to feel the flight impulse. "Are you going to beat me up again?"

Lala didn't acknowledge the comment. "What are you going to do with the cat?"

"Pet it," I said, gathering my arms around the animal and, opening the sliding glass doors in the room, walking out onto the porch. Only the rain knocked on the door. We stood in the water from the winter sky for a while, me petting the cat. When the feline landed on all fours Lala and I began to maul each other romantically.

The rest of the night remains in fragments. I slipped my hands under her shirt in the dark basement while footsteps pounded on the floor above us. I tried to take her shirt off, to fuck her in the cellar, right there. She pushed my hands away and said, "No." I turned, not angrily, but like someone who'd finished with, and failed at, a risk with a ninety-nine percent chance of failure attached to it to begin with. I ran upstairs, maybe looking for the cat again. The wine, whisky and beer went magma in my stomach. I carried drunkenness with me like an igloo.

We met again in the bathroom. I kissed her between every couple of words she tried to speak.

"Gabe ... I think we ... should try and talk ... stop it! I want to be the one in ... control this ... time."

"Exactly. Yes. First-rate idea. I need some beer," I said, taking a mood swing for the manic. "And a cigarette." I turned from the neck I'd been kissing and ran into the kitchen, groping for beer among the million condiment bottles in the fridge – the bottles spilling and rolling onto the floor – while simultaneously trying to light a cigarette. She leaned against the sink in the bathroom where I'd left her, trying feelings out on the face in the mirror. The party slowly drained off. I found a beer.

The minute she moved out of kissing distance she became extinct. I went to the living room, where a maniac with a pig shave sat staring at his hands. The brother of one of my roommates, he was training for the army in Esquimalt, taking some unarmed combat course. The guy stared at the palms of his hands like they were privy to knowledge he wasn't. He was adjunct to his hands. I sat down beside him and took a long drink.

"They make me do a hundred push ups on my fists. They make me stand still and punch me in the stomach. I have to keep standing straight, but the straighter I stand the harder they hit. If I complain or grunt I have to do another hundred push-ups."

"I don't get it," I said. "Why do they train you guys? They should just send in the air force and strafe the shit out of everything."

"But they need us to go in afterwards as an occupying force. Without us they can't win."

"But they can occupy the place with anyone once everyone's been bombed to death. They could even use pacifists, for God's sake!" I stood up. "You're wasting time with this stuff."

He shook a muddled head angrily, glared at me for a minute. I stepped back, swamped in his savagery. He returned to his hands.

The party came to a last stop. Guests disembarked, haphazardly, through the front door. Bodies leaned heavily against the railing, some smiling, heads fallen forward, others with halos of sweat shining from their foreheads. Poor boys who didn't shake their dinks hard enough had spots of pee the size of quarters on the front of their pants. All of them left soiled, with distressed livers, stains either of liquor, puke or food covering their clothes.

Lala slept with me, as it turned out.

"No. I want to be in control."

Naked and rough-housing, we pushed each other around, palms to the chest, banging into my bookshelf. The sour lining of alcohol unshakable from our mouths. I got her out onto the porch, into the cold rain. I tried for tactile sex, our bodies falling together like freight. I tried for two forms streamlined down to muscle, arching from each other, glandular, feral. No more of the personality business, no more traits, distinguishing features. But she shivered in the winter and put a stop to it, arms locked to her chest, fists against her cheeks.

"No," she said. "Forget it." During the five second walk back to bed we took totally separate routes, through totally separate regions.

She kissed me on the neck and I took her face in my hands and tried to nudge it down, down. She took her hands off my face. And when she finally went down it was brief, despite my attempts to keep her going.

"Not tonight," she said. "Tonight I want to be the one."

"Control is something you take," I said. "It's not a word. It's an action." And I pushed her over onto her back.

She was too dry. Long ago, our first time around, she'd close up in an unyielding fist, as if her biology had its own programme, neither of us able to dope out why. Tonight it was probably a result of confusion, drinking's dehydration, our bodies forced into positions we'd long since weaned ourselves from.

"Don't," Lala commanded.

"I'll find something," I said, getting off the bed, drunker now than at any other point in the evening. I went into the kitchen and came upon the bottle of olive oil, carried it back to the bedroom with me, parted her legs.

"I don't know," she gulped, but I was already doing it, pouring the olive oil in, the open neck of the bottle at the edge of her labia, inside a millimeter. And then I had her turn around on all fours. "You said you didn't like doing it this way. That you felt like you were degrading me." She reminded me of an old admission.

"It doesn't matter anymore," I replied.

"No," Lala predicted. "I guess it won't." Then she turned around, pushed me onto my back and climbed on top.

Afterwards, we lay entwined. My head rested below the hollow of her throat.

"Tell me," she said. "You used to love me?"

"Yes. And you loved me?"

"I loved you like a favorite song. That you never get tired of, though you play it over and over again. No, I loved you more than that."

"How much?"

She chortled. "I loved you more than Einstein loved the atom."

The darkness pasted itself to my lips, eyelids. The sheets, being the exception to my blindness, lay like fields of snow.

"And you?" she asked. "How much did you love me?"

"I loved you more than myself."

"That's lame."

"I loved you," I said, thinking. "I loved you more than Hitler loved exterminating races."

She turned to face the darkness, her essence one of pure exhaustion. "I always think nobody could say things like that. That their mind would stop the words from coming out. Gabe ... only a monster uses the Holocaust for that kind of comparison."

"I was just being accurate."

"You asshole," she said. The sweep of her blinking eyelashes tingled on my neck long after the lids had closed.

"I wish," I sighed, her fingers pressing down on my arm. "I wish I had something definite to say about that."

Over two years ago now. I haven't had sex since.

Lala left the next morning to return to San Francisco. She died there. San Francisco is where Lala became dead or where she engineered her death – a death, like her life, untranslatable with ambivalence. She shacked up with a boy, a greasy-haired thing who provided her with the old woebegone mattress they slept on in the kitchen of her tiny apartment. He was someone, mutual friends later informed me, who treated her very poorly. This came as no surprise. What did surprise me was when one of Lala's old cronies in Oxbow said that Lala had written her saying she didn't love him. *She didn't love him.* That might have explained her suicide to everyone else's mind, but it wasn't Lala. If Lala went with someone, had sex with them regularly, boredom and pity played no part. *Lala never lived apart from love.* It was her peculiar syndrome. Through the act of being unfaithful she proved her love to herself and to you, carrying the guilt afterwards like a four-leaf clover. The perfect nude, Lala put nakedness on rather than uncovering herself. On the other hand, she told me once that infidelity let her experience a nudity that left her stripped down to a fundamental love. Even when in the midst of open betrayal, her lips panting with lust against the neck of the temporary tryst, uninhibited, out of her head with enjoyment of the fuck, she never lapsed out of love with you. Quite the opposite, actually. The emotional difference between her one-night fling and her long-term lover realized itself only through constant testing. And so, I can't hazard a fiction to account for her last months. Either she posted lies or had changed or was already dead. Maybe she understood, finally, that all styles fitted her incompletely. And what real thing of Lala jumped her from the bridge I do not know.

Shortly after the night of the party, I sent Lala a letter bursting with information, guilt and misgivings. The envelope came back to me with an added cat-scratch on the front: *Return to sender. I'm dead.* The letter, naturally, was unopened. The handwriting needed no verification. I can't remember now whether I'd dated it before or after the time of her death.

The Tottenfoggel Hotel was Chinatown's charnel house, the roost where pigeons went to die, the place where bygones were truly bygones; it was a lesson on the secret death, the death you can keep hidden for years, for longer than time. The Tottenfoggel Hotel stood for the perfection of disrepair. Jazz notes scattered from the speakers of the Chinese grocery stores and butcher shops one floor down as if the musicians hadn't yet had time to nail them down. You breathed up the merchandise of spice shops.

And if I was lucky it was night and I would be upstairs in the Tottenfoggel Hotel, on the top floor in red brick. I'd walk on tiptoe across a carpet of hollow, flimsy pigeon bones, stirring up the old feathers. I'd clutch an umbrella of dope smoke among the broken glass, cracked plaster, pitted wood floors. The ceiling above me was caved in from water damage. In narcosis. In a place where the immigrants had gone to smoke opium after months of carrying railway ties or placing posts in the Empress Hotel's foundations.

Most of the top floors of the buildings on this block waited in emptiness. Pauline (down with her boyfriend's pickup to help move me home) and I balanced on brick walls, carrying flashlights and whisky, a little bag of grass. We saw the carcasses of cats, rats, and the ever-present pigeons. We came to love a glass door with etchings of birds and flowers in it. Pauline found a pile of yellowed writing paper that she took with her. Dreams came in wireless through these walls, remote as ham radio. There was nothing left to renovate.

We sat on an old brick balcony facing a derelict courtyard. Too dark to see anything except what fell between the flashlight's beam. I turned to Pauline.

"I saw Lala last week." Whispering in the dark. "I think for the last time." Pauline said nothing. The flashlight played across the household relics in the courtyard, a washtub, a water pump, a tricycle. "She asked me how much I'd loved her." Pauline leaned her head back and drank, a line of bubbles rising in the bottle. "I want to tell you what I wanted to say to her, but didn't." Pauline lit a cigarette and passed it to me. I took a deep suck. "I wanted to tell her, to say to Lala, that I loved her more than I could."

I love you more than I can.

Fear is its own childhood sweetheart, coming around passively, brutal as pigeons shitting on cities. I go visit a doctor who has elbows full of psoriasis, the way I also have psoriasis on my elbows. Psoriasis comes for me once a year in a little annual event, an anniversary of sorts, and always when things seem to be at the best. Psoriasis is my fair-weather friend.

The doctor doesn't seem nervous enough for a psoriasis freak but that's what he is. A chain link fence around the home; inside: a large white dog called Piranesi by his master. The white dog holds mountains, sheep and a contempt for wolves in its blood, memories coded away in the genes that no fence, city or dry dog-food can erase. The dog rises massive, taller than me by a good two feet when up on hind legs. But the teeth are soft, almost bovine, and look clumsy, made more for crunching bone than tearing flesh. My life will maybe owe its continuity to this morphological detail. "Come on in," the doctor says. "The dog shall not bite you."

"Are you sure?" I ask.

"Let me call my daughter. She will help us."

The daughter comes down to try and hold the dog but she's a match-stick compared to the animal. The mastiff shrugs her off the moment my feet defile its territory, and attacks. It's waited for this moment all life long. Even with the two of them acting as buffer, interposing their bodies between myself and Piranesi, I'm thrice bitten. The world wires down around me, becoming all claw, fang, fur, growl and irrationality. The fence towers too high for me to vault. I put my back against the wall of the house, keeping the dog in sight. The teeth leave my left hand mangled, my right arm scored with a careful imprint of the dog's dental pattern. Every hole oozes blood, which stains my shirt, runs down my forearm. The doctor and his daughter race headlessly around, trying to keep the devil from mauling me. But they are only as successful as humanly possible. Still, if not for them I'd have my jugular rent from me. Someone finally opens the door to their house – the wife, I think – and I sprint up the stairs. The dog chances one last sinking of its teeth into my heel. I bequeath my shoe to its appetites. Not satiated with the offering, it snaps at my sock. But for the grace of my reflexes there go I. Then I stagger inside, wild-eyed at all the blood on my hands. *All the blood on my hands.*

I am now terrified of dogs. Add it to the official list.

After the doctor's tetanus shot and biblical oath on Piranesi's disease-free veterinary record we become seated before dinner. My left hand can still manipulate a fork. Frank is a good doctor, an old DP Hungarian like my deadified father, another refugee of '56. Canada offered asylum. He brought a violin along and a silver stethoscope that belonged to his Jewish father, murdered in one of the Nazi concentration camps. Speaking for the dog, they all apologize. I tell them I can't leave their house until the pet is dead. All laugh except me. Frank, as a friend of the family, lets me come to his house whenever my problems require a physician. This way I avoid the clinic lineups and waiting rooms that the proletariat must suffer. We sit down to dinner and Frank starts in on his favorite topic: Marxism.

"You know," he says, brandishing a chunk of sausage on the end of his fork, "I don't understand these Marxists." He lets words fall and spit from his mouth as he chews loud and wet. "They say that if Christ foresee all the bad things done in his name he would not have live. You can say same for Mister Marx."

We nod like trainees. Frank never attends church but still insists on his Hungarian mother's Catholicism. Arguing with him at this point is like arguing with notes erupting from a musical instrument. And all I want to discuss is my spermatozoa!

"So they talk about the harm certain people in the Catholic church have done. But look at what Marxists did! They say those weren't real Marxists, that they didn't do good Marxism. So, I suppose, what some of the popes did wasn't Catholic either?"

He stops to swallow.

"Bad Catholic popes, you say, like bad Marxist Stalins. The Inquisition, the Gulags, forced starvations, purges," he gestures with encompassing arms, "all the same kind of things. But they don't blame Mister Marx for Russia or China or Cuba, oh no, they blame leaders. Marxism is still okee-dokee. But they are first to lineup to say Catholicism is bad because Inquisition and witch hunts, not because of bad Catholic leaders. Those Marxists make one law for themselves and one for everyone else. And then. . . ."

He swallows again.

"Before *Perestroika*, they say at least there still was food," he roars. "Then why not say that at least before the British left India there is peace. I think they forget the millions who die of starvation in the twenties because of Communism, or die now because Communism couldn't leave anything behind, like at least the Tsar did. These revolutions last as long as the previous regime's treasury, no longer, and when they collapse? Chaos. Why don't they say instead: at least before the Tsar was killed there is food. And what they did to Eastern Europe, to Hungary! *Uramisten*! *Szegény hazám*! Pass the *kolbász*, please."

We offer heaping plates of pig sausage, potatoes, home-grown yellow paprikas, pickled beats, cucumber salad. He refills and continues.

"Hungary had a Communist after the First World War, you know? Yes, Béla Kun." He belches, mouth stuffed past the safety valves. "Didn't even last a year! But long enough to steal as much things as he could and run away and leave the country in shit."

"The treaty of Trianon! What a tragedy! Two thirds of Hungary's land taken away! Fifty percent! Ridiculous! Name another country of such misfortune. Land was given to Austria! And they lost the war too! Why do the British and Americans and French decide to give them our land? And Romania. A shameful thing. Romania: the first to join the Nazis and the first to traitor. As a reward, they get Transylvania. Two million Hungarians live in Transylvania. The largest minority population in Europe. But do we ever hear about that? Oh, no. Never." Pickles crackle cleanly between his teeth. "Under Ceaucescu's regime and the current one Hungarians persecuted. Not allowed to publish in our language. Our signs taken down. We are blamed whenever problems happen for the country. An old man killed for talking Hungarian in the street. You know something?"

Yes, I do. He's going to tell me about how ethnic Hungarians in Transylvania retained their culture better than the rest of Hungary did.

"They speak better Hungarian there than anywhere."

"Really?"

"Yes, really." He nods and spears a fork through a hunk of *kolbász*, lifts it, spears it again through a pickled beat, a potato and a raw carrot, puts the whole smorgasbord into his mouth. My hand still throbs. The dog's teeth flash in front of my face, white, pure, strong. My arm registers every tooth mark like a new tattoo.

"I not excuse for what Horthy did with the fascists. You know Horthy came after Béla Kun? But Horthy died with nothing more than what his father give him. Yes he had an estate, but he didn't use his politics to make money." The doctor blusters. "And he never stole. Yes, he was a fascist." The doctor stops eating and stares out the window. "He killed my father...."

"Everyone blames Hungary for siding with Germany. But what choice do we have? Tell me? Side with the Communists, the Russians? We see what Communism do after the First World War. The Germans kill Jews in their camps but the Russians kill everyone in theirs, including themselves. The Germans gave us back Transylvania. Who should we choose, which side? What choice did we have?" He rants on, but his voice has lost all conviction. In the name of the Father ... I think of that prayer we all recognize, religious or not. "What choice did ... my people ... have?"

None, I think to myself. Except maybe to fight them both, I guess. But that would have been suicide. Not that suicide's necessarily the more evil of the three choices.

After dinner ends we retire to the living room and Unicum sipping. He asks what brings me to these straits.

"I want to have a sperm test."

"What?" he says, leaning forward, very interested.

"I want to know if I'm impotent."

"Why?"

"It worries me," I say, lying. "I've had ... well, chlamydia two and a half years ago and I'd like to know."

"Come with me," he says, rising.

Byzantine iconography adorns his room, back from times when artists went anonymously. One of the bedroom windows covers its cracked pane with duct tape. The bed is walnut, king-size. Hand-painted urns and vases from Transylvania top the dressers and night tables. He looks outside the bedroom, down the hall, nervously, for the approach of his spouse, and then quickly reaches under the bed's mattress and pulls out a scientifically thumbed-through best-of '82 centerfold collection, and takes a glass vial from a medical kit at the foot of the bed.

"Go into the bathroom," he says, slightly embarrassed. "Don't wet the pictures."

What have you made me do, Pauline? I think. I nod at him all the way while backing into the bathroom, smut rag in one hand and test tube in the other.

Pauline's boyfriend gripped my neck in his hand while I stared side to side like the last of the mad scientists. Shadows on the walls outside Pauline's mobile home paled in comparison to us, while a bright light on the end of a stripped and bitumen-cured telephone pole raved mad with wattage. The summer mosquitoes winged it.

He was a strange gent, Pauline's boyfriend, or, as of about ten minutes before, her ex-boyfriend. In the space of ten minutes he'd gone from belonging to lonely. Inside, Pauline growled, throwing his clothes out the window. The windy night lifted the clothes into the air, pulled them along the ground. The wind had a body to roll.

My arrival came on five minutes too early. I mumbled hello and he pinned me to the trailer by the neck. We stood like that, until I gave up on trying to escape and hung down my head, looking up at his face from under my eyebrows. He turned his profile up at the window. "Crazy bitch," he said, and shrugged. The animated and bewitched laundry and the curses of Pauline scrambled out the open window beside us, the clothing itself bolting from Pauline's wrath. The gentleness of his hand bewildered me. I experienced no difficulties. The choke-hold was a contradiction: true in form but lacking in content. Some errant articles of clothing twined around our legs and the night sang lyrically as bluegrass. "I'll never see you again," he said. "You were like a brother who embarrassed me." I turned my head from him, offering my best side. "Forget those stories I told you," he went on, not knowing I'd never taken them for gospel. "But let me tell you. Selfishness, that's what cowardice is, the ultimate form of selfishness."

Then he let go. His hands dropped to either side like the bride of Frankenstein. I found him unpredictable, but he knew my next moves, all of them, in succession. My body suffered from adrenaline, a high-octane that hits the joints but quickly atrophies the muscles. Clothes jumped around in the wind, striking-out like kung fu.

The boyfriend watched Pauline's white hand flashing at the window. He walked back to his truck. My face turned away from him but my eyes tagged along. "You'll never change," he yelled back to me. "That's one thing to be sure of, anyway. That's one thing." His truck moved without landscape, bottles in the back rolling together, irreconcilable bedfellows.

I squatted down on the rocks and rested my chin in both hands. I could smell the dirt under my nails, my face tired and bored as a bloodhound's.

In Hungary I met a cousin who wore his pants around his narrow chest. His black beret looked tattered enough for the poor in spirit, and the undershirt seemed to have sometime or other been loaned to teething puppies. His face was sunken, slim and pathetic, mooncalf eyes drowning in eternal dissatisfaction, like he'd missed out on his due, like all he could think about was what he didn't have, what he didn't get. He was a thirty-five year old virgin through his own fault, ordinarily nothing to be ashamed of except his stack of porn magazines neared to bursting the roof. He ate with a suicidal mania, huge gibbering mouthfuls, but never gained an ounce – metabolism like a blast furnace. Instead of cutlery, a spade and pitchfork rested to either side of his plate.

This cousin of mine lived in Miskolc, the grim industrial heartland of Hungary, where the tastes were right-wing conservative to an extreme working-class degree, little Hitlers hitting the barbershop for their weekly buzz-cuts. His house was completely empty except for chairs, a table, pictures on the walls and the girlie mags. He spent most of his time sweeping up. On about a common ancestor, he pointed to an old graphic of her face, behind a cracked pane of glass. "She was Dutch," he said. "The genius."

"What do you mean she was a genius?" I asked.

"Well, a genius. It was recognized. Everyone in the town knew. I inherited it from her. Maybe you got a touch of it, too."

"But how did she prove it?"

"Well, she was a genius. You know, the kind of person they call a genius? A very gifted person."

"But how can you tell if she didn't prove it in any way?"

"No. Everyone recognized it. They all knew her as a genius."

He couldn't understand my confusion. For him, the blood he carried, the genetics, justified his self-opinion, proof enough. He tapped me with those horrible, insane eyes that said we were bonded, part of a process. I got fucked in the ass every time those eyes leeched me. I wanted to knock him to the floor, to perch on his ribs like a two-legged nightmare and scream obscenities into his tiny, frightened face, to herd his wasted nakedness through the streets of Miskolc with bullwhip and buckshot, to see the look on him when I did that, to smash with the truth.

A fool's errand. I sat by the table and shook inwardly, outwardly, beside windows covered with wax paper to prevent peeping from the street.

"Does that drunk guy still live next door?"

"Shhh," he said, putting finger to lips. "Yes, he still lives next door. Just released from jail."

"What happened to him?"

"He killed a woman who lived down the street. He banged her head against the telephone pole outside my front door until it split. I heard the whole thing. Such a tragedy."

Lifting the espresso to my lips I dipped the tip of my tongue into it to scald. I glowered at him, much as Pauline's boyfriend had looked at me.

My cousin had the sorrow of mourning on his face, but resigned, as if there was nothing he could have done, nothing he could do.

"Luckily, I managed to sneak to my door and lock it while he was hitting her. Then I felt safe. But now they've let him out. So make sure he doesn't hear us," he said.

I rose from the table to leave, noting his attire. At the next costume party I shall debut as him, easy.

When Lala got back from her transatlantic sabbatical, and she and I restarted our relationship, we tried regulating sex with condoms instead of the pill. Condoms give sex a polite formality that's worth investigating. We rarely failed to take the brief pause from foreplay to put one on, to capture the moment in latex. My preference tended towards sheep-gut prophylactics, but as a sex ed. teacher once told me, "They didn't do the sheep much good," so how the Hell could they have helped Lala and I? We were far inferior to sheep. No, it had to be artificial for our sakes.

By then, I'd moved to Victoria and was beginning the second year of my ultimately fruitless attempt at a university education. I think I majored in Geography. Odds are it was Geography. Or Sociology. Or Environmental Science. One of those types of courses. But it could even have been Canadian Literature or Women's Studies for all I know. Mostly, my time there frittered away in a medley of shooters. It was a golden age for shooters. I remember them all: blow job, orgasm, prairie fire, rusty nail, paralyser, cotton swab, fuzzy nipple, sex on the beach, hot dog, arsenic, hemlock, cyanide. The list of cocktails read like poetry business. I even snorted tequila a few times. It cauterized my sinuses. I had it all then; I was flying business class. In the end a dean's vacation in the middle of the third year terminated my calling to such hallowed life, to the ivory towers of higher learning. I went home to Oxbow and never came back, got hired at the pulp mill and the pay-cheques annexed my life. But somewhere in the vacuum between starting university and leaving it came a second phase with Lala, which lasted all of one semester. She liked to call it the second coming, but I was trying to keep my mind on acts of love and leave off the negative influence of raunch and religious profanity. This was the brand of wagon I was on: a bumpy ride, no seat belts. Lala was free to do as she pleased. And she did.

I managed to sneak through my first year, and went back to Oxbow for a summer of student work at the Pulp Mill, earning money for another round of tuition and booze. The ringing phone wrecked an otherwise perfect December. It began with something that clean – a perfect electronic blip. I picked it up. "Hello?"

"Gabe? It's me, Lala."

My heart went through the floor like barbells. "How's your leg?" Her laughter splashed.

"It's fine, Gabe. Do you want to meet sometime? I've been here for two weeks. I'm working at a language school, teaching French. Do you want to meet sometime?" She repeated herself, still laughing. Outside, some teens had tied a toboggan to the back of a station wagon and they motored on it, two riding at a time, faster than fifty kilometers an hour, back and forth along the street. Their total scream influenced me adversely.

"I'd love to."

From there on down the road was steep, stony and buttered with vaseline.

Who would have thought, second time through the mill, that Lala's and my sexual, emotional and culinary proclivities would come under arrested development. Lala behaved like a totalitarian.

Forget that. Lala truly sought a male mother: me.

The spontaneity of attempted rape caused our first divorce. Our second death would come from the opposite source: unremitting repetition.

Eight beers later I wish for the friendship of dilaudid. I've finally gotten in touch with Pauline after hours of trying. She won't answer my questions in full. Since conversation can't happen, I drill her on her present situation, on the what-you-up-tos, the with-whos, the whereabouts. Her monosyllables trickle through ice: nothing, nobody, nowhere, gotta go. Most likely desensitized by narcotics, Pauline regresses to flower child. Her talk, when she's like this, makes me lonelier, so I put down the phone on her niceties.

I set up the chair under the lamp: a kind of wooden wagon wheel hanging from the ceiling. The fake candles on its perimeter are actually electric-powered glass bulbs. Pauline talked about buying some velvet Elvis paintings, but it's too late for new decor now – the apartment has grown sacrosanct around me – even though Elvis's overweight Vegas years are my favorite. That great big stoned mass of crooning succulent fat with the white suit and rhinestones represents something flawless: the quintessential idiot. No ambiguities bungled him up then, no hidden possibilities. He was plain to see. And Elvis's lean younger years could never have hoped to match that level of refinement. I'd love to have the Vegas Elvis as my mascot. I'd get him to burble some nonsense every now and then. I'd get him to sweat for my friends. I'd get him to be beautiful.

Positioning myself under the lamp, I kick away the chair. The first swing into the dark stretches my wrists like putty but as I proceed my muscles grow accustomed to the strain. I kick my legs forward and then back. The lamp performs like a perfect vehicle. Flakes of plaster fall from the ceiling into my hair. I'm a swinging chimp. But I don't chatter for fear of waking the neighbors. My pants and underwear slip halfway down my ass from the performance. But I just keep on swinging and swinging, getting the lamp rocking around. One thing you can say for the seventies, they built things tough. Maybe they expected someone to innovate sex hanging from this lamp. My navel puckers, sending waxy kisses to the fans. I wish I had a tail to hang from; it would free my hands to open beers. But slaving away to this motion preempts the importance of drunkenness.

I'm maintaining a grip, waiting for the roof to cave.

I met Bill one time before the shoot-out in the shower.

The siren on Number Nine went off and I participated in a communal groan with the rest of C crew. Then I stumbled into the chamber behind the calendar stacks, safety goggles on, caught in boiling steam, sweat soaking through my pants, shirt, socks.

It was the saddest thing when a machine had a wet-end break. The whole perfect production stopped and we were left with the pieces. We had to run. Pick up the airhose. Blow the break out of the stacks. Pull the larger slabs out from under the rollers. Spraying stove oil at drums moving at thousands of feet per minute and the stove oil coming back into your hair, mouth. The boss ran down from his office, job security depending on getting production back quickly, every second a loss of a hundred dollars. But sometimes the machine was down and down and down. We'd thread the sheet through and in fifteen minutes the paper was being flung in every direction again. So much paper you couldn't push it all down into the beater pit before the next break. You ran back and forth from the stacks to the winder to the reel controls. The stacks jumped and shook around you like a deranged priestess. Red hot scabs spat off the rolls right onto your skin, burning holes in clothes. Twelve-hour shift and no time to sit down once. You'd walk out with spring-cushion knees and eat your lunch during the drive home.

Some massive chunk of paper had gotten stuck under the safety guard right at the bottom of the calendar stacks and the old Italian (that's Forty-Four Magnum Bill don't you know) was shouting: "Salami bitch! Salami bitch!" I'm scraping the stacks, all the while being hit with jets of steam so hot they scald. "Salami bitch! Salami bitch!" Every other swear-word was enunciated correctly – Fuck, cunt, shit, cocksucker, etc. – but nobody ever taught Bill how to say "son of a bitch" properly, so he had his own little syntactical invention.

Later on, when everything was running on schedule again, I took a break from rounds and went into the doghouse. Bill sat there smoking a cigarette. "You know," he said to me, "my wife always tells me to quit smoking. 'Stop those cigarettes or you'll die.' And I always tell her the same thing."

"What's that?" I asked, getting a glass of water.

"I tell her the graveyard's full of people who didn't smoke."

"And what does she say to that?" God, I'd make such a good straight-man for a comedy routine.

"She says I've lost my love for life." And he thought deeply on this.

Ever since the night of the attempted burglary, I've been Pauline's sugar daddy, but without the benefits usually incurred. In fact I'm more her private benefactor, a patron of the opium arts. I buy out the tab she's run up in the two weeks previous to events in the widow's home and bring her money so that she can get her narcotics. This ends Pauline's need for larceny, or so she upholds. My mill workers' wages are plentiful: I've no car, no wife, no kids, no mortgage, and, most importantly, no ambition – none of the regular expenditures that most of my coworkers ill afford. I budget a shoddy apartment, rust-trap car and the rest is for feeding the fire. I easily keep up to Pauline's dealer's prescriptions. And the amount she takes never rises. Strangely enough, it never rises.

Pauline enters the house with a cigarette at the lips, dangling it like a handkerchief she might have dropped in the more correct seductions of one hundred years ago. She carries a load of unfolded laundry just taken off the line in her arms, an impression of the wind still in the clothes. Pauline's face wears winter well, nothing but fair health and the bloom of youth to her countenance – certainly no longer the look of a committed junkie. I sit in a niche of shadow, where two walls meet. Her eyes tilt. Everything about the day outside spells a world of calm. I tap a roll of bills on the tabletop.

"Hi, Pauline." I tap the bills again. "Latest installment."

"Oh hi," she says, dropping laundry on the counter. "I didn't see you in your dark little corner of the world. Just put the money on top of the fridge. I'm going to fold these clothes."

"Cold to be hanging laundry, no?"

"Well ... sunny so I thought ... just such a beautiful day that I wanted to hang laundry. Save on the meter too. Who knows?" She swishes past, down the sardine-can hallway, into the innards of her mobile home. She laughs. For some reason, she laughs. When putting the money on the fridge I notice there's cash still there, bills that look conspicuously like ones I left, the same denominations. I rearrange the fridge magnets. "Pauline?" A mumble carries from down the hall. "Are you okay?" I ask. "I brought the money, but you don't seem too worried, y'know? Is everything's all right? I mean with the drugs and everything? Want me to bring more coin?"

"Why not make us ham sandwiches?" comes her answer. "Just stocked up the fridge." She sings Christmas carols out of season. I reach for mustard, avoiding Grey Poupon to grasp the French's.

"Make sure you use the French's," she yells.

"We're made for each other," I murmur.

Ever tried putting on makeup when there's stitches in your eyebrows and bandages on your face? When you're patched together like some book of psalms? I did once. It was three years ago. I had no spokes left in my wheels. Lala and I had broken up once again; in the course of the negotiations she'd delivered me a few roundhouses and haymakers, a few clotheslines and body slams, perhaps even the deadly, flying scissor-kick. I had returned temporarily to Oxbow to convalesce, before taking another year-long shot at university. Pauline was mixing drinks in her kitchen.

I wandered asocial and melancholy through Pauline's trailer.

I took off my clothes except for underwear and socks. It began with the greasing up of my body with cold cream. I even spread grease over my underwear until the yellowed cotton clung to my skin. I was so lubed nothing stuck in my hands. When the cold cream ran out I used vaseline. After my whole body, from hair to toes, was covered, it was time to do my face.

First the lipstick. I was careful not to press too hard on the places where my lips were swollen up. In any case, it went on crookedly, thick – a botched smile, but the only smile I had. The teeth behind it sat sorely in their gums, a few of them chipped.

The mirror was a womb for me.

The lipstick finally broke off against my lower lip, a big glob of red on my chin. I sipped from a whisky-sour, leaving a kiss on the rim of the glass.

Next came the mascara, in making the mask. With some help from the bruises around each eye, the eye-shadow may as well have been tar, slathered on. Meanwhile, I spoke a little. To myself. To steady my hands. I kept hitting the stitches with the eye-shadow, looking for infections.

"I'm waiting for the director to show up," I said.

Next came the rouge, the blush.

"With the black and white film," I continued. "And a wedding dress, of course. And a great big fucking dildo. Yessiree bob. That's the ticket."

I pulled off my socks and took another drink. Then I put my foot up on Pauline's dresser and began to paint my toenails pink. "No, that's not the ticket," I said, shuddering. "I just don't want to die. Please."

When finished, the nails on my hands received a thick coat of red polish. Then I began to hair-spray my hair, and kept going until it was wetted-down, my face sticky and solid from the drying lacquer.

Hope somebody finds this funny, I remember thinking to myself.

My face like a side of pork. My hair like a boxing-ring mop. The cosmetics melted into petroleum on my sweaty body. Pauline's dresser was a mess of chemicals, the doily on it stained irreparably. My whole system, outside and in, was a carnival gone bad. The face in the mirror seemed too much happier than me. I'd temporarily retreated to Oxbow to play out some strange tendencies. For homosexuality? Transvestitism? Did I now require a sex change, or just run-of-the-mill emasculation?

Say what you will. It's your interpretation, so tell all the lies you like. Be my guest. You see, I've sworn an oath to always speak the truth, even put my hand on the Bible, whatever that means, but I'm afraid I can't answer any self-reflexive questions. I'm no expert witness on myself.

I watched the sweat bead and drip down my face, carrying everything with it. The corner of my eye saw Pauline in the doorway, drinks in hand, looking at me. But she didn't come into the room until I slapped my face and body flat on the glass – whether I tripped on the rug or threw myself into this enthusiastically remains the subject of much controversy – and slid down the mirror leaving long streaks, the kind of move you expect from a walrus starring in *Wild Kingdom*.

Pauline couldn't help but laugh. When she came with the make-up remover and cold cream I think I started to laugh with her. She even took polaroids. "Nothing could be this bad," she said. "You're like a Bergman flick: so depressing you're funny." Then Pauline kept on laughing and passing a rag over my skin like a shoe-shine kid.

I haven't looked in a mirror since.

My father christened me Gabe because he didn't want his son's life tainted by an old-country moniker. He avoided scandal like herpes. But sometimes, some very select times, he'd bare his blackened and silver-capped teeth and talk about the case of worms he developed on the ocean crossover from Europe to Canada. Just to amuse us kids, he'd pull up his shirt and distend his big hairy beer-gut to the size it had been when full of wormies. But only rarely did he communicate so vigorously. In general, his misanthropic tendencies stayed pretty much under the covers. He named me Gabriel after an angel neither of us had an inkling of, that neither of us had met or even considered. I do not gamble, but odds are he still hasn't met the angel, though he's a doornail in the house of death. (My mother – living an entirely different story – still believes Gabe an English adulteration of the Hungarian name, Gábor, but my father altered the birth register without consulting her).

He had chronic temper spills. He'd just click. For whatever reason. Too long in the car. Irritated by me underfoot. Me bugging my sister. Too many friends over at the wrong time. The suddenness of his bouts always surprised me: amenable one minute and murderous the next and amenable again in five minutes. Driving in Vancouver one time he stopped the car in the middle of the intersection because someone behind was incessantly honking. He got out of the car, went over, hauled the other driver out, held him by his shirt down on the hood and screamed at him: "Why are you honking at me!" My sister and I, at mother's request, had to get him back into the seat. All the drivers around us had stopped to watch. Another time a waiter brought him cream instead of milk in the restaurant and he yelled: "If I drink this my asshole is going to fire like a machine gun! What are you thinking, you fucking faggit?"

When I was a kid he always apologized for getting mad at me by telling me I had such a good nature, such a wonderfully forgiving temperament. In this way he reinforced and praised my ability to take abuse.

Bill traveled like a simple terrestrial with somewhere to get to. You see, I gave him the money he asked for and a little kick in the ass: "Don't call back unless you've got some good stuff. That story about the river just doesn't wash, bud; sorry about the wordplay." He tried to dog paddle for it in the freezing river. Naturally, he went under and filled up his lungs two quarters. He must have taken drowning lessons at some point. Then Bill thrashed back up for a snatch of air and submerged again to fill his lungs another quarter. Came up for another grunt. After a while his wife, sitting beside the stream, swam back in and saved him, towed him to shore. But she left Bill spluttering on the bank and ran away.

"I'll call you when I find her again. Good-bye, Gabe."

So, for a while Bill disappeared from my horde of annoyances. Then my phone patched him through again, and we spoke, wretch to wretch.

He used the five hundred dollar money-order I sent to purchase a used car. He kept the bright red three-inch pumps his wife left on the edge of the flood, and touched them sometimes for psychic guidance. The South had so many arteries. Her destination was Mexico, he figured, and was sure he could cut that short, head her off, that sort of thing, if only the cops delayed her occasionally for speeding. There were moments of irresolution. When he saw a golden retriever trying to fetch the rock a callous owner had thrown into a creek, Bill almost broke down with futility: no more of this pilgrimage. Other times he felt he'd lassoed tomorrow and broken it in. Sometimes these opposite emotions came and went less than five minutes apart. On the phone he told a mean sob story.

"Don't give me the run-down on your 'feelings,' Bill. After all, feelings ... well, they're nothing more than feelings ... even feelings of love.... You are pure mission," I told him, "not a simpering man. Just the facts."

"Okay," he'd say, going on, staid but with a stuffy nose. He met up with her in Portland, Oregon. When I think of this location now, my adam's apple always goes "gulp."

There was a promising knock on his hotel door. Bill hadn't been in for more than twenty minutes. He answered it. She took two steps in, shook his dumbfounded hand and then turned to slam the door behind them in a big-business kind of way. Before Bill could consolidate she picked the shotgun up off the bed and loaded it. He stood transfixed.

"Why don't you sit down, Bill?" He sat. "Pretty hard to play Russian Roulette with a double-barrel, eh?" She looked deep into the barrels, holding them right to her eyes like binoculars. Bill got grabby for something, anything. She put the gun under her chin and pulled the trigger. Nothing. She pointed it at him. Bill's testicles crawled up into his body like a pair of snails. Nothing happened when the firing-pin clicked its sequel. "Let's face it Bill," she said, "your gun has no bullets. What kind of hotel is this?" his wife asked.

"We are getting close to California," Bill eked out, some kind of yogurt in his pants.

"Don't follow me anymore," she said, taking the gun.

The next day someone had paid his hotel bill and left a book of matches with a note scrawled in it: *Don't be a silly-Billy. Go home.* The picture on the pack of matches showed the Golden Gate bridge.

"I need money for a new shotgun," Bill groveled.

I prepared the cheque, more exuberant about Bill's quest than he'd ever been. I tried to pep-talk him the whole time. "Don't be disheartened," I said. "She's smart, but you're smarter."

"You really thinks so, Gabe?" he asked.

"Damn straight, Bill. You'll get her yet."

Once, Lala and I had fastidious sex in the front seat of a car. More accurately, she took pleasure and I experienced it on my knees, my face between her legs, the rest of my body scrunched into the hollow under the steering wheel. Storm showers outside and she'd left the window down. Rain blew in the open hole, drenching my forehead and hair. Pollen from Butchart Gardens' flowerbeds permeated everything. The back of the seat lay horizontal and Lala arched her back on it. I concentrated on the clitoris, as per her directives. After letting out a series of linked O's, Lala pushed my head away for seconds and then pulled my face up to kiss me.

The second time Lala and I went out I tried very hard.

It is, of course, nighttime. I have a rifle. Moments of lucidity wither to nothing. My breakfast, lunch and dinner today consisted of dark chocolate. Clouds scud over the moon. This scenario needs only trenchcoat detectives with gullible partners. To paraphrase Obi Wan Kenobi: sometimes the dark side takes the cake. The door opens. The cur trots across the sights of the cocked rifle, but the all-season Christmas lights above the door shine directly into my eyes and hamper any chance at aiming straight. This must be accomplished with one bullet. The rotted fence leans at a forty-five degree angle in the unreliable earth. The dog sniffs out a spot on the concrete where it will leave a fecal signature. At the moment I've finally fixed the beast in my sights it bolts upright and dashes into the grass. I dismiss it as a flashback or flaw in the scope, because wiener dogs aren't bipeds yet.... Perhaps it is only a clear-cut case of momentary demonic possession. My luck: the one time it suddenly decides to defecate in the grass instead of the driveway, I happen to be aiming at it. Fortunately, its absent sense of smell lets me ignore the wind's directions as I sneak to new positions. The wind's wild at this time of night. The dog trembles under the weeping willow, square in the cross-hairs, when a tough feminine hand drops on the barrel and rips the rifle from my grasp, and so disarms the sniper.

"What the fuck are you doing?" questions my older sister, Katy, machete in hand. My father, when we lived at Oxbow's eastern end, slashed trails through the sticks with that same blade.

"What about you?"

"The dog is mine," she says.

"What?"

"I want to kill it."

"What?"

"I've got my reasons. You stay out of it."

"I've got my reasons, too."

"Well, whoever gets to it first then," she hisses. Putting the gun-strap over her shoulder, she goes to the hole under the hedge which the dog slunk through.

"Wait," I plead, getting up. "I don't want a competition. How about a fifty-fifty split. I kill half and you kill the other half."

"A bit player is all you are to me."

The hedge rustles. Katy lifts the machete to chopping height while I part the leaves. A freed robin takes wing and my sister's machete cleaves empty air. In the distance we hear my mother calling the runt's name, nails scratching the stairs as it responds. The dog has proved itself an escape-artist, pulling a Houdini while Katy and I bickered.

I don't think Pauline imbibes, injects or inhales narcotics of late. I make weekly support payments but it feels like a tithe because no visible evidence of my largesse crops up.

My stepbrother, his son and I go up to her trailer so I can drop off the latest installment. As far as brotherhood goes, myself and my legal sibling experience no fratricidal impulses. Approximately four years younger than Katy and two years younger than me, he came with Benny like a car option you can't say no to. Benny's first wife died giving death to their second child, a daughter. Since my stepbrother and I rarely speak, we rarely argue.

Pauline sits on her deck thumbing an old scrapbook filled with wedding photos of her parents. Against the images' black backgrounds the wedding dress looks sparkling white, the father's face distended, equine. Dry leaves pour from a rip in the sofa Pauline and I placed on her porch. She pages through the scrapbook on that couch, joint dangling from her lips. When I mean she's avoiding drugs I refer strictly to hardass narcotics, the golden ambrosias: morphine, dilaudid, cocaine. Smoking a joint is just another cigarette to Pauline.

My stepbrother's boy lacks judgment. Fire recoils from his touch. He bruises the earth when he falls. He sneezes and the wind catches influenza. He'll outlast life like a chunk of rebar. The years might rust him down but nothing else will wear him. He can dip his honey-spoon directly into the beehive.

In a flurry of creased leaves Pauline jumps down off the porch, lifts the kid, launches him into the air and catches him, joint dangling all the time. The wind rifles through the scrapbook's pages, left to flutter on the boards beside the sofa. I say hello to Pauline. She winks at me. I go inside. The heap of money on top of the fridge hasn't decreased, the pile a quarter of a foot deep with untouched fives, tens and twos. I drop on the fresh bills and wander outside, my left ear twitching. How'd I come to this shyster situation? Who wrote chump on my forehead while I slept?

The kid plays on the edge of Pauline's lot. My stepbrother refuses a drag off Pauline's joint. "Come on," she pressures.

"Well, it's been a while," he says. The wind lets it rip across treetops. My stepbrother inhales, then blue smoke pumps from the two holes in his nose. The kid finds a beer can and throws it against the ground. His face awry, my stepbrother looks at the joint pressed between his fingers like some strangeness scraped out of his ear, obviously not recognizing the weed from previous experience. He shrugs, hands it back. Pauline turns quickly towards the kid.

"How's the mother?" she asks.

"He doesn't have a mom," my stepbrother says. "My son wasn't born of woman."

"Was it a she-wolf?" Pauline quips sarcastically. "The antichrist come upon us?"

"No," my stepbrother grins, watching his son. "He had a mother like a nine-month incubator." He looks down at the toe of his boot, suddenly crestfallen. The river runs a peculiar chatterbox that only stops once a year with the winter freeze, when eagles come and peck at the salmon trapped in the ice.

Pauline glances in my direction. "How's that?" she asks my stepbrother. I ram my hands into my trouser pockets, ignore her and begin performing triage on the garbage therein: wrappers, half smoked butts, matchboxes, expired pieces of ID. I place one of my ears against the wind to catch their words streaming past.

"One day she asked me what I thought of abortion. I told her it was none of my business. Said if I was for abortion I was attacking my rights, as father, to the child. Shit, I don't just want it to be the woman's choice. It's my kid, too. I couldn't agree with that. On the other hand, if I fought against it I was telling women what to do. She accused me of looking after only my own interests. I laughed and told her that was what abortion was all about in the first place: looking after your own interests. It wasn't my business. I told her I'd just make sure the person I slept with didn't want an abortion, either. Then she told me the business by pointing at her stomach. She didn't use too many words after that."

The kid waddles around the trailer's backside. I've found an old phone number for Lala's mother in my pocket, written in Lala's hand. I check for spelling mistakes to stop the ache in my fingers.

"I went home and talked to Dad. No way she'd marry me, she said. Not a chance. We'd only fucked once and I guess my performance wasn't worth a lifetime commitment. Next time I saw her she was drinking and smoking. I couldn't stop myself and I smacked her lips halfway across her face. Shouted that if it was my choice I'd never see her again. But she had something that was half mine. Then I promised to look after her for the next nine months, give twice what they gave her at the supermarket. She could go back afterwards. She wanted another two thousand dollars for 'the hassle and pain.' My Dad lent me that, too. The price changed to three later, when the puking started. I'm still fucking paying for it, had to move back home to save on rent!" my stepbrother winces. "Kids don't come cheap."

His son's wail comes up like sirens.

Around back, the child has fallen onto broken glass and cut open his hand. Blood runs down, entwining his arm. My stepbrother holds his child and Pauline scoots for paper napkins and band-aids. I guess I typecast the kid all wrong; there's no invulnerability clause written into its lifetime.

My stepbrother blabs on the ride home: "It's funny. That joint didn't have any weed in it at all. Nothing. I wonder what she was trying to tell me."

I hold onto Lala's mother's phone number and wonder myself.

In Hungary they schedule shock-management courses for train drivers because multitudes throw themselves in front of the trains every year. After the fall of Communism (and probably before, but the girls in the Kremlin prettied up the statistics), Hungarian suicides shot to the top of the charts. I met a railway engineer in a bar, both of us sincere with alcohol. "I've hit four people," he said, leaning on the formica. "Four of them. Two women and two men."

He ordered more shots of Unicum for us. One of Hungary's most famous poets, József Attila, killed himself by train early in the century. "Squished by the locomotive." Ever since then many copy-cat Hungarians have followed suit.

Sometimes I think I'd like to be a trend-setting, society-page suicide too. How to influence people.

"You don't know what it's like," the engineer said, talking of that moment when you're hooting along the tracks, sucking juice out of the day, feeling just fine, and a shape flickers in the lower register of your eyesight before you feel it, a tiny bump immediately swallowed by the train's unchecked forward motion. "Then you know, or, with my luck, you know it again." Just when you'd almost totally filed the last trauma away like an unopened letter, someone jumps in front of your train again, suckering you into being their executioner. "The worst part is you still have an arrival time to meet." There is no broom to sweep up that kind of mess: a suicide leaves too many corners to get into and out of. "You arrive at the station and call the police, the ambulance, the railway office, then run back to the train to make the next stop." You dream of a brake that's retroactive, that compensates for every split second, so that anyone falling in front of the express waits for the impact in vain, because you've stopped dead. You want to counteract Newton's laws. "I'd get out of the train, help them to their feet and under my wing. I'd take them all in if I could," he said, "enlarge my house, make it a place to stay alive in."

"I always arrive late to the train I want to jump in front of," I told him. "Or the train knows I'm coming and rearranges the schedule. Or it leaps up into the air, way up high, over my body and lands on the other side of the tracks." I spoke to him about Lala, who didn't want me anywhere near France, who'd sent me by proxy – through the mouth of a friend – an express invitation not to attend the party.

Halfway through my story he put his arm on my shoulder and his head on the bar, eyes open. "People kill themselves here all the time," the train driver said, tilting his cap back. "If suicide is an art-form, Hungarians are the trail-blazers. Don't get discouraged easily. Life is not something you add water to and stir." He advised: "Change." The train engineer listened to me stack word on precarious word, building my tower of babble. I had nothing to fear; he hadn't had a reason to be bored or sleepy in years.

Too bad talking about it never helps.

Lala's and my two relationships have fused into one passionate war. I regard the year she spent in France under cease-fire or temporary truce. (Funny how a full year always came between our meetings – between the first relationship and the second, and between the second breakup and that final meeting at the party – as if the cycle of seasons was trying to tell us something). I spent that time in university, drinking my way in and out of hangovers and bedrooms. Nothing lasted for very long: neither the bedrooms nor the hangovers. I've alphabetized all the names and places, that much I care to remember. But I won't be an informant any further – enough names named already.

While I couldn't stand Hungary for longer than the month of August, Lala so loved every one of her 365 days in France that she only returned because Dad cut the funding. In Europe Lala fucked around with ski stars and harlequins, the jet set and the destitute. She learned to juggle in Paris, how to toss a suitcase out of a ground floor apartment so it would crack open with clothes like a jack-in-the-box. She learned how to use a razor blade on a man's face. She learned the running of a perfect bath, how to stand when they toweled you, how to avoid slipping on bars of soap. When we returned to each other she brought many gifts. She was a magus, myself a Herod. I had no directions to give except ways to lose tiredness and introspection for an hour or two.

In short, my dowry promised nothing. I had buried my talents. Sometimes I spent whole nights digging for them in her, but that woman was hardpan.

She also came back semi-professional with violence.

"Funny," she said. "We used to scream at each other twenty-four hours long. After he slapped me this one time I didn't talk again and he went to sleep. I looked at his face and realized all along he'd just wanted to sleep, just wanted me to shutup so he could pass out."

Sometimes you buy rotgut. Sometimes you do. Not only when the account's low but when the mood returns after a long absence and you race to the beer and wine store for a bottle or, better yet, a cardboard carton, of some plonk only possible from the Okanagan. You drink it. Your stomach becomes a distillery, your head a boiler room. You grab hold of the refrigerator and hope it's not on castors. Your veins run dry. You tend towards that big cry ten years overdue. Understand? Make no mistake, it's not as sexy as it sounds.

The bottles assembled around us in various stages of emptiness. We'd put out the money and were now getting reimbursed – guzzling in the kitchen while my roommates were out on the town.

"With the frying pan ready," Lala continued her story, "I went out into the lobby and filled a plastic bowl with ice, then went into the bedroom. I dumped the ice on him and he shot out of bed. But, you know, using the frying pan was beyond me at that point. He started screaming at me all over again. I screamed back. Told him to 'use the door' and threw his luggage out the window after him. Clothes everywhere! It was tremendous," she hiccuped. "All the lights coming on like after a black-out," she hiccuped again for punctuation, took another swig. "People hollering in French all around. Nice little midnight apocalypse. The *maître d'* pounding and pounding a broom on the door. My boyfriend bent down in the rain trying to put the suitcase back together. I realized the next morning it was my suitcase I'd thrown out by mistake. He slept in the train station and found panties instead of the usual underwear. I took him back after he told me how he was born in a police cruiser. Made him promise never to hit me again. He never did."

I lurched towards the bathroom but tripped on a bottle underfoot. Groping towards the counter for support, my hand landed in an unwashed plate of leftover sweet and sour pork. Lala hiccuped, lifted a pale hand to an even ghostlier face, and burped a laugh.

"You know, I learned something from him that night."

"What?" I yelled. The sound of my piss interfered with the discourse.

"You can hit someone. I'd never considered it an option before. A good little smack upside the head."

"You don't believe in Heaven and Hell do you?" I asked, coming out of the bathroom.

"No," she said, smiling and milking the bottle for dregs.

Sometimes the telephone rings like a cultist, killer or census-taker at the door. I sit and watch, sometimes twiddle the end of my nose, flip a coin, sometimes pull the connector out of the wall. I even cut the line with scissors once, pretending to act out a spy thriller. I should then have taken the chord, made a noose and hanged myself from the ceiling lamp or showerhead, but the idea of such wild-west or expressionist melodrama brings me either tears of laughter or a snort of contempt. Adults must conserve their suicide attempts for when the stocks and bonds go bust, when terminal lung cancer sets in. They must leap from the tenth storey, preferably through glass. I got as far as the noose.

I will pick up the phone this week only once, Tuesday, tenth ring of the hour between two and three. Putting the receiver to my ear feels like putting my head into the MGM lion's toothless mouth. Frank the doctor calms me with the Hungarian accent that makes his English sound garbled, though his grammar is nearly flawless. "My friend," he says, "you have wonderful sperm! Wonderful! You will make great Hungarian children!"

"Thank you, Frank," I return. "Thank you for this and all the other things you've done for me."

"Anytime, my friend," he drawls into the receiver, as if from horseback on a wind-swept plain before a flamingo sunset. "Any time at all."

Now I have to make a call outward, to Pauline. I get her answering machine. This saves me many a dramatic gesture. For example, had she been home:

"Pauline?"

"Yes?"

"This is Gabe. The doctor graded my sperm double A."

"Right on!"

"Why is it so important? You know how embarrassing it is to ask the doctor to check your sperm?"

"I just wanted to know."

"Why do you always have to be such a stranger?"

"Look, Gabe. I wanted to know if you could make kids because I want to have them."

"What bearing has that on reality? You know I haven't had sex in years, not since Lala."

"One hand job from me, baby, and you'd be ship-shape."

"Pauline, do you always have to be so fucked? Tell me the truth. Why did you want me to be sampled?"

"I guess I wanted to know about VD too."

"Well, everything's okay. But what difference does it make to you if I have herpes or something...."

And that would have been the conversation. As it was, I speak only the facts into the phone: "Hi. This is Gabe. The doctor loves my sperm. Good-bye."

Go figure this: one time on a certain farm I pretended to dig for gold but unearthed a goat. My parents had gone off on ostensibly the one and only dirty weekend of their marital career, consigning my sister and me to a week of apples and crazy chickens, dogs that spent their days outside, territorial bulls guarding pastures and a fat and thin farming couple.

I didn't wear overalls, only got my hands dirty in jest. For breakfast the rosy-cheeked matron fed us a mixture of Rice Krispies and Cornflakes. Her husband gave me an old collapsible army shovel his grandfather had used to dig himself a homey little hole in the blood and gore of one or another of World War One's permanent fronts. A good shovel, its end came to a point, probably to eviscerate enemy with if they ambushed you while you dug out the latrine. The old man drew maps for me with Xs on them and no north, south, east or west whatsoever. I'd climb what fences needed climbing that day and dig a shallow pit. Finding no treasure was the thing, to be assured of nothing; success came with digging three feet down to confirm this expectation.

The map he drew in the chicken coop made me lose my nerve forever. Between putting bad eggs into an egg carton the old farmer pulled out a carpenter's pencil and sketched some geography. The stink was terrific. The stubble on his rounded, bony chin shone white like nails. He wore a long extinct cowboy hat with a ripped brim, strap dangling under his chin.

"You know," he muttered while doodling, "my wife cheated once. Back when we lived in the USA. Some poet guys who used to do drugs and travel in boxcars. And me overseas with the military, in Korea. I told her to write me love letters. Instead, she bought a car in San Francisco and shipped it over with drive-away. The car showed up totally trashed. She didn't care, invited the two beatniks who'd driven it for dinner and they decided to stay. In their spare time they were a couple of queers. Freeloaded for two months, swigging wine and doing God knows what with each other and her. They took turns writing me letters on Benzedrine, letters all one unbroken paragraph, no periods, just commas, typed on rolls of paper towel. She'd sign. Best damn letters I ever got. Wish I could meet them. My wife said they both had goatees. Course, I'd probably boot their balls so hard they'd fly out back of their assholes. Maybe I'd kiss them though. Ever kissed a man? Don't worry, I ain't about to molest you."

He finished sketching and tapped the pencil against his teeth. "Yeah, best damn letters I ever got. I wrapped 'em all with a piece of ribbon my mother wore in her hair. Great ribbon; I got memories of it too.... Anyhow, sitting in a foxhole in Korea, I figured it wasn't my wife on account of the typing. See, she doesn't know how to type – a dead giveaway. They gave their names as Jack and Neil. Could of been phonies though."

He went back to the rotten eggs. "Yep, best damn letters...."

I took the map and scrammed.

It was a map for closed eyes. The X marked a spot in the center of recently plowed field. Dust filled my pockets and shoes. I climbed over the fence with the shovel balanced on my shoulder. A row of dandelions straggled along the thin shadow of the fence's railing. The place to dig couldn't have been more obvious: a mound of dirt just ten feet from the fence. Never before had I found such a definite place. Normally his map was a vague blueprint that my imagination brought alive, always fifty percent in my head, following it the way you jump from floating raft of branches to floating raft of branches in the brown river after the storm. I hopped from one instruction to the next on the crumpled napkins he traced my inspiration on, the map nothing but lines for tampering with. But today left no chance for invention, everything laid out so carefully.

The mound of dirt looked like a pillowcase stuffed with live sparrows. When I speared my shovel into the top of it the earth buckled under me.

I put the point of my shovel straight down and almost leapt on it before noticing a tuft of hair vibrating between the soil. I staggered back. The goat struggled free, threw off a coffin of earth and stood, blinking red eyes in the sun. It had a filthy white coat, probably aswarm with lice and tics happily free of the burial. Its horns were just stubs, like wax candles after the power comes back. When finished blinking, the goat gave me a comprehensive once-over and walked off towards the chickens.

I recognized the goat from the fold. Despite my disappointment at finding something at the end of my shovel – because I hate surprises – I managed to overlook my own concerns to wonder what the old farmer had in mind when burying the beast: perhaps a hatred or horror squirreled up for so long it had outgrown all usefulness and now came out rotten and absurd, transmogrified into goat.

His wife called. We all ran to eat. During dinner the old man tried attracting my attention by glinting light off his fork into my eyes, but hunger overruled all distractions.

The goat showed up again in a riverbed, where running water widened and pooled for a time before continuing. You could have cut me up with a knife and fork. Its back legs stuck straight up out of the water. The river passed the goat by on either side like a circle around nothing.

Clad in underwear, I crawled along the river's surface, dove down and unhooked the rope attached to a sack of bricks on one end and the goat's neck on the other. The two of us swam ashore. Trout glinted silver as they shot off in the waters. A chorus of toads croaked.

The goat shook itself off with civility, took its dapper goatee and trotted off into the forest. I waited for the water to evaporate off my body.

Getting back to the main pasture I found the goat lovingly rubbing its face into the seat of the old man's pants. The old man was trying to plant carrots and no amount of his back-handed slaps stopped the animal nudging him off balance.

The couple's farmhouse had an extra large ketchup tin with dried flowers sticking out of it on a stripped, cedar shelf and a stained, hand-sewn table cloth, intricate as the past, tacked up to the wall. Light struggled past windows onto photo albums antique unto themselves. Nobody remembered the names or faces therein. You counted the folds and wrinkles on the old lady's face and came to some kind of age span. But for a better guess you observed her behavior. Every time she pulled a cigarette away from her lips you witnessed a movement adjusted by every other person she'd seen smoke. If aware enough to catch the nuances you knew exactly the low-down types who'd influenced the style of her smoking. In the morning the old man swaggered into the kitchen the way some forefather once had. The couple were parrots: in every movement a thousand inflections, predecessors guiding their efforts. The cumulative centuries of breeding, forced on them for free by genetic imprints, combined with their "lived" years to jerk their behavior over. And they also had wills to appease. Distilling the three elements let you count the years these old people had lived like rings in a stump.

The old man swore he'd taught Satan some tricks. "You taught him piss," his wife said.

In the forest leaves slid along my cheeks. Rain sloshed in my gum boots. The storm had finally arrived. Waves of a nearby pond ran skittishly, in a series of broken lines critical of each other's advance. The flats of mud lay barren at the edge of the pond, long grasses hissing snake-pits of noise. Black clouds marched along the ridge, thundering in their boots. An eagle flew like a jackass in gale-force winds. A flotilla of ducks surfed the waves.

I'd seen the old man disappear into the forest, a coil of twine around his shoulders. I tailed along furtively. If he'd had eyes in the back of his head he would have worn spectacles there too, horn-rims circling the skull. Trees and weeds parted for him. I wormed my way into thickets he slid through without a nick. He kicked the goat ahead, moving its stubborn hide, the storm a sound in the dark at the top of the stairs.

He hanged the goat from the branch of an arbutus. Without protest – the goat didn't kick, didn't emit bargaining, but rested its eyes, tongue lolling. The old man was gaunt as beef jerky. His spine hadn't yet calcified into an uncompromising pipe. He climbed all over the tree, up and down it, without catching overalls on branch or leaf. He surveyed the goat spinning on its hempen necktie, then gazed behind himself, right at the place I hid, right at me, then left.

I climbed the tree, took the jackknife from my pocket. Laying on the branch directly above the victim, with one hand underneath where my blade bit the rope, I severed the hangman's line. I thought I might hold the goat up by the rope. That's inexperience with gravity for you. Both animal and I dropped from the tree. I bruised my tailbone and water poured from my eyes. Not a breath of spirit to me, I couldn't stand. The goat survived fine. Its life gelled with good fortune. Looking me in the eye it just acknowledged predictable fate, me being the executor for this current round of saving grace.

I ran back to the farmhouse, entering the back way, through the cellar. The old man sitting by his fire didn't raise chin from chest. The goat stood on its back legs outside the window bleating forgiveness and entreaty to the drowsy old man through the glass.

One balmy day the old man came out of a black spell (he'd spent most of the morning in the garage, coming out occasionally to smoke, control some fit of exasperation, then returning) and shanghaied me into accompanying him to town. Our relationship – passive outside the goat – implied that in other matters we would be gagged by politeness, friendly even.

He owned a barely serviceable pickup truck, one notch over unsalvageable and degrading at the rate of uranium. We rode the wreck into town to pick up groceries, the steering wheel twirling as if nothing more than an excuse for show and tell. Juicy bugs blew up colorfully against the windshield.

Halfway there he started to sing the praises of speed bumps. The suspicion of an offing came to me. From then forward I was sensitive to everything.

"You know, Gabe, I love speed bumps. They're an excellent thing."

"Yes, I like them, Mr. Carter."

"No more beautiful a clanging, Gabe, than when a car with a shallow muffler meets the resistance of a speed bump. It is my private church bell. You a religious boy, Gabe?"

"No, not me Mr. Carter."

"You will devise your own religion, son. Believe you me. You will devise it. Everyone does. And you might call it politics, or reason, or facts, or theory, or common sense. You might even," and here he shifted down for drama, "call it murder. We all need something to rage against. If you don't have something now you will later. Hopefully your rage will find a constructive target. Mine has. I guess."

"Anyhow, your reasons will arrive," he continued, "be they flawless or absurd. Carry things out. I personally love speed bumps, the way they curve like a mound of dirt, say, in a grave, love their smoothness. You know that kind of asphalt molding? Boy, Gabe, I even love the colors they paint them. That traffic-sign yellow. Sometimes they're white. Know what I mean?"

I think at that instant I had temporary omnipresence of mind. We stopped for gas. While he went into the bathroom, I opened my door, leaned out, and saw the goat – a leather belt wrapped around its mouth to stop the bleating, wired to the chassis of the truck, riding dangerously close to the ground. I jumped out of the cab and crawled underneath. He'd wired it in five places. I didn't care how long the old man took in the bathroom. The goat said as much as hello to me. I opened my jackknife and inserted the double ends of the wires into the socket where the blade used to be. A corkscrew in reverse, I unfastened all the fetters and dragged the goat out from under the truck by the belt wrapped around its mouth. This accomplished, I slipped the belt off and fastened it – end in belt loop making a choker – around the goat's neck. Everyone in the gas station stared while the goat fought against leaving the truck. Couldn't that animal tell the difference between its Samaritan and executioner? It remained true to the old man past the brink of sanity. I tugged until the goat heeled and then we took a little constitutional along the highway. The day was made for walking your goat.

Perhaps the old man knew a shortcut, or maybe he took the long way home. Perhaps he flew that truck like a space-age shuttle. Maybe he mapped the last frontier along the way. What does it matter? He reached home way before we did, with groceries and other provisions. I thought he'd hurl a mouthful at me but I was getting to realize this would never be the case. He wanted me to frustrate him. Love and hate played at odds in that brain. I don't know if he wished to tilt the balance or maintain it. I let the goat go. Of course the beast ran right up to lick Mr. Carter's hand. Dust in that old man's face no river could come between.

He drew water from the well. The well was an old miracle: nowhere in the vicinity could you get water in such quantity and purity. He wore a pajama top and some old greasy trousers held up by suspenders but sagging nevertheless at the belly, covered throughout with bread crumbs that he'd peck at with a wet fingertip, place between his front teeth and click away on. Strands of hair poked between the buttons of his pajamas. Dew evaporated into the morning wave of heat. His bumpy face sprouted patches of beard. He spoke passionately, seeking publicity for his soul, while I held the jug for him to pour water into: "Don't steal nothing from me when I go, son. Take my grave to a swamp and lay it out there, lining it with the bones of a mangy goat. Put me down among the rot and decay of the swamp. And don't – do not! – whatever else it is you do, don't let my wife scatter her indignant tears like seeds across my buried bones. Because you know they'll grow into plants and the plants will have roots and the roots will tell my bones the newest news and I will know the passing of seasons. I want no more seasons, son. You get me? And don't plant no fancy-schmantzy decor at my head. Two twigs held together in the shape of a cross by a rubber band will do. And that goes for the rites as well. No Goddamn rites for this geezer. You find out when I'm dead and you haul off into my room. I'll be light as sun-dried shit by that time so you can just grab me by the hair in one fist and drag me outta those god awful winding sheets and keep right on dragging me out the front door, straight to the forest until you come to the first patch of muck, then scrape a couple three feet down. Hold me over the hole by the hair and drop me in like a sack 'a potatoes. It don't matter what position I assume, or how many Goddamned bones ya break. Then you can cover me with horseshit. Just yourself, mind you. No mourners! Not that anyone would come anyhow. And when you're done tamping down the horseshit and planting the cross you can go and fuck off yourself. Now make me a promise, boy."

I crossed my heart and carried the jug of water inside. My sister sat in a swing that hung from the overreaching arm of an apple tree. She sang a song in a flat, off-key voice.

Later that afternoon mice sabotaged the kitchen. Mrs. Carter, slumped on a stool, ate strawberries with whipped cream. My sister and I had already finished ours. I felt strangely happy, very much a young man, watching, with the other two, mice chew holes in sacks of flour. We all felt super, on the receiving end of the best injections.

"I keep telling him to put out some poison but he just won't. Then I've got to crush them with a broom, which ain't so bad really. I like it. Hands-on. Doing the job yourself. But for Christ-sakes that old man of mine's a real asshole," Mrs. Carter said.

Our brown room had curtains thicker than the skin of a purse. The light went off and you saw symmetries of black. Nothing parted for footsteps. You negotiated every article, the floor boards following every movement with percussion: their way of complaining.

I crept over to where sister slept. "Hey," I whispered. "Hey!" Louder still.

She rolled over, away from the yellowed wall paper. "What? What is it? What do you want?"

"Do you hear it?" I asked, my face upturned towards the window. For a moment pure silence came into hearing. Then I noticed – but only me – the reverberant bleating of the goat. My sister heard only the swish of drapes on the wall, the creak of the floorboards under my shifting feet.

"I don't hear anything. Go to sleep."

"No. Come with me." I pulled her out of bed by the wrist. She didn't recoil but didn't help either. She moved only after hitting the floor, groaning, and got into her clothes. I already wore mine.

We went out through the kitchen. White mice scattered in a bubbling carpet before our feet. The moon rose, half-formed as my sister's consciousness, still troubled by sleep. I had her by the hand.

I knew the sound's source.

We came alongside the well. Lifting off the cover we both heard the goat screaming, the sound of thrashing in the water like the turmoil of a million fish. My sister's eyes filled with moon, a reflection broken only by flocking clouds.

"The goat," I said. "Help me pull it up."

The bucket was light and empty.

"I have to go down there," I said, "to get it."

My sister grabbed me by the elbow. "I can't pull you up. You weigh too much."

The old woman's voice hit us, I think, long after she'd released it because when we reacted she stood silently in the kitchen doorway, watching us, a nightgown wrapped around her fat body. Gray hairs trailed over and behind her head like smoke from chimneys under winter, the rest of her censored by darkness. "What are you two doing?"

My sister ran to her. The old lady walked with her over to the commotion. By now, she'd heard the goat's distress also. So, of course, she scrounged up a flashlight and reluctantly agreed that I should descend, never once mentioning her husband.

Blue ripples traveled up the stone sides of the well-mouth. The moon glared into the hole. Perhaps some birds flapped past. My sister's and the old lady's grunts, as they lowered the bucket, changed to ghostly chants in the hollow confines. Even the goat's splashing and bleating took on the character of a soft summons. The bucket plunged in stages as the rope went from slack to taut and jerked my body. I thought for sure the bucket would snap off its rope. Some kind of phantasmagoria down there. I never wanted the rocking motion of the bucket to change.

Arriving at the goat I had to slip into the frigid water. Blood cubes rattled in my veins. I felt hooked up to a car battery. All the sensations experienced on the way down gathered like fire and leapt straight up and out of the flue. I quickly got the goat straddling the bucket for them to winch it out.

The old man turned up once the goat and I had been snatched from the jaws of the well. Mrs. Carter wrapped her robe round me but I still ached with cold. The goat, on a broken leg and in primitive shock, limped towards the old man, trying to look attractive and graceful. "What's happening?" he asked.

"Someone threw the goat into the well," she snarled at him. They communicated without mercy.

"It must have fallen in," he decided loudly.

"But the top was on when we got here," I corrected.

He glowered at me then, chin raised to the moon like a headhunter. No one has looked at me in that manner since. For some reason, though, it didn't scare me. He fondled the underside of my chin with fingers rough as a rasp. My exclamation had breached the contract. Suddenly he shifted his head down and looked penitently at the old lady. "Harrumph!" he said and stomped off towards the barn.

The old woman set the leg of the goat in a splint. My sister and I stared into the goat's nostrils as it screamed from the pain of the leg bone's broken edges meeting. With the last tie on its splint fastened, the goat hobbled off in the direction of the old man.

Shivering, I wandered off after it. My sister and the old lady watched, blank and uncomprehending, not privy to our little theater of cruelty; the house's screen door slammed behind me. The goat yowled with every attempted step on its broken leg, until it just gave up altogether and held it in the air, tottering on three. I knew the goat's perverse guidance system would lead straight to its would-be murderer. We walked through clods of a recently plowed field while stars winked over treetops.

The old man was brewing musty mushroom tea over a fire. The goat hobbled to him and pushed its head under his unfriendly hand for a petting. "Ever done psilocybin, Gabe?" the farmer asked. He proffered a tin mug, motioned to drink up, and I gulped the hot, fetid water, tasting topsoil and humus. He sipped his like Earl Grey at the parish picnic and patted the goat's head two or three times before clubbing it aside with a clenched fist. But the goat hung around just out of arms' reach, totally infatuated. "I learned about mushrooms from those letters the beatniks sent. Nothing like sitting in a steaming jungle, ninety or so percent humidity, in some dang-blasted hole you clawed outta the red clay and reading a letter that's supposed to be from your wife – though you know it ain't – about how good a time she's having smokin' wacky-tabacky for the first time and doing funny mushrooms." For a while nothing occurred, not even a rustle from the bales of straw we sat on or a clang from the bell around the goat's neck. One side of the barn wall exuded a fairly satisfactory glow. The old man starting to cry and the rain to fall happened in tandem. "I normally make a pretty peculiar soup out of these 'shrooms," he roared through tears. "But for that you need a great big goat bone, and you just won't let me take out this damn animal." The goat had inched closer and he conked it on the head again; now the bell clanged. The goat instinctively relied on its broken leg to recover balance and it howled long enough for my gaze to descend its open throat and travel the length of its intestines twice around. Continually sobbing, Mr. Carter blubbered on: "That's the recipe for magic mushrooms those guys gave me. I tell ya, Gabe, there's nothing like reading a letter from your wife – though you know it ain't her – when your buddy's just been blasted to dingleberries by shrapnel and his eyeless head falls into your lap and you stop shaking it awake because you realize it's ridiculous with no body attached, and look down to see your thumb stuck in the eye-socket and you can't get it out and you jam his head between your knees and pull until your finger'll break; it's like some wedding band the skin's grown over, and you trip up among the corpses, falling on mangled friends and get up and shake and shake your hand to get the head to fling off but it won't and those Koreans open up with a new salvo because they see you still alive, so you forget about the head and drop among the dead and all you think of is your wife shacked-up with two weirdos who're typing you love letters...." The old man buried his head in his hands, still crying hysterically, only interrupting the emotional outpouring to sip tea. Years later I would bring this up at a dinner conversation as my definition – in the classic sense – of the word "bad trip." The goat limped up to him and licked the tears away with a tongue floppier than a Christmas stocking. The man lifted his head and stared the goat down: "They woulda made magic mushroom goat's head soup outta you."

The goat bleated the equivalent to "I love you, you sad old bastard." Little by little, we behaved more and more like hippies.

"Figures the one thing in the world that loves me also happens to be the one thing in the world I want to kill." He dried his raw red face on a worn flannel sleeve. "Funny how my wife has nothing to do with it anymore."

If the fire under the teapot ever transferred to the bales of hay only our dental records would have identified us among the barn's cinders. I placed my hand on Mr. Carter's back to make his sobbing subside. The goat snapped at my hand – jealous I guess. In a flash, the hallucinogen communicated what Mr. Carter needed: to slough-off a painful history. I reached up, grabbed the zipper hidden in my hair and pulled it down to my crotch. The goat followed suit and our skins fell to either side. I stepped out of my skin as Mr. Carter, and the goat stepped out of its own as Gabe. We found the old man's zipper and helped him out of himself; there: we had a new goat. Gabe spoke: "Mr. Carter, we are reinventing your religion." The goat bleated in the affirmative. "Religion should free you from love and hate, not help them fester," Gabe continued.

"No," I (or Mr. Carter) said. "It's mushroom tea that transcends love and hate." We three laughed while I again pulled my zipper down, reappearing as goat. Gabe unzipped and Mr. Carter emerged from the folds. The goat became me. We lost no body mass in the process, and howled at each metamorphosis, a million laughs kindling an unprecedented warmth, mouths open so wide our jaws nearly unhinged. In the end only dental records identified us.

My parents fetched us some few days later. The mister and missus stood at arms' length from each other beside the hood of the car. My father and mother took their hands. As we backed out the car, my father said to the old man: "Thanks again, Gabe."

The time had come to fling holy crows and mackerels and shits from the mouth.

Discovering that we kept the same name threw me for years. But now I know better, knowing as I now do that my father either mispronounced Giovanni for Gabe mistakenly (though I don't see how even a complete dimwit could do that) or with malicious intent, to screw with my mind, already so susceptible to demonic coincidence. Probably the latter, knowing Daddy-O. Only 55 years separated my person from myself, the time between his gripes and mine. No, definitely not. Saying 55 years makes me immodest and a liar. A much, much smaller lapse of years delayed the merger of our psyches.

I intend to obtain a monopoly on the wiener dog's execution. I have a little capital, good looks, intelligence, charm.

Workers are painting the house across the street. Never have I seen more haggard lackeys. They keep repainting the same wall and occasionally a window, while the woman who owns the house adjudicates from the front yard, trying to inspire them. It is obvious she despises them thoroughly. If they sat in electric chairs she'd happily pull the lever. Meanwhile the painters tell each other jokes, admire the horizon, try to appear flippant, but the wind carries their fear of the housewife to Katy and me.

My sister straddles the fence and rejects my two hundred dollar buy-out. My mother spent all morning French-braiding her thick brown curls into chains fuzzy with wires of hair that wouldn't be co-opted, braids that would restrain crash test dummies.

"I can't take your money," Katy says. "Your dirty dollars make me sick."

I remember, as a child, being in Hungary with my sister, when we knitted laurels for our heads, daubed our bodies with red clay during games of *ipi-apacs*. We were in concert almost constantly. I remember her falling out of a sailboat into the reeds of the Balaton. The reeds terrified us both, their lurching, their consortium of leeches and carp gone mental from the liters of human urine entering their gills daily. But I leapt in after her and gripped the supportive reeds until someone threw us a life jacket. I remember the wickedly spiced Fisherman's Broth they brewed for us, putting the fish-head's in our mouths and nearly choking from the laughter. Our parents photographed us arm-in-arm with fish-head's on our outstretched tongues. We were primates, really. After eating that soup we swam with perfect form. You swallow your enemy's heart and the next thing you know you're a better person for it; not very Christian, I admit, but I'm the soul of indiscretion – agnostics can't be choosers.

"You are filthy," my sister labels me, "with the blood of Lala."

"What?" I say in disbelief. Somewhere along the line my sister and I dissolved our amicable union.

"Everyone knows she killed herself because of you. You let her get raped."

"Raped? She wasn't raped. She poked the guy's eye out."

"I'm not talking about that," she said. "You raped her. And everyone else."

"What are you talking about?"

"All the humiliation she endured going out with you, everyone knowing you didn't stop them from trying to rape her. And she let you have sex with her afterwards! How do you think that felt for her when you appeared together in front of people? When everyone looked at her it was like they were fucking her as well. It's your fault."

No pieces of silver for this lady. She straddles the fence above a meticulous flower garden, her hair in French braids. My sister pries open the places where I keep the sensitive documents.

"Fine," I say, dropping my head, cramming dollar bills pell-mell into my pocket, letting them tear. "I'm sorry." I turn around. Katy grabs me by the back of my collar and pulls my face in towards her chest. I put my arms around her neck.

"That chlamydia infection I had," she squeezes my head against the hollow of her throat. "I'm infertile. And that fucking dog can't help not having kids."

There you have it.

En route with Pauline to Lala's mother's in Portland, Oregon I sit on my sunglasses. Suburban Doberman's cruise gracefully into neck-and-neck competitions of speed with the car, but at seventy kilometers per hour we elude them all. Birds of prey turn up ungratefully, as if scorning the wind that bears them. Pauline and I eat potato chips and smoke Marlboros past the border crossing. The song on the radio is a revamped oldie that Pauline chants the original lyrics to. Soon as you hit the States there's nothing provided for you but gas station pitstops. Signs grow thinner along the highway. Pauline holds the map.

"Why are we on this journey?" is Pauline's opener.

But before answering this I ask about her needs: "Why the snit when I said I was going?"

"I consider Lala a friend, too," she brightens.

How many boys have put a gun to their heads at such an answer? I confess in turn: "I want to know if Lala's still alive. And if so, what's all this tomfoolery with death certificates."

Pauline: "Okay. I'll tell the truth. I want to come because I'm in love with you."

"Don't make fun of me," I say. "I'm not in the mood."

Co-piloting, Pauline turns the map with the motion of the car, as if manipulating geography, as if we stood still and she steered the land past us. Pauline takes trees, lakes, highways, beasts of the earth and air, and the hills into her two fists. The wiener dog can wait.

It's hard to drive without looking once into any of the mirrors. Blind spots rain all around.

Portland feels like a place where old men build secret organs in their attics but never play them for fear of talent scouts and the curse of fame, where all the criminals are really one man with several disguises, where panhandlers have day jobs. Everyone listens to songs in private that they'd be embarrassed of listening to in public.

Pauline and I rent a room in the motel hinterlands along an avenue dedicated to overnight accommodation. They used one architectural blueprint to build every motel. When we come back to this paved stretch at night we try the key they gave us in any number of locks in any number of motels before great coincidence pinpoints our room. We have to remember contexts to find the way home: the half-painted fire hydrant, the variety of fins on the back of the manager's car, the knife and fork in the buttonhole of the drunk sleeping on the public bench.

Yellowish light seeps into the motel room, everything as threadbare as herring. We open a bottle of whisky and turn on the television. Pauline insists on an Edith Piaf special. So we listen to Piaf bellow. Later we'll eat hamburgers as if it was the most natural thing in the world, Pauline breaking her vegetarian creed. At night, wrapped in gamey sheets, my tongue picks through stray tastes of bourbon inside my mouth.

Lala's mother lives in pre-fab housing near factory rail-yards. Her house is its own worst enemy, eating itself to death. Some people must live in such hovels all life long. I saw her last at the funeral, where us ritual-mongers attended the gravediggers lowering an empty – my hypothesis – coffin. Lala left neither note nor corpse; a passerby saw a blonde girl fitting her description fling herself from the bridge, but not clearly enough to help the cops come up with even a composite photograph. In fact, the cops had to describe Lala to this woman, who then said: "Yep, that sounds like the one." Lala could have at least left me a forwarding address. A chain link fence separates the road from the rail-yards, where black and gray workmen can occasionally be seen between cast-iron rail-cars, boilers, stacks and tanks, as they slog through snow and mud, changing points on the tracks.

I rap on the door. Pauline stays in the car. I peel the price tags off the store-bought flowers and knock and knock but no one answers. I go around back. A rusty swing set perturbs the backyard with slow creaks. Due to medical complications, Lala's mother became barren after her only child. By the time my knuckles tap the back door someone opens the front entrance. My representative, Pauline, gets out of the car and distracts the homeowner long enough. I retrace my steps at a run. Light rain fizzles around us.

"Jessy?" I say.

"Well for saint fuck's sake!" she snarls.

Lala's mother was a castaway: hopelessly overweight, addicted to television and welfare, uneducated, defeated, with a face like a white steak squished against glass. My love for her is lewd and endless, but restrained. We had only met three times. Lala and I visited twice from Victoria.

"Hi. I wondered if … oh, wait … here." I thrust the flowers into her face. She took hold and let the bouquet hang at her side. Her bathrobe ajar, the flabby tops of her breasts shone like an unpowdered nose. "I wanted to come in. I mean, I was in the neighborhood … just wanted to see how you were doing. I haven't seen you since…."

"The funeral."

"Right. Want to talk?"

"About Lala?"

"Yes."

"What's to say? She's dead. You killed her."

"That's a lie," I say. "A horrible lie ... okay, misunderstanding."

"Go away."

"First tell me something."

"What?"

"Is Lala really dead or just making it look that way to make me suffer?"

The door slams in my face, the lock snicking into place. "I'll be back tomorrow," I yell, kicking at it and almost falling when my toes go through the swinging doggie-door. Pauline shoves me along to the car.

Once the car turns over Pauline nudges and says, "Look!" In the window Jessy is having nervous conversation on the phone, eyes on us.

The road to salvation tonight involves liver damage. I stare at the fluorescent curtains through the neck of a half-empty bourbon bottle. The motel rugs remind me of shed skin. The highway map walks out the door in the cross draft to find some place roads don't encompass, thinking of unkempt meadows. The neon signs up and down the motel strip outside flicker a little comforting morse code.

Pauline combs her long black hair. The brush disappears into it, black into black. Sometimes she gulps down a whole glass of whisky without giving lips or throat time to consider it. I think I have to use the facilities, and cast my eyes to the ground when passing in front of the mirror. This motel inspires a tasteful kind of vertigo. I pull my trousers and underwear right off, and leave my shoes on to make the going rough. I promise myself the reward of a good shit when the work's done. The whisky tries drowning me in a flood I must drink myself out of. The universe continues to conspire against me.

The muse requires me to puke a little bit. It's good to empty the stomach somewhat, make more space available for fresh spirits. I puke on my pile of shit for no other reason than to connect with meaninglessness. Sometimes you must make a god of absurdity. Otherwise you're doomed. The scanty patch of vomit pales in comparison to the large offerings I used to stage when first enrolled in the notorious school of alcoholism. I decide not to write home about it.

I brush my teeth, careful to turn my head towards the sink.

The phone rings. Pauline answers, talks a few seconds and replaces the receiver. Coming into the bathroom she announces: "That was Lala."

My mouth hinges open; my head jerks up. Spittle mixed with toothpaste slaps against the sink's porcelain. A jackboot kicks a door open in my brain. I remember an October day long ago, with my mother cutting my nails while friends watched, chewing their own nails, all their faces expressing hunger. Everyone concentrating except me. I watched my father yellowing away in the sunlight that overtook him on a lawn chair. I think again of something like that, something like my father, a face to which light is detrimental.

Pauline laughs behind my back, unaware of the joke's tactlessness until I pull my head back and slam it face first into the mirror. I feel glass splinter under my skin before I hear it. Pauline stops guffawing on the second head-butt into the mirror. Before she intervenes I pull the bottle of whisky back over my shoulder in one fist and club the jigsaw reflection. Broken glass and grain alcohol spatter the walls. Still hitting the wall behind the mirror with the bottom of my fists, Pauline pulls me to the ground and shoves a towel into my mouth for me to gnash.

"Two years without looking into a mirror," I say, spitting glass and wiping blood off my eyelids, "until now." Pauline drips iodine onto my cuts. "Who was that on the phone? Really?"

"It was only me." She shrugs.

The bedsheets surprise us, not only because they're a white ghost's wardrobe but because they will not break. Someone cleaned them on us. They stiffen over our bodies with starch like old brick. I put my lips to Pauline's. She kisses me but in a fashion I can't replicate. The way she kisses me precludes my participation, lips in combinations that stall all returns. Pauline leaves me lukewarm. "You never said good-bye to Lala?" she asks.

"No I didn't," I reply.

"Either you say good-bye or share her with me," Pauline decides.

"But if you share it means that we divide her up. And I choose the parts of her I take and the parts you're left with."

But I am not quite yet the volunteer.

I have to go back to Jessy's, the way I always return to Lala, like a dog to a flea in its back: risking spinal injury just to snap at the itch. There is nothing for it this morning except to leave the sagging bed for well-traveled clothes. Pauline is already up, sweeping glass in the bathroom. I open my wallet to check the price of breakfast. The shadow I cast has its back to the wall, in sackcloth and ashes, waiting with wisdom on its lips: *You've starved in front of banquets, frozen to death before seething ovens, blessed and spat on by everyone you met.*

Bacon and eggs later, Pauline and I are driving towards Jessy's place. Pauline will drop me off and come back. I don't want her in this. I am either going to turn up Lala's body or stop rooting around in her grave.

Jessy tells me to come in. I hadn't even knocked. The yellowed lace curtains quiver from her touch. The house smells like a downtrodden pet store.

I remember Lala's and my first visit, when Jessy's second husband took a leave of absence from daily rounds of marijuana cultivation and psychological abuse to run for president. I guess he hasn't made it there yet because nobody's seen him since. On meeting me, he remarked: "Well, you're cute." He never directed another comment my way except when leaving: "I'm going off to register my name in the vote." He even got a couple, I was later told, mainly from his personal pool of addicts. Jessy said to us after he left: "He's gone off to find a prostitute. He once went away on business and his friend set him up with a prostitute. Don't ask me, I just know." Unfortunately, looking at Jessy, and knowing her, I couldn't fault the candidate for that.

I am inside the home. Jessy calls me by name. I go into the kitchen, expecting what I see.

Jessy's fat, lumpy, white body sprawls in a rocking-chair installed in the unused kitchen. Pillows prop her back and she's inside a sleeping bag zipped up to her armpits. Her hair is either slightly matted or slept on, gray curls dry and unsympathetic. Four reproachful cats sit on the arms and headrest of the chair, their tails keeping time. The television blares with muzak: a soap opera. Jessy has lived like this since I've known her, even while cohabiting with the candidate. The VCR tapes a soap on another channel that she'll watch later, before the game shows air.

"Nice face," Jessy says. "What happened to you?"

"I needed some more bad luck," I reply, waiving the questions.

"So you decided to come back," Jessy purses her lips. "I thought you might."

"Look, Jessy, I'm not here to piss you off."

"No, but that's a side-effect of you being here. Can't you leave my little girl in peace?"

I sit down on a chair, lean forward, put my elbows on my knees and stare down at my shoes. Then I look up. "I can't," I say.

Someone is building a storm out of me. I slap my palms together and glance at the ceiling. I must look very bucktoothed saying the things I do. Or like a larvae on a dance floor. "I can't forget what she did to me."

"And so you want to be with her, to try and pull off a different ending," Jessy comments. "My girl's finally happy. Can't you make that your happiness?"

"If I could manufacture happiness you think I'd be in the self-loathing industry?" I reply.

"So what do you want?"

"I want out." She begins to laugh, slowly, warmly, without a trace of sarcasm. "What?" I ask.

"You want security! To know what's up next. To be able to count on yourself. To live up to some example. That's what you really want, isn't it? Poor little boy. Don't you know that the last thing you should count on is yourself? Besides," she looks straight at me, "you can't build castles out of shit. All Lala ever really wanted was for you to fall in love with yourself so that you could finally fall in love with her. So you got scared and couldn't help. So you started looking to make yourself foolproof. You know what one of the last things Lala said to me was?"

"What?"

"'I cheated on him so he'd never have to worry about me not being attracted to him and going for someone else.'"

"That's complete hogwash," I say.

"But it was one less thing to worry about, wasn't it?"

"No. I always thought that if I could step outside of myself and make something right, just once, she'd stop cheating."

"So maybe she gave you more excuses to think about yourself."

"This is going nowhere."

"So what do you want, then?"

"They took my pride, for starters."

"They?"

"Lala and all involved."

"You gave it to them! You think you'll prove something to yourself if she comes back?"

"No. I'll prove things to her."

"You couldn't. You have nothing to give, you never did."

"No.... You're wrong. I was trained to give. Give 'til I'm dead."

"Oh, Gabe," Jessy rests her eyes. "My girl's resting finally. That's all I can tell you. You're going to have to be happy with it unfinished. Uncertainty is what Lala left you. See? She's still pointing you in the right direction. Maybe the next time someone wants to hurt someone close to you you'll be able to help. Or maybe not. You can either use that uncertainty to free yourself, or you can let it fuck you up. Knowledge itself is useless; realizing you're a coward doesn't give you the means to stop being one."

I rise, button up my jacket. The animals on the rocking-chair sit still as effigies. Jessy looks at the blank screen as if there's finally something on television.

"Don't think anymore about Lala. Lala said good-bye to you a long time ago."

By the time I return to the motel the party is swinging, the light of our room stained with smoke. Bottles line up along the outer edge of the window sills. Voices and music bubble together in an incredible stew of argument and casual conversation. Some people sit on the hoods and roofs of cars like dissatisfied, muttering Buddha's. The music flows like cement from the party. Someone must have brought a stereo and a song with one, long, endless guitar bridge between verses. The frightened tenants of the motel peer past their curtains. The nexus of this party is our room.

Pauline is in the corner talking to some guy. The party seems full of neo-hippies, defending their trend by pointing out their heritage: "My parents were hippies. I always grew up as a hippie kid. I've been dressing like this all my life. Want to know what my parents named me? It sure isn't Christian."

The rest of the crew dress in black leather or overgrown lumberjack plaid. The requisite nondescript ones are present too, in running shoes and clean, properly fitting jeans – always the most dangerous because they have no pretentions and therefore never bluff. The place steams with body heat. The film on the windows is full of names, loves and slogans, as printed by fingers.

"Hi," says Pauline. "You finally made it back. I passed by while you were walking back from Jessy's place, but it looked like you needed it so I didn't stop."

I have not been drinking. I have flogged myself with weeds taken from the wilds. Actually, I've been playing Red Cross. I come into the bathroom where stand two boys. One of them is pushing thirteen. The other, his brother, leans over the sink and bleeds profusely from the face. Sometimes he finger-paints a little Mr. Yuck into the blood on the washbasin. His clothing has tears.

"What's that you got in your fist?" I ask of the younger, obviously frightened, boy.

"My brother's teeth," he replies, tears in his eyes, a smear of blood on his cheeks.

I take the older boy over and sit him on the toilet. "Who did this to you?"

"Some asshole," he says, making vocabulary somehow out of the gaps in his mouth.

"I think we should go down to the office," I tell them, "and get some band-aids or something." The little boy goes and stands beside his brother. He looks at him.

"Why didn't you hit him back?" he wonders. "I always thought you knew how to fight?"

"Look!" the older boy, spluttering blood at the mouth, yells at his younger brother. "Can't you stop with these fucking questions!" He grabs the kid by both arms. "I didn't ask you to come here! To follow in my footsteps!" He lets go of the younger brother and wipes his face with the palms of his hands, reopening fresh wounds. He stands and crosses one arm over to hold the other dangling arm by the elbow. "I'm not your role-model." He turns to me. "I don't even like looking at that punk!" He flicks a hand out and slaps his little brother across the face. The kid falls backwards into the shower and rips the curtain from its rings. The little boy grabs a faucet for support and the cold water turns on and spills all over him. "Do something different," the older brother yells.

I jump in between them.

"Suck off a purer source!" The bloody-faced boy yells over my shoulder. He lurches towards the door and walks out, leaving a bloody hand print on the wall to mark his passing.

I pull the little boy out of the shower and hand him a towel.

The kid and I sit on the roof. I feel bad about giving him a beer, but he wanted it. I don't really care, anyways. We are hidden from sight. He gives me a cigarette. He offers condoms as well, but I decline. There's a part of that boy that's fifty years old and dying fast. I find myself with the urge to sniff rubber cement. It must be either the presence of all this youth or the general chaos. The last time I felt this way was in Hungary. The kid and I try to tell each other jokes but we've heard them all before.

When the police arrive we poke our heads over the edge of the rooftop. The police raid the party. It's bedlam's grand reopening. They smack people on the heads with clubs. The manager chips in with a baseball bat. Our guests jump over the balcony onto the roofs of cars, denting them in. A boy runs out without any pants or underwear on and falls down. Below us, on the balcony, the cops and the guests flow together like square-dancing.

"Hey! Look!" The little boy shouts, pointing and standing up. I look towards where he indicates and recognize his older brother's shirt. A scuffle underway, and a policeman is on the ground. The brother plants the toe of his shoe into the policeman's face. "I knew it! I knew it," yells the kid, jumping up and down. "I knew he kicks ass!" Then the kid – before I can stop him – is off and clambering into the whirlpool of bodies. I lose track of him, stay on the rooftop. It's a beautiful thing that Pauline signed us in under aliases. I let the thought of action without responsibility, risk, consequence or penalty sink into me. It feels fine. Then I go back to the show with the cops.

The next day, Pauline, her bruised face in makeshift bandages of Kleenex, her belly pregnant with hangover, asks me, as I stop the car to give her a breather from motion: "What did Jessy say about Lala?"

I smile and breathe in the sunlight, groggy from sleeplessness but without a trace of alcohol poisoning. "She didn't say much," I reply.

"Is she alive or dead?"

"Never existed," I say. My feet sink into the rest-stop's grass. A drunk sleeps, his back against the outhouse. In his dream they are serving him the seventh course from a five star kitchen. I wipe off my pants and adjust my crotch.

I first began to suspect my phone wished me ill when it and I occupied the house in Victoria. I had some friends over. Lala was regaling them in an uncharacteristically talkative moment. The phone rang. I picked it up. Lala continued the tall and short of her tale. The call was for me and I can only remember that the person on the other end of the line was dear and that I hadn't spoken to her in a long time. While

Lala entertained I began a conversation with this person. After a few minutes Lala broke off her current tale, turned to me, and slapped me hard. Everyone stared. I quietly said good-bye to the person on the other end, telling her I would call back. Lala went on with the story as if nothing had happened. Everyone in the room looked jaundiced.

Afterwards, I asked Lala why she'd done that. "Because you interrupted me," she said.

I remember another argument my parents once had. We sat in the living-room having a glass of wine after dinner. Soon as the argument started it was like I didn't exist. It had to do with the advent of Katy's menstrual cycle. I remember the argument not only for its intensity but because it was the first and last time my father ever referred to sex, either the organs involved or the act itself. He laughed at sex scenes in movies, but gave no commentary. Sex talk was his private malaise. My lessons on biology from him amounted to how to gut a fish and a ptarmigan. Which was fine as far as I was concerned. His theories on that subject didn't hold my interest.

As usual, my mother spoke in Hungarian: "George?"

My father lifted his head from the wine he'd been staring at. "Hmmmm?"

"Katy had her period you know."

My father put one finger between his belt and gut and gave a small wince, as if something pained him. He looked at me, and then back at my mother, cocked his head slightly sideways, and raised an eyebrow.

My mother didn't even twitch in my direction. "He's old enough to hear this. He's twenty years old for gosh sake," she said.

My father coughed.

"Well," my mother continued, "she's ashamed of it." As she spoke, Mother rose slightly forward in the direction of my father, as if forwarding the problem to him, or as if it was his fault. "And it's nothing for her to be ashamed of. It's a beautiful thing, really. It means she's a woman now."

"Yes, of course." My father lit a cigarette with an angry flick.

"And I'd like to have a party for her. To celebrate it. To celebrate the fact that she's a woman now. Nothing big. Just the family, maybe one or two friends. It would help her deal with it. Show her that it's a good thing. Not something disgusting."

"That's just a great idea," my father replied, using words so saturated with sarcasm they never got off the ground.

"Pardon?"

Sarcasm wasn't my father's best known sport. At heart, he was Hungarian rural stock, known primarily for direct address and incandescent rage. He rarely had a need for sarcasm. It was an urban trait he didn't have the tools for. It shocked me as much as my mother. "Pardon?" she repeated.

"Have you gone insane?" he asked. "Who ever thought of such a stupid fucking idea." My father only swore at fellow motorists. I'd never heard him swear at home.

"What do you mean?" my mother replied, losing her temper.

"What do I mean!" My father rose from his seat and walked swiftly to the window, and then turned on my mother. "What do I mean?! Sure, let's have a period party. Yeah, that's a great idea. While we're at it why don't we have a 'wet dream' party for the boy and celebrate that one as well?"

"Now just a…." my mother interrupted.

"Yes. It's a great idea. We'll invite all the neighbors and they can ask Gabe here: 'So Gabe, you had your first wet dream. Tell us about it. How does it feel to be a man?' And Gabe can answer, 'Oh yeah. It was great. I had this dream about this woman with great big tits. And she gave me a blow-job. And I came everywhere. It was fantastic. I woke up and there was semen on my bed! I love being a man.'"

"Shut your mouth! Don't talk in front of Gabe like that!"

"Yeah, we'll have the neighbors over and Katy can tell us all about the blood coming out of her vagina. We'll sing a few songs. I'll hand out cigars. Katy can show us that she knows how to use a tampon now. You know, what they call an in-home demo. We'll have a few drinks and then you can bring out the cake. And the cake'll be in the shape of a … cunt … yes, with strawberry jam in the middle or ketchup or something. And you can dish out great big servings of cake coated in red stuff. And we'll laugh and hug Katy and pat her on the back and just have ourselves a little menstrual jamboree. We'll get the full story on this sexual 'coming of age' thing, both perspectives, male and female. Christ! I've never heard of such a ridiculous thing in my whole life! Are you the same woman I married? Are you? How can you even think of such a thing?"

My mother and I stared at him. We'd been used to his explosions before but nothing of this magnitude. My mother had breached some forbidden zone of conversation. She calmly put down her wineglass and looked at him. He glared out the window. She rose from her chair.

The next evening, dinner occurred at the expected hour, though my parents were not talking. Dessert was not something my family ate. It was reserved for guests. So when my mother mentioned dessert, it amazed all three of us kids. But she told us the dessert was only for her and father. When the dishes had been cleared she told us to leave. My siblings and I stuck around, outside the kitchen, waiting to see what would happen. My father, too, waited to see what would happen.

I couldn't believe the cake my mother brought out. It had shaved dark chocolate for pubic hairs, a cream-colored icing, and right down the center, between two rounded labia of pastry, was a thick layer of red glaze, or jelly. My father stared at it, his knuckles turning white as he gripped his coffee-cup.

"*Bon appetit*," my mother said.

My father just stared at the cake.

My mother cut herself and him a piece. "Now, we are going to celebrate," she said, taking a large bite out of her slice. "Mmmmmm, sure is good! What's wrong, aren't you hungry? Or can't you handle it? Don't tell me that someone with an imagination as vivid as yours is scared of a little bite of cake? Come," she said, proffering a bite on an outstretched fork, "not even one itty-bitty little taste?"

My father grabbed his fork and began shoveling the cake down, not pausing. When finished with his slice he made to leave but my mother just shook her head. "Oh no, there's more where that came from." She cut him and herself even bigger slices. The cake-eating became a contest. They had almost finished the whole thing when my father started groaning. He rushed past us to the bathroom, where we heard him retch. My mother calmly finished the last piece and, putting her knife and fork at the five o'clock position on her plate, took a sip of her coffee.

Katy had her party. An aunt and, I think, a cousin took part. My mother talked to us about menstruation and sex. Everyone was uncomfortable and that made for a solidarity that gave way, eventually, to a type of relaxation. My father sat in the corner and attempted to sell himself back into our respect by flashing encouraging smiles. Mother talked without heed. It was the only parent/child sex-talk I ever received. I think it made Katy less self-conscious, but, for all I'm insensitive to, it could have done the opposite. Menstruation was not a frequent topic in our home after that. I don't think the talk really helped any of us kids at all. Katy had her chlamydia infection a few years later, and I've been fighting the various STDs off and on as well. Despite my mother's attempts at educating us, we all remained dunces in the field of sexual relations. We were all trial and error, but had no one to blame except ourselves. Mother's years of troubleshooting came to a close that night. We'd have to make up our suicide notes without her ghostwriting now, in our blood not hers.

Think of a captain, any captain, and you have Lala's dad. Think of a compass surrounded by magnets, what the needle does, and I won't have to say any more about who he was. Except: cruel, mixed-up, avaricious, unloving, selfish.

Lala went home one day. This was on our second swing around the bend. Her father had recently moved to Vancouver from Oxbow. His latest wife, number four, had managed to convince him to start over in the big city. Lala's dad had been starting over every minute of his life, starting over so many times and so rapidly that "new start" was synonymous with "failed again." The eyes on this man were a brilliant green. There were creatures swimming in them, creatures unknown to humanity. Those uncanny eyes: I never believed they actually belonged to him, was absolutely positive they hadn't been his to begin with. Three wives had left her father already. There were many more out there. Once in a while he'd have a nervous breakdown and do something funny and/or interesting.

Mounting the stairs to her father's apartment, Lala heard a crash on the street. It was five o'clock on a late October night. People didn't make many sounds in the neighborhood at that specific time. Only the cats slouched about, silent, all eyes. Sometimes an automobile rattled down the strip like a thing made entirely of tin and spare parts. Empty rubbing alcohol containers littered the back alley. But that could have just been coincidence. As she kept mounting the staircase, her leather-soled boots clopping on the stone, Lala heard another crash, but kept up the time of her footfalls, thinking nothing. She could be hopeless sometimes. How do I know this story? I know everything.

When Lala opened the door to the apartment, her father stood in his underwear, with a baseball cap on his head to keep the hair out of his eyes. He also had on one shoe, no socks and was pulling the couch towards the open sliding doors that led onto the balcony. Lala noticed a coffee table and recliner missing from the room's usual furnishings.

"Hi Dad," she said, smiling a nervous smile that always managed to look condescending.

"Nothing is as it should be," he said, grunting and exerting himself over the couch. "I wish I wasn't a paranoid-schizophrenic sometimes," he continued, after moving the couch halfway out onto the balcony. "But there are people indigenous to imbalance, God help me." He lifted the edge of the couch onto the balcony's railing. Lala waited just long enough. She grabbed onto the other end of the couch.

"What are you doing, Dad?"

"You have to help me with this."

Lala didn't like the direction of the "new start" so far.

"Also, do you realize this is the month your mom left me? This is also the month your other mom left, too. Then there was that third one. Now your fourth mom is gone. Ergo: I relapse into paranoid-schizophrenic mode. And thus the furniture must be disposed of."

He was only having a nervous breakdown. It happened every year on the anniversary of his two divorces. October was his alter-ego month, when the evidence that all were abandoning him became convincing.

Lala looked down at the splinters of the two previously departed furnishings. The eighth floor looked on a long fall.

"Dad, why don't you bring the furniture inside?"

"Because, as I've already told you, I must not. Grab that end and pick it up."

"By the way, you're an asshole, Dad."

"That's exactly what you'd like me to be wouldn't you? But I'm too great a guy. Now, if you don't pick up that end I'm not going to let you leave. I'm going to lock you in a closet. I won't let you go to the bathroom."

He never teased. Lala bent down and picked up her end of the couch, and pushed. The two of them rushed to the railing – like daughter like father like daughter – and watched the couch tumble down and disintegrate on the sidewalk. They stayed for a long time with chins propped in their hands, elbows resting on the railing.

When his wife walked in they'd just thrown the love-seat over. Lala perspiring and scared. She knew that when the furniture was done she might be next.

His girlfriend – Lala's fourth mom – walked in with her children. "What's going on?" she asked, looking balefully at Lala.

"Where the hell have you been?" shouted Lala over the sound of her father squealing, "Whoopee!" from the porch and the crash of an eight-piece tea and jam set on the sidewalk. "How could you leave him when he's like this!"

"I don't know what you're talking about," the woman said, pushing her curious kids' faces behind herself and backing towards the open door. "We just went out to a movie. I told him that's where we were going."

"Call an ambulance or the police then, please," said Lala, sinking down into one of the dining room chairs and rubbing panic-stricken hands together. But the police had already arrived. Lala had disliked the cops since the night of the blond. Now she'd have to go through another cross-examination.

I arrive home from Oregon to discover my sister's been in a near-fatal car crash. My parents' Monte Carlo is a scrapyard heap. Also, the dog's tail is broken; it wears immortality on the splint.

I visit my sister in intensive care. She forces me to draw the curtains around her bed. I hold her hand and coo mollifyingly.

She confesses: "One night I'm coming home and I see the dog pissing in the street. Can you believe that? Shit. Normally, the only thing that gets it out of the yard is some bitch trotting by. And, for once, the car purrs silently. It couldn't be better. I take aim, hit the gas, turn out the headlights. So dark I never even saw it move. I was," she pulls her pillow under her chin, "so sure I couldn't miss."

Somehow the dog passed between the wheels of the car. She only managed to hit its tail. Because of her ecstatic focus on the dog she ran through the fence straight into one of the maple trees in our yard. My parents charged her with drinking and driving. The dog knows better.

"I'm done with the dog," she says, snatching at my sleeve and ripping off the cuff button. "I'm not going to let it kill me. I'll adopt children if I have to. You should try another solution too."

I depart, relieved to be unrivaled.

There is more than one way to be a eunuch. First you swim up a personal shit creek. Then you have to have a certain knack for inability.

This is something you're born with, or something you work very hard to cultivate or, in my case, a little of both. The rest follows matter of course. The blame comes on and you point a fat finger at yourself to fix the verdict for the failures you've accomplished. You hibernate through spring, through summer, through autumn, and in December you decide to hibernate the rest.

I could hear yelling from around the corner of a hedge. Some kind of crowd. When they came in sight, I saw a group of people standing in line. Some men held back the crowd. The rest of the Hungarian folk market consisted of peasant women, in black shawls and embroidered skirts and blouses, selling table-cloths and pastries. Buried in the dirt up to the neck, in front of the crowd, was a chicken. It swiveled its little bite-sized head to avoid the glare of sun, but there was no shade for it anywhere across the sandbox hemming it in. It talked to the crowd in chicken language.

Someone stepped forward out of the crowd, and one of the boys running the show tied a blindfold around his head and put a metal rake into his hand. He took faltering steps over the ground towards the chicken, blindly swinging the rake just over the surface of the ground.

"What's going on?" I asked someone, but they looked at me like I was too stupid to warrant an answer. The guy in the blindfold stumbled around swinging the rake and almost stomping on the head of the prize. Finally, one of the gameshow hosts called: "Time's up." They took off his blindfold and collected a ticket from the next person in line, getting the blindfold and rake ready.

Someone finally let me in on the rules of play. The person who rakes the head off the chicken gets to take it home and put it on the perch in their larder. Nothing like opening the larder to say hello to your dead pet chicken, sitting on the shelf without a head and without a feather on its body, its puckered chicken-skin covered with goosebumps the size of nipples. Hey, chickie, chickie, chickie.

"Oh man, where do I get my ticket?" I asked.

It figures: during my turn with the rake, an animal activist ran out of the crowd. I was kind of malingering in one spot, not moving much, just sweeping the rake over an area like a scythe. I was the grim reaper of chickens and thinking of all the times Lala and I had held a wishbone between us and the thing cracked right in perfect half along the joint.

I heard a yell from the crowd and someone pulled the rake out of my hands. I had just enough time to pull the blindfold off my head to see the last three centimeters between the rake and my face. I went down in the dust, feeling blood on my fingers and a hole or more in my head. Why do they always hit me in the noggin?

The crowd's feet stamped all around me, trampling on my head. I tried to look up but too much blood clouded my eyes. "*Kapd el! Fogd meg aszt a faszt! Az anya picsája*!" The crowd scrambled to nab the activist, who swung the rake to keep them at bay. Finally, he just started to run through a small forest on the edge of the market-grounds, everyone in hot pursuit, intending to break both his arms and legs, if not his neck. Nobody gave a thought to me except for a few kicks in the side from people wanting to join in the chase. "Get off the ground," they yelled. "Anyone who lays bleeding on the ground like that deserves to be kicked!"

When the thuds of feet on my body stopped, I wiped the blood and dirt from my face. Laying dust-covered on my stomach, I looked up at the head of the chicken, which had somehow survived the riot. It cocked its head at me like I was some new kind of oddity. Over to the east I saw the crowd of locals like some medieval witch-hunt leaping through the wheat after the activist who waved a glinting rake way in the background and hotfooted it towards the sun. Together, pursuers and pursuant weaved an S in the wheat and disappeared near the horizon. Then I reached over and twisted that spindly neck of the chicken right around.

The night of our rotgut reunion in Victoria, Lala and I stopped talking about France to make classic and elegant love, with a pinch of speed. Nothing explicit about it: two bodies, nudity, a rush of sheets. I kissed her first and afterwards she bowed her head, flashing through our history fast as a drowner. I lifted her head, daring enough for a second and even a third try. Under the edge of the V-neck sweater she wore without a shirt I found a shoulder so round it looked chewy, tempting bites. But ever the weakling, I just grazed my mouth on it. The third time our lips met she joined in. Why not? Apart from the obvious, that is.

Soft breasts in a burgundy bra: for all the world they fitted there like alliteration, every part of her so filled with possibilities I couldn't picture all her anatomy at once. You could isolate and spend years resourcing every square inch of her physique. Kissing, now naked, we walked out one of the kitchen's four exits into my room, me plodding forward, her backwards. Our heads aslant in the kiss, we both had only one free eye; the tongues made slippery work, and keeping four left feet and twenty thumbs in sensual play is no junior patrol. But she seemed more proficient at movement. I let her lead. We didn't go astray.

Then into the sheets to love ourselves and each other the way proper missionaries should.

A word-of-mouth bulletin of some perverse discovery on the beach goes door to door in Oxbow. Within minutes I telephone Pauline. More minutes pass before we come to a spot which has attracted onlookers. The ocean is really calm today. The fog rests lazily on it. You can't see for miles.

On the edge of the shoreline, in the inter-tidal zone, lays a dead killer whale. Someone has modified its body. I suppose an environmentalist would say "desecrated" instead of "modified," but environmentalism is a belief system about which neither Pauline nor I speak easy terms. I would prefer to call what they've done with the whale art. A sculpture. Perhaps performance art. Or an installation piece.

Yes.

The whale looks like something they've shot out of the sky.

Branches prop up each appendage. Someone has painted its eyeballs a gruesome shade of pink, put a party hat on its head. What looks like a massive joint (made out of an enormous number of rolling papers) filled with dry seaweed sticks out of the blowhole. But the most stunning aspect of the whole piece is the large heart chiseled into the blubber, which has an arrow through it, and contains the words, 'Popeye's Mom,' the whole heart painted the same shade of hot pink as the eyes. Large oily drops of sprayed color run down in long drip marks from the heart carved into the belly of the whale. Hasty work, no doubt, done by journeymen or junior graffiti artists in a moment without manifesto. I try to decide on the statement they attempted. Maybe they wanted only to upset the *status quo*.

Perhaps the whale did it to himself. The leviathan's magnum opus. The final testament. In that case, it would have to be called performance art.

Totally.

The second week's sexual itinerary – after the resumption of Lala's and my coital association in Victoria – began with kisses in the kitchen, again. Lala marched me into the bedroom, as before. Nothing seemed premeditated, yet. Following foreplay, initial entry and five minutes of a basic front-stroke exchange, I carried Lala – I had to, her legs were locked around my waist – to a low chair in the living room. There she straddled me while I sat in my regular couch-potato slump.

The second week's menu happened because Lala came on Tuesday before noon and I offered her food: an omelet. The first mistake was telling her the ingredients: mushrooms, cheese, onions, green pepper. She wrote them down on a matchbox fished out of her back pocket and turned a deep shade of embarrassment when I asked why, her shrug similar to a twitch. The sunlight smelled bad that day – rank as burnt skin – but the warmth overjoyed our joints, seized as they were by weeks of fallen barometer.

"I need things," Lala said. "In France I stayed with three families. The first two fathers wanted nothing but sex with me. The third had so many mistresses he didn't have time to give me a glance. Like my poppa back here," Lala snickered. "So I stayed, at home away from home."

"And the mothers?" I asked.

"Their dining rooms doubled as slop kitchens."

"Like mine?"

"No, like my mother's." She laughed, then got serious and said: "Only mothers give you more than sex."

I turned, aghast: "You've had incestuous lesbian experiences?"

Lala jumped onto my back, kissed my neck and then stayed there. "Only with you," she said and sang, to the tune of Elvis's "You Ain't Nothin' But A Hound Dog:" "You ain't nothin' but a warthog, rootin' grubs all the time...."

I flipped an omelet that twirled six times before landing back in the pan. Lala let out a little drum roll for added pizzazz. I would have piggybacked her over hurdles.

I need things: exactly what she said.

The second week's avowal turned out to be, I love you more than fungus loves feet.

Bill takes the muscle out of my bank account. He phones me from San Francisco and the background music suggests a cheesy strip bar, the patrons hooting for hooters. O Bill, I think, how you've devolved. Nor does he sound lucid, only caught in the rain. He loved his wife. That's bonafide truth and that's why he tried to pop off his foot. Now he reviles her thoroughly. Understandable reassessment, I think.

Only, something has changed. He had attributed their current differences to her betrayal of his thieving ways and his need to be revenged for it, but this odyssey is putting him through some kind of personal revival, of which one part is the realization that his wife doesn't hate him as much as the condition of their married life. "You can't really blame the blind," she told him in San Francisco during the incident I'm about to relate, "for their blindness, or the stupid for not having brains, or the unfeeling for their emotional discrepancies. But sometimes all you can do is run them through. What do you want me to do? Live with it too? You think I can heal everything? You think I've got some gene-splicer? Even if I had the tools it would take too long. Fuck off, Bill."

And all he could say was: "Since when do you use words like 'gene-splicer?'"

"Been doing a lot of reading on the road, you know."

And certain transformations took Bill by surprise. For one thing, he'd learned how to speed and ignore the tweaks of conscience. The feeling that he was on to something heinous came to bug him less and less. So he actually managed stay on her rubber tire tracks before they'd even had a chance to cool and harden. Ever since Portland her taillights had more or less stayed within striking range but Bill had yet to attain the nerve needed to become a drive-by hitman. He kept the shotgun under the level of the windshield, and stalked her to San Francisco.

Bill had the unmitigated heedlessness to book himself under his real name in the same hotel as her. The bluntness of his purpose made him myopic. Despite the blunder, he stayed unnoticed. She didn't say, "Come out, come out; I know you're in there," when she walked past his room. For once, he'd managed to get somewhere unbeknownst.

Eventually he stopped with the disguises, the push-ups and sit-ups, re- and unloading the shotgun. He stopped striving for excellence, went over to her hotel room, knocked – she answered – and offered himself as dinner companion for the evening. She looked down at her sneakers. "Motherfuck, Bill. If I didn't know better I'd swear you wanted my body."

"Let's not get carried away," Bill assured her. "I just want to remember why I decided to kill you."

"Because I was a company informant."

"No," he shook his head confusedly, "that doesn't seem valid anymore."

"Okay. Let me freshen up. I'll come over to your place."

"Fine," said Bill, dazed.

They went out to dinner, a steak and lobster place. Bill took a comb, ran it under the tap, and slicked his hair flat onto his head, found his wedding suit in his luggage, took it out of the rubble. He'd lost so much belly his belt didn't have enough holes.

Most of the meal passed in soundless bites. Bill doubted the waiter's taste in entrées and didn't follow his recommendation, so his wife got the better meal by faith. Though this wounded Bill, the tears began sliding down not his but the wife's cheeks.

"I'm scared of you Bill."

He sat back relieved. "You sure don't seem like it. What about getting into my car in Seattle? What about that, that, that fucking two-barrel roulette back in Portland?"

"I'm desperate, you degenerate! I want you to stop chasing me. You're sick in the head. Why don't you stop?"

"Because you ruined my life you bitch," said Bill, snapping the napkin from where he'd tucked it into his shirt-collar. "Or you ruined something."

Her voice cracked with tenderness. "And what about my life?"

Bill dropped his features.

"I'll see you in Mexico," she said. "I'll be there first." And writing her name down on one of the cloth napkins she left with the words: "Maybe the drive will cheer you up. Maybe you'll like Mexico. But that's where I intend to stop. I hope you can make up your mind by then."

Bill got stiffed with the bill.

Dilaudid was the third who walked the road with us. One of Pauline's friends worked at a pharmacy in Vancouver and the supply came in philanthropic quantities, at a low, low price. My dog wiggled along the road in front of us. Under the love of dilaudid, the world became all blissful.

Lala had been living in San Francisco for some months now. We'd had the last sex I'd ever want again.

I'd just left university and was in a nirvana of joblessness, on a hiatus from everything except the glorious slumming of sheer existence. Pauline still had her job as a night-watchman in an office complex; but she freeloaded, punching in and then going to a nearby bar or my apartment, returning to work only to punch out. The boyfriend was weeks out of her life.

In the early evening of a balmy Indian Summer day we'd decided to partake in pills and a walk of the dog. The clouds weren't sails or white horses but black and blue bulkheads. But what could I or Pauline do? Chiefly, dilaudid does away with annoyances from without; everything else about it is an insignificant drawback or health hazard. Pauline and I ambled in a boulevard of dust. Every synapse in our minds took its time with input and output, every response coming out relaxed. Our eyes sat pretty.

Pauline had to shit. Dilaudid usually affected her so. It produced nausea in me. I had to be outside and walking or constantly have to swallow little belches of puke. We were out trekking because of me. Luckily, Pauline brought along a couple wads of kleenex. She disappeared into the bush. I waited while deer flies buzzed around my head. Normally, I would have been in a panic, swinging at them, a rabid windmill, but I just watched them land on my bare arms and then snuffed out their disagreeable lives with effete slaps of my hand. Afterwards, I examined how they looked pulverized on skin. This aroused paternal instincts. I wiped my arms off on my pants.

When Pauline had come down we couldn't find the dog. It was up in the woods eating her shit. We found him there, a beard of crap hanging from his chin. He sucked the log of shit in with a great big slurping sound, his mouth in a sharp triangular grin somewhere between pain and bravado, as if saying: "I'm tough, I can take it." He panted and vacuumed Pauline's shit into his mouth like a portable defecation receptacle, ravenous for feces, sucking it back like a shit cigarette and altogether overdoing the theatrics. Pauline and I both had to kick him in the head to make him desist.

Some scenes even dilaudid can't mellow.

The third week's sexual itinerary: Lala insisted on the kitchen for starters. I was unmotivated and her stubbornness almost lost me what half-hearted erection I had. For one thing my roommates were at home, albeit sequestered, studying behind doors. I'd uncovered a hidden exhibitionist in Lala. But I let myself succumb. We left clothes on the floor. Lala did her patented walk, led me to the bedroom. I lay above her on four points: elbows and knees. Then she wanted to be where the teevee was. "We've already done this before," I said. "Time travel does not titillate me." But out we went. The staccato of Trixy's typewriter in the next room offered me a tempo, so I gave Lala a staggering thirty-five thrusts a minute which, of course, made my orgasm certain in a devastatingly short time-span. By then, totally impassioned – this flaunting of common decency ain't a bad racket – I sucked on her nether regions for a good while.

In this fashion I set myself up. If not for innocence, I might have known better.

The third week on Wednesday Lala refused the salad I made: no egg in it.

"It had egg in it last time," she yelled, slamming her fist on the table.

That night her stomach would not stop rumbling from emptiness, keeping me awake, sipping warm water.

The third week's avowal: I love you more than fungus loves feet. I love you more than hatters love chemotherapy.

The crazy man who lived on my grandmother's street carved pictures into anything scarred by the blade of his knife, trees for instance. And the pictures he cut were folksy: a little girl giving a straw bouquet to a wolf, or three dwarfs standing on stones, or donkeys kissing during a dance. Everybody said they knew the extent of his madness. His features were so sunken he couldn't make facial expressions.

My grandmother, great-grandmother and great-aunt lived next door, along with my mother and her siblings. They avoided him on the street. The children watched him read some novel while balancing on a fence woven out of fallen twigs and sticks. Occasionally he'd put down the book and play out the last bit of dialogue he'd read. Once he cradled an invisible but sweet prince and whispered: "Goodnight, li'l fella. Goodnight." Once he appeared in front of my grandmother, sitting in frayed clothes on the fence of dead branches, picking scum out from between his toes using a knife with a serrated edge, and told her about all his enemies. But then he smiled like a rain-split cherry and said: "Ah, but my sweetheart, how I'd bend over for you."

You guessed it: he owned a beautiful, white, long-haired dog that he tied to a tree and skinned alive one starry summer night. My grandmother stuffed all the stricken childrens' ears with cotton swab at two a.m. The feckless matriarchs sat up that night gulping quantities of brandy. The dog wouldn't stop howling.

The next day, my three ancestral matriarchs in high command, the villagers took the psycho down to the river, to perform a ritual usually reserved for unwanted kittens. Even with the last flurry of bubbles he tried to convince them of his sanity, or his enemies, but this only caused five of the thirty or so hands pushing him under to reconsider. The three ladies stayed until the end. Necessity sure does invent some mothers.

My father came back from his home number two, wife number two, son number two, and then we sat with him at dinner. I was younger then, and it's easier to entertain and forget the criminal element in others when your mind's still relatively pliable. To this day I don't know if anyone but me knew of his other life. Even calling it home number two, instead of home number one, suggests a certain inexcusable faith life has failed to cure me of. I still have scars from the time he ran over me with the bicycle.

I'd try to bring up the other life when he least expected it.

We were planing wood in the workshop for a new bedroom in the basement. "Dad, about that ... thing...." That's how I began, hoping he'd leap to fill in my blanks.

"Hand me that piece of wood," he commanded, easily heard over the buzz of the electric planer. I held on to the long board coming off the machine, reached behind me with one hand and grabbed the stick he'd requested.

"Don't you think we should talk about River City?"

He handed the stick back to me and we lifted another piece of wood onto the machine. "Make sure you put that stick back where you found it, cause I'll need it again to push this wood through." He flicked on the machine.

"So, as I was saying. I'd like you to answer some basic things for me. I just don't understand. Why don't you get a divorce?"

The board came off smooth and stripped of splinters. He disconnected the extension chord and the machine hummed lower and lower, stopping. "Okay, grab those boards," he said. "Let's get them in fast. I don't want too much rain on these. It'll warp them."

Another time we replaced the muffler on the car.

It was still raining, like it hadn't had a chance to stop since last we talked, months ago. I lay under the chassis because I fit more easily, and squirted lubricant on the exhaust pipes and bolts, permanently bonded together by rust. "Dad, I know you don't like me bringing up that other town," I started, handing back the WD-40. Kneeling down beside the body of the car he peered under with a flashlight. "I'll never tell anyone. Don't worry. I won't tell ever." I thought I saw a nearly imperceptible nod, to concur, but in hindsight I realize he just inclined his head inward to pass a wrench.

"Try those bolts again," he suggested.

"I want to know...." I grunted, pulling on the monkey wrench. It slipped off and I banged my knuckles against the body. "Fuck!" I cursed, picking up the wrench to try again. "I just want to know, Dad, how you feel about me knowing. Doesn't it bother you?"

"No, that wrench isn't going to work. It's too short. You can't get any leverage on it. Let me get you a bigger one." His flashlight clicked off and I watched his feet walk around the car, heard him clanging in the trunk.

"How does it feel to have two wives? How do you justify it to yourself?"

He came back and bent down, handing me a larger wrench. "That one should do the trick," he predicted. "When you're done getting that off come into the shop. I'll get everything else ready."

"Dad, could you answer one question?"

"Sure."

I had oil on my face and I stared into his flashlight like we'd reached some border checkpoint past which I was not authorized to go. "Who do you love more?"

He smiled. "Yeah, it does look like this rain's going to clear up."

Another time we went on a family picnic: fishing rods, mother, sister, father, dog.

I'd purposefully set myself up close to the old man. My sister stood lower down the shore of the lake, happily looping a Muddler Minnow forward and back to tease the trout. So many fish crowded the lake I wondered why we needed fishing rods at all – a flat shovel would have been enough. "Dad why don't you ever answer my questions about that thing that happened to us up in River City?"

"Goddamn!" my father delightedly yelled, the tip of his fly rod bending down.

After he reeled it in and unhooked the flapping prey I took another crack. "It's not like I want to make some kind of prolonged debate about it. I just want to talk a little. I'm a bit confused about where me and the rest of the family stand."

"You know," he said. "I never really believed that home-tied flies worked as well as store-bought ones but, shit, the fish are just eating this one up."

I felt like walking over and snapping his rod in half, but he would have broken my neck with a flick of the wrist. He could have drowned me in his spit. Everything about him seemed invincible and invulnerable, especially his mind. "So I guess you're just never gonna tell me?"

I felt my mother behind me only after I'd spoken. "Tell you what?" she asked.

"About his affairs," I answered.

"Look at these beauties," my father beamed, holding up the fish he'd caught. "What?" he looked at us tiredly. "You've got to admit they're impressive."

We had to.

So I had strange imaginings: daydreams, daymares. I've selected two from the many. Here they go:

1) The judge stares at my father while he sits in the witness box. "Tell us about your wife," the judge demands. My Dad reaches forward, fingering his tie.

   "You know," he replies. "I bought this back in 1963 for fifty cents. Check it out, judge, pure silk."

   "I don't give a rat's ass about your tie," the judge says, magisterially, "I want to hear about your other wife. Please discuss the matter at hand."

   "I think I also bought a pair of shoes with it," my father says, after a minute of reflection.

2) Nazis torture my father. They put his head in a vice. "Tell us about your oder vife."

   "Do you mind if I have a cigarette?" my father asks, his arms and legs stretched out and tied down. In response, the Nazi interrogator presses his cigarette into my father's stomach.

   "You vill tell us everytink you know about your oder vife!" the

Nazi shouts, tightening the handle on the vice squeezing my father's skull.
"You don't have any aspirin, do you?" my father asks.
When they take him to the edge of the acid bath the Nazi barks, "Dis is your last chance. You must tell us about your second vife, you bastard polygamist. Vee vaunt to know everytink. Everytink!"
My father looks into the scum floating on the surface of the liquid in the bath. He thinks for a minute, very hard. "Normally I like my baths a bit cooler. In fact, if there was more time, I'd tell you about how I used to refuse to get into the bath as a kid. But when in Germany do as the Germans, no?"
Splash.

I don't know, apart from such nightmarish scenes, how my father's two-timing affected my thought patterns and therefore behavior. I would like to say they messed me up, but I haven't discovered any pattern in my activities to support this. Sometimes thinking about it puts me in a bad mood and then I'll have a drink or a toke. But sometimes I think about it and go out to pick flowers or help old ladies cross the street. I have my moods, my unexplainable whims.

I never found out, for reasons of the above, if my father considered what he did wrong. Not that it makes a difference. It is one thing to know that the way you behave is not the way you want to behave, and it is another thing entirely to switch that behavior over – Lala's mommy taught me this. Moving out of the house helped me ignore his comings and goings. To him, it made no difference. He was the same during dinner as before I changed address. Then my father died and his secrets became enigmas of the most endurable kind.

On the 105 bus up Andrássy Boulevard I watched the decaying Austro-Hungarian mansions slide by – balcony's supported by massive columns, ringed with arcades, decorated with Germanic looking gods and goddesses, some of them with elaborate paint jobs on their exterior walls, arabesques and scrolls, triangles and neo-baroque glory, gold, crimson and silver, every building sad-eyed in the grime. They were neglected, disparaged publicly as excessive and then moved into by the cutthroat communists when nobody was looking. I hadn't shaved in a week or eaten much; I wore my clothes three days in a row. I blended in.

Nine a.m. and our bus traveled towards Heroes' Square, my favorite spot, where scruffy eastern European boy-wonders skate-boarded in and among tourists. In the center of the square stood an angel on top of a pillar, ringed down below by statues of Hungary's greatest kings and leaders.

Nine a.m. and no somebodies sat on the bus, just me and the city laborers. They stank of double shots of cherry *pálinka* and the chemical sourness of the green beer they tilted back at *Moszkva Tér*. A heroin addict told a friend of his – perhaps also a junkie though not of as sordid an appearance – about injecting rainwater when no other fix became available. I stopped listening to his story – too mythic for reality – and concentrated on the workmen instead, one of them telling a joke.

"Three neighbor farmers – an Englishman, a Frenchman and a Hungarian – get a wish each. The Englishman goes first. He looks out at his bare pastures and old worn-out bull. 'I wish for a brand-new, beautiful cow for my fields.' Poof, there it is. The Frenchman goes next. He looks at the Englishman's shiny new cow, udder chock-full of milk, already attracting the bull to beget some offspring, and he says: 'I wish for a cow as beautiful as the Englishman's.' Poof, there it is. Now the Hungarian gets to brooding. He looks out at his fields, at how empty they are, how devoid of promise. Then he looks over at the fields of his French and English neighbors. He feels envious of how good their farms now look with the beautiful cows in the middle, of how prosperous they now seem, and he hates their superiority over him. He raises his voice to the sky and yells, 'God how I wish that their cows would die, die, die.' Poof, two dead cows, and everyone back where they started."

The two drunk workmen howled at this, knowing full well how to laugh at their own expense.

Fourth week's sexual itinerary: "Lala, I don't want to go down on you," I said.

"You did last time. Do it now."

We'd been to the kitchen, bedroom, done the chair. Lala urged me to get that rhythm back. The bones in my pelvis creaked, the flesh upon them bruised. I did not want to go down on her.

"So, I did last time. So what?"

"I need you to do it."

Sigh.

During the fourth week's menu Lala dumped an omelet into the sink because it didn't contain the latest addition: anchovies.

I began to make very careful shopping lists.

Fourth week's avowal: I love you more than fungus loves the foot, than hatters love chemotherapy, than parasites love hosts.

I attended my father's funeral in River City. I had kept careful tabs over his final years, and already knew whose house the body would be in, the names of the mourners or, more accurately, celebrants. As far as my mother was concerned, I was merely going to River City to sort out and sign papers for the body I told her they never found.

The undertaker was perhaps too understanding of my dilemma when I explained all to him at our private rendezvous. I hated his hands on my shoulders – they'd fondled too many mortal injuries, full of a craft I detested. Of course, he took all major credit cards. I was responsible for replacing on the corpse that false mustache my father pasted to his lip with gum arabic the three days per week he decamped to River City.

The party was, appropriately, an extravaganza: all the photos and portraits wrapped in black cloth; the glasses, cutlery, bowls and plates dulled in gloom. They must have prided themselves on their humor because the food was burnt to a fine black crisp. The wake was a good theme party. Father reposed in the center like a lid to the coffin he satiated, hands folded across the chest in a foreign configuration. The mustache intruded on his face – an uninvited guest, like me, a wake crasher.

A man in the corner doubled over at a joke, tears gumming up his eyes.

The hostess, widow number two, praised the body's reconditioning, the undertaker's superlative job. She pointed to various parts and said: "The fingernails, look how polished they are!" Upon noticing me, she left off.

"Excuse me? Do I know you?" Her son, breaking off from a group of well-wishers, came over, a xerox copy of his dad, unlike me, in matching but authentic mustache.

"Uhh, I worked with Joe here," I replied to the question. He stepped forward and pulled my boutonniere out of its hole.

"No, you didn't!"

"Yes, I did."

"I don't think so, I knew everybody who worked with my Dad and I've never seen you before, buddy." He slapped the end of my nose with the orchid.

"Oh, well," I suppressed a sneeze, "I worked with him in Oxbow."

"Is that so?" he laughed. A millisecond later those gathered around laughed in support of him.

"That is." I nodded, countering their laughs with a toothy grin. A small circle of miners closed around me, obviously in complete solidarity with the boy.

"Can you prove that?" he whispered.

"Yes, I can," I squeaked.

"What's that?"

"I can prove I knew him."

"How?"

I wheeled and ripped the bogus mustache off my father's head.

"You know," I tell Pauline, "if my dog wasn't a boy I don't think the urge to kill it would overpower me so."

"Don't discriminate," she says.

In the anthology of our afternoons there file pleasant climes, untroubled skies. Before the near-miss-rape-trauma, Pauline, Lala, Pauline's boyfriend and I sat in lawn chairs and sunglasses and the dust billowed through the unfinished trailer park. I was still incognito to Lala and the boyfriend, just plain likable in fact, though Pauline knew me exactly. The theme for the afternoon centered on picking up people in bars.

"You know," Pauline's boyfriend said, sipping the margaritas Pauline and Lala had devised, "I knew someone once."

"Oh, that's nice," Pauline interrupted. "You know," she turned to us, "I knew someone once, too."

Her boyfriend pretended hurt feelings. "Shut up," he scowled. "I knew this guy once who used to go to bars and, after a few drinks, would walk around and find the best-looking girl in the place, walk up to her and ask her out. If she turned him down, the standard thing, he'd go, find the ugliest girl in the bar, and try again. He always got laid, anyhow. And once in a while, every once in a while, he'd get the good-looking chick."

Lala laughed at him. "I used to do that, too. I always called the ugliest guy the pig-fuck. Go straight for the gold and if that doesn't pan there's always the pig-fuck."

Hilarity gutted all of us on that nice callous, sunny day, a day done up for this kind of mercilessness. "Isn't the world cruel?" Pauline asked. "It makes no concessions when it doles out the gifts.

So selective."

That's the truth, but nobody replied.

Fifth, sixth, seventh week's sexual itineraries: Kitchen, bedroom, teevee room.... I made the mistake in the fourth week of letting Lala give me a blow job after I had gone down on her. We went back to my room and had cute sex. By then I felt servile. We had sex at least every second day, if not more. The ritual cast itself in lead. I tired of the kitchen, the bedroom, the teevee room, the same rotation, the same methods of fore- and aft-play, but the more discontent I showed the stauncher Lala became, the more she seemed to thrive on the process.

My roommates caught us a couple of times. Trixy walked through while Lala straddled me in the teevee room. I looked at her, shrugged my shoulders and she rolled her eyes. Luckily, Lala began adhering to certain time schedules, so the roommates knew when to be scarce.

"You can always leave me," Lala threatened, her father's green eyes seemingly borrowed for the occasion, "like you did before."

"No," I lied, weary and vanquished, "it's fine. I like it."

Fifth, Sixth, Seventh weeks' menu: Mostly I took to avoiding meal times. Either I planned my eating around her or we went to restaurants. In restaurants, for some reason, Lala consented to any fare, reading the menu like an unrecognizable chart, her face completely bewildered, a bit bored. Eventually she told me to order for her. The rare passerby could see two figures, one dribbling ketchup on the other's fries, through the diner's plate-glass window.

Somewhere in the sixth week Lala came over for dinner and I had lost the pine nuts for the pesto. I went crazy searching for them, climbing up on the counter tops, spilling containers of flour and sugar, ransacking the cupboards, throwing boxes of cereal and macaroni onto the floor, searching in places where I knew for fact that pine nuts would never hide. Any peeping Tom would have instantly recognized me for a spaz in action.

By the time Lala arrived I stood over the stove, hands on either side of its white surface, my face red and sweating. Lala sat down in the kitchen with her leather satchel. "I lost an ingredient," I told her.

She reached into the satchel. Everything I needed was there. "Probably the pine nuts," she mumbled. "They're easy to lose."

By the end of the seventh week, on a Monday afternoon at four o'clock post-coital time, I began reciting the avowal: I love you more than hatters love chemotherapy, than parasites hosts, than dogs their bones, than beauty queens flattery, than spinsters their homes, than the torturer groans....

Lala whispered to me, in a sultry tone, her fingers tight in my hair: "You forgot that fungus loves the foot."

She got out of bed, put on her clothes. I closed my eyes so I wouldn't see her go.

My grandfather always drank the cream off the morning's milk and left none for the family. He hogged the butter a neighbor lady brought for the kids because he felt the skin loose on his frame. "I didn't bring it for the lord of the house," the neighbor lady later said indignantly to my grandmother. He padlocked the larder because he said the kids were eating up his paycheck. "Don't let them out of the house then," he said when my grandmother told him the kids needed new winter coats. He sold her heirlooms to buy polluted real estate near airports. "I didn't do anything when he withheld what I needed," my grandmother said, "but when he took from the children then I divorced him."

My grandfather vows that he sent half his monthly paycheck to the family following the divorce, but his net income amounted to what would now be eighty dollars a month. Nobody in the family prides themselves on him.

My grandmother worked graveyard shifts in a transport factory, her daytime employment being bookkeeping. My great-grandmother raised the children – my mother and her brothers, sisters and cousins

– in the house owned by my grandmother's sister. It was a nice matriarchal trinity with the drawback that none of the children could relate to men after that.

Stalin's reign had just peaked. The bread was made out of corn and when broken open the dough flowed out the middle. Soldiers impounded anything the government needed. The times bred new tsars, with different names and ideologies but really the same agenda: acquisition of wealth and empire. Nevertheless, my mother remembers only joy, because they had a big yard to play in. They were constantly ravenous, verging on cannibalism, sleeping nine to a room. All those siblings grow wistful when they talk of that period. "All the happiness you need is within you," my mother says.

Times like that I wish she'd had an excessive, ennui-stricken American, I mean Canadian, childhood. Something fouled.

Lala and I baited bats. Dusk came to the football field. Cones of light from street lamps illuminated myriad insects. The roach had just been stubbed on Lala's tongue and swallowed. She reached into a bag stuffed with wads of bread and threw a wad skyward. A bat swooped down without much stability and snagged the bread from the air. It flew like two hands struggling to get into one glove. In a circular underhand, Lala tossed another wad, a new bat jumping at the chance.

Lala said, then: "They're more beautiful than birds."

The bats had the candid faces of wolves, sharp teeth estranging every smirk they made. When one flew perilously close Lala wished her hair was long enough to snare it.

Lala found more words: "They're mammals, like us. They're ugly and barely fly."

When I saw my father put a cigarette out on the dog's back one night while it sniffed at his socks I felt no anger. Father was watching teevee, but he looked up and noticed me. We understood each other. It was the closest I ever felt to him. What he'd done meant more than if he'd admitted to loving me, a veritable *tour de force* of camaraderie. The dog wept. My father lit another cigarette and winked. I got us a couple of beers right away.

At the end of the eighth weeks' sexual itinerary my spirits and erection drooped. We'd gotten far as the teevee room when things wilted. Lala flopped up and down on me for a few minutes like hot-wired jello before I retracted completely. She stopped, sat back on my knees. Minutes later the tears came out, predictable as constellations.

"You're supposed to love me no matter what."

"Lala…." I couldn't reach out to her, my hands pinioned by exhaustion, partially of the libido, partially of the will. "I can't. The same thing all the time. What happened to you in France?"

She slapped my face. "What happened to me before France?" she accused. I pulled my knees up to my chest and she dropped off onto the floor.

Pulling up her panties, Lala never took her eyes off mine. Looking at her ribs made me cross my arms over the folds of my belly. I counted the bones in her torso like moths inside an airtight jar. Her eyes never left mine.

So much for the first two months of the second round with Lala. My roommates approached me after they noticed Lala hadn't been around for some time and gave me storm warnings. Trixy banned any more public displays. For shame, I thought, for shame. The other one (who, for the sake of convenience, I call the Unknown Roommate and think of as swathed in bandages from head to foot) supported Trixy's views.

After her and the Unknown Roommate laid the law down, Trixy and I sat for drinks. She knew I was a slut when drunk. We decided to sleep together that night, just to show no harm's done, our sex a bit slapdash, more convenience than attraction. Trixy kicked me out of her bed afterwards, saying it had no room, but I knew what was true: two in bed tend to sweat and Trixy had no desire for fluids other than the byproducts of sex.

I saw Lala only once during the next three weeks – an unexpected and unwelcome visit in which we had a slight tiff over my sleeping with Trixy. Lala expected me to remain faithful, though she never came around.

Lala's half-time visit gave a sampling of the violence that she'd employ as the solution to her problems with me, a foretaste of the second break, which would feature not only an outburst of rage but just punishment as well.

Though I cheated on her with Trixy, and the friendship between the two girls was waxing, Lala would never know the exact identity of that ephemeral darling. The infidelity hadn't been easy but it was a job well done.

When Lala walked in on this interim visit, her face was ghastly pale. "Ten guys in ten days. Not bad, eh Gabe?"

"Well, it's better than me Lala; I've only had one girl in the last two weeks, but man was she hot!" My admission was one way of pouting. Lala didn't appreciate the adultery, pointing out that this wasn't hypocrisy or double-standard on her part, but that her infidelities overhauled our relationship, while mine marked it for death.

"You aren't capable of polygamy," she said, "because you can only be with one person. When you cheat it's not so much a cheat but the beginning of a new loyalty. I'm the one who always comes back. Your desire is so primitive, so clumsy, it can handle only one object at a time."

"Nah," I said, chewing air, happy with the upper hand for once. "It's your desire that's got the problem. It's so thin that without constant testing you can't prove that it exists. You're not even sure of love's presence. You have to go out and have a one-night-stand just to remember that you have feelings at all. You call my desire primitive? Yours is retarded. It only exists in the process of violation."

Trixy sat uncomfortably with us during the whole argument, eating Kraft dinner with ketchup, keeping her eyes on the food and glancing sporadically at the television news. Just to thwart Lala a jot more, I leaned over and shouted, "Trixy!" She looked up, rattled. Then I kissed her flagrantly on the smacker.

I was turning back with the triumphant smile when Lala lashed out. Whatever the instrument of her wrath, my skull won out. Glass rained around me, blood flowing into my eyes. Seconds after the impact I felt rich and strange. Then a terrible pain opened my head and I dropped right off the chair, probably down to my knees. I managed a glimpse through the blood cloaking my eyes: a broken wine bottle in Lala's hand. I reached up and felt the gash. Macaroni fell out of Trixy's open mouth.

Lala turned and threw the broken bottle into the lidless garbage can with an elegant whip of the wrist. "Two points," she said, then walked past me as by some different mother's son. The door swung open behind her and winter stepped right up.

Lala's face formed a grandfather clock, lists of behavior on it instead of Roman numerals, one long hand ticking them off in a daily cycle that made me her cuckoo.

A great-aunt of mine crammed as many cigarettes into her day as would fit. She'd light one, put it down somewhere, light another while going to the kitchen for wine, lay that beside the other to smolder in the ashtray, and light a third while drawing the gauzy, floor-length drapes across the French doors to the balcony. So many cigarettes burned at one time in the apartment that I took up the habit to avoid breathing all the second-hand smoke. I remember modeling for her delight the rows and rows of old furs kept in the wooden armoires, pulling old ticket stubs and forgotten lipsticks out of their pockets.

She needed supervision around the clock. Old age brought her wholesale into a mindframe of megalomania and paranoia. She wouldn't let the postman in because he could be anybody. "How can I tell it isn't a robber?" she said. Then, because he couldn't get my great-aunt to open the door and sign for it, she had to trip down to the post-office and collect the money. This in turn made her accuse him of being rude and unthinking.

We went walking to ram fresh air into her, which meant a bronchial intake of something without tar or nicotine every seven or eight sucks to the cigarette. She breathed through fiberglass. We walked along the Danube and she pointed out the boats churning up the Danube. Once in a while a hovercraft zoomed past towards Vienna.

"Look at all this dogshit!" she moped. "Name another race of people who could live in such filth! You should write a letter to the ministry of tourism telling them you're an English tourist and you're appalled."

"I don't know if they have time to read those kinds of letters."

We arrived at a dirt parking lot just before the Árpád Bridge. Squatting drunks looked up at us from gutted mattresses, dirty bags full of pop cans and beer bottles in front of their feet, faces browned, weathered and unshaven, skulking around as if it was the chic thing to do. It might have been; you know those Europeans. They could have been high society, for all I knew, out for a night of acting cool. They stared at us through their eyebrows, chins stuck to their chests.

"Look at them, sitting in all that garbage. It's just what these people need. They elected the communists back; they deserve it."

"Please." I didn't know how to say "pipe down" in Hungarian.

We approached the foot of the Árpád bridge on the Pest side. The street lamps shone distantly now. Graffiti on the concrete slabs of the bridgehead drove points home: "no power for anyone"; "Gypsy-free zone"; "long live Nazism"; "anarchy does not mean chaos." The anarchists and skinheads vied for control of the city's free propaganda space, painting or modifying each other's slogans. "Homos die!" became "Homos die after the Nazis."

"You know why nobody has any pride anymore here?" my great-aunt asked. The colorful lines of spray-paint simmered in the darkness and the cherry on the end of her cigarette glowed. Trucks and cars hauled muffled sounds above us, past the girders and cement, on the other side of the bridge's ceiling.

"Could you not tell me why?" I pleaded.

"Because of Trianon...." I swung and grabbed her shoulders. She had a cigarette in her teeth nothing could dislodge.

"I know: Trianon, Trianon, Trianon. I've been hearing it all my life! No wonder I learned how to complain. No wonder everyone's learned how to complain!"

"Let go of me!" She squirmed her shoulders out of my grip. Granted, I wasn't locked on all that strong, but it was still a snappy wrestling move. Traffic rumbled at even intervals above us every time lights changed from red to green someplace else. She stumbled on an abandoned tire and landed on her ass, the cigarette still between her teeth like a prize possession. "All this dirt and garbage," she execrated. "Nobody cares."

"Tell me another country that lost as much land as Hungary?" she asked, spitting on her finger and trying to rub dirt off the palm of her hand.

I bent down and took her hand, pulled a tissue out of my pocket. "I'll tell you one," I replied. "Austria: they lost Hungary and all that she owned plus some others." My great-aunt wrenched her hand away. "No! You listen to me," I shouted. "Hungary lost everything long before Trianon to the Habsburgs. And you know that!" I lunged for the escaped hand and got it; she squirmed but I was ready for her this time. I spat into her palm and started grinding the kleenex in. "And I don't want to hear about what a proud nation Hungary was. I don't want to hear no crap like 'Rump Hungary is not a country, / whole Hungary is Heavenly,' or about how shitty they've made life here. You know why this country doesn't have any future? Because of this constant living in the past, obsessed with failures you can't turn back the clock to redress."

Wherefore comes my problem, I thought.

I heard her cry and relaxed my grip. She trembled while lighting up the next in a series of cigarettes.

"I'd like to go home now. Take me home." I helped her up, convincing her with mild words to retrace our steps along the Danube. I loved the smell of water, feeling the river in the air against my skin. She whispered as we passed the bums: "The only good thing is that they don't sit with the Gypsies; at least they have that much pride." I held her elbow and tried to distract her. Wildly lit casino boats full of mafioso and executives floated by on the Danube, drifting downstream. I asked her for a cigarette.

She complained about her people most of all, the wrongs done by others second: like many Hungarians. Me for instance: first I complain about myself, then the rest. And I am Hungarian. So there you go. What more proof do you need?

Teenagers drank beer and necked on the flights of steps leading down into the river. My great-aunt and I turned away from them towards her smoggy apartment, where there would be no power, none of the switches working. Someone had redirected our light. "Nobody knows how to do anything right in this country," my great-aunt wailed. I crawled into bed.

Lala tapped at five in the morning, just as the sky came into focus and chirping sounded from the trees.

I didn't know where Lala had vanished to, thinking maybe she'd been on the receiving end of sex in one place or another. She blasted through the door with the mark of other bodies on her, talking about a drunken binge, about trendy nightclubs, flat shoes, upsurge of dance music, running into "cute" boys. She drifted like a car on black ice. She wore a slinky black dress that made her want to wiggle.

Lala came pouncing onto me, pinned my arms under her knees. I didn't bother to struggle.

"I'm not sorry, Gabe. I'm not sorry for smashing that bottle on your head. But I am back."

I noticed her hand gripping a silver flask of liquor with someone else's monogram on it. "Hanging out with the sons of notables, are we?"

"I suppose you think I should apologize, but I'll proposition you instead," she slurred. A strap slipped down Lala's shoulder. She held the flask across her belly. The cold of her bare feet made itself felt through my shirt, her face mottled and puffy, eyes delirious, knuckles bloody.

Lala took a swig from the flask, belched fermented air over my face. "I met a man," she said, "with a Victorian house. He wants me to look after it this summer. We could try." Lala weighed on me like a bag of feathers. "We could live there." The hand holding the flask pulled the dress-strap back onto her shoulder. "We could … you can try it. If it doesn't work come back here. Come back in the fall."

"Okay," I said, not flinching when she raised the flask.

Pauline rolls up her sleeves to fork and spoon her five-minute macaroni. When I notice that the track marks have healed I throw a little conniption.

"Where's my money?" I scream, throwing the glass of wine against Pauline's head.

Pauline responds by dumping a plate of hot macaroni and cheese into my lap. We would have made a tremendous sitcom couple. I fall onto my knees bailing hot macaronis from my thighs. My burnt palms will require ointment.

"Sorry about the cheap theatrics," I say, getting out of my scorching jeans hurriedly. "But you told me you were buying. I want to know what happened to the money."

"What do you think happened to it?" Pauline yells, throwing polaroids at me.

The photos document the finale to Pauline's drug addiction. Spread before me are five discolored polaroids that look taken through yellow curtains. In each photo but the last Pauline stands on a twilit wharf. The sea rolls, strangely empty of vessels. Nothing proves that the pictures have been snapped by human hands, the composition so off-kilter. I have to turn most of them crooked to frame the viewing angle. Waves in the photo crash up through the burnt wharf's planks, wetting Pauline, plastering the skirt and shirt to her skin. The twilight saves the photos from being wet T-shirt shots. Her skirt is long and trails in the wind, a flag made of shirts given freely off my back and stitched together with the time spent on all those labor-intensive shifts hustling broke on paper machines nine and ten. She holds an upturned shoe-box above the waves. Ampoules, syringes and plastic bags flow in every direction, covering the sea's surface.

In the last polaroid she's tied to a chair with chain. The yaw of her mouth and eyes spells freedom, the beads of sweat on the face spell release, the twitching muscles, liberty. The photograph is all foreground, taken through a pipe, though I believe I recognize the chair as one the old Soviet lady tied me to.

"When were these photos taken?"

"None of your business," snaps Pauline, snatching them one by one from my hands.

"What about the money?"

"I spent it! Now get the fuck out!"

I comply.

Summer poked its head out of winter's grave and received the all-clear. The property's arbutus trees and flower gardens covered the base of a small hill which the three-story mansion crowned. The heritage house's view stretched over Oak Bay and the Olympic mountains across the sea. I took advantage of my valid student card to get a government sponsored job with the university for six weeks, editing the manuscript of some hockey-puck writer working under the pseudonym Marcus Antony. The job description insisted on my role as editor but I just typed, which suited me because I didn't have to think. Also, the seven hours a day the job paid for compressed easily into two or three actual hours of work. Lala invested in welfare and the black market employed her as a waitress. The heritage house was rent-free. I stayed though Lala had been forbidden guests. There was something good about fucking in the owner's double bed. Though, considering the sex, I don't know what exactly gave it that quality of goodness.

The nights spent on the heritage steps smoking, drinking wine and confabulating resist comparison. After all, there must have been good times: nobody puts a finger into the meat grinder without expecting a little sausage.

If only not for that torturous sex.

I grew up under conditions straight out of Eastern Europe, conditions never strange or demeaning until the West won out over my conditioning. For example, children roamed naked on the beaches until the age of eight or greater. Nobody considered covering the asexual nudity of the child. Pedophiles were rare as platinum deposits. Our behavioral boundaries were reinforced with corporal punishment. My sister told the school principal to fuck off once. My father whipped her without conferral. I was caught stealing and my father placed strategic bruises all over my ass cheeks. This was not an extraordinary development, not an insult to my subconscious, not something that would emerge later and turn me into a crank on the witness stand with a penchant for repressed memories. I don't look back on it bitterly at all. You know the rules before setting out to play. In terms of father, I can't think of things I did wrong that I didn't receive proper justice for afterwards. Except for tracking him down.

But when that bitch on the verge of a nervous breakdown, Mrs. Monash-something, stood me up in front of music class for talking when it wasn't my crime and slapped the motherfuck out of me, that's different. I didn't deserve that. I'm going to exhume Mrs. M. one day and make toilet seat covers out of her carcass.

My mother gave us fifty cents for every Transylvanian folk song we learned. She never let us forget that we were Hungarians living in Canada, though Canada took up equal space in my brain and soul in terms of heritage. She told us England wasn't part of Europe. Canada had no ties to Europe other than through us. We were the cultural moles, the intelligentsia. My mother had a film projector and a million Hungarian folk tales for it. Every night before we went to bed we each got to choose one folk tale and she projected the maximum goodness and innocence a race can have on the wall in front of us. She told us stories whose plot contained our blood like a heart.

Other things Lala did to crap out my mind the second time. Happily starting my fifth or sixth drink beside the bar she'd come up to me like an investigator, eyes large as pies, full in the waters of shock. "That guy there," she'd say, "won't bug off. I talk to him and he tries to kiss me." This type of information regularly crashed my fragile drunken joy. I never knew what was expected of me. When I said I'd talk to him she held me back. When I shrugged she left angrily. I wondered whether she wanted me to breast feed her or not. I looked down at my meager male tits and her sullen face, shook my head, shrugged, took another drink. I remember once actually getting mad enough to confront the offender. He didn't know what I had accosted him for. I believed him because he was scared. We scared each other, like looking into a mirror after you've forgotten about the Halloween mask on your face. Then I became paranoid of Lala hoaxing me. That's when I suspected she sought a mother's succor. Lala began spending inordinate time giving me oral sex as if looking for mother's milk. Our time together began to terrorize my digestion.

I recall going out once with our occasional friends: Sean and Laura. When necessary, their company was available and usually worked fine. But mostly, when they phoned, we couldn't think of a single use to put them to.

Sean was a long tall caricature with a wraparound grin care of Lucifer and company. Laura turned out to be the kind of person who would save herself first, which made me sympathize with but not like her.

The nightclub held no attraction for anyone but sailors, strangers with knives and impossible trousers, people with legs furthest apart from each other at the knees but ankle-bones meeting, giving their legs the shape of harps or hearts. I found a clutch of lilacs on the floor, festooned with yellow lace. The bartenders never knew your name, no matter how hard you tried to befriend them. Steel-nerved, they tipped their hats and lifted their bottles. None of them jumped when glass hit the floor. They all had fallen arches, you could tell. A whole different mythology came calling at these crossroads. You'd ask the waitress for a date and she'd say: I reserve my luck for other occasions.

So doped up were Lala, Laura, Sean and I that figuring out the nightclub was like piecing shredded documents.

Minutes after arrival I sat. Lala and Sean went off for drinks. Laura looked into the bathroom. Under these lights, every cocktail glowed phosphorescent like liquid neon. They left me in the seat because I had become a passenger. Lala returned with my drink. Oh no, I thought, she's into that smile again. Her mouth started up: "You know what Sean said?" she conspired, handing me my drink.

"I can hazard it without much risk," I answered.

This offended but didn't stop her. "He said if Laura wasn't here he'd ask me to come home with him."

"Are you a Puritan?" I asked.

"Why?"

"Because your hand is on the cigarettes and you've got nothing fun to say."

Lala stared at me. I stood by, awaiting further clearance. Lala blew her nose at me and stormed off. "Let's be fair," I commented to the waitress.

"Pardon?" she said.

"Another large one of these things, please. It needs less fizz too."

She took my order.

Sean stood at the edge of the dance-floor. Laura came back and I leaned in towards her. "Laura?"

"Yeah?"

"Sean said that if you weren't here he'd try and fuck Lala." I put a hand to my mouth like a school-marm. "And," I said, taking the hand away from my prune-shaped lips, "he tried to kiss her. Oh my, can you imagine such a thing?"

"That fucking little cunt," Laura said, madly searching for Sean and Lala.

"Quite so," I said, taking a stinging drink of whisky. "Yes, yes. Quite so. Mmmmm?" I took a long drink. "I couldn't agree with you more Laura. Yes, yes."

Laura jumped up from the table. I think Sean got it across the face first. Then Lala. Things began to settle for me. I was enjoying, for once, a shrewd diplomatic immunity.

I put on the mustache; the ends were long and wobbled on my face. "Notice the resemblance?" I asked them. The miners were dumbfounded. The guest list buzzed a bit. The widow's slice of cake slid off its plate. Still wearing the false mustache, I reached forward and rearranged my dead father's hairdo. "I don't know about the barber around here," I said, "but the Oxbow one did things differently." The silver strands of hair on my father's head indexed the hard times: one for the miner trapped under rock whom father dug out and mothered until he died; one for me fallen off a clothesline onto an iron railing and pissing blood all the way home due to a bruised kidney; one for the helicopter counter-rotating when, in panic of death, he laced his running shoes in preparation for jumping out of the helicopter before impact; one for 1956 and the revolution he declined; one for teaching my sister how to hail a taxi and nearly getting beat up by the cabby. How many more for the alternate family? His head grew a silver grapevine of minor calamities, a sterling trace of two families' history.

The other son stepped forward. "You're called Gabe."

"Yes," I said. The mustache slid down from my perspiration, almost into my mouth. A woman fainted and guests fanned her with handkerchiefs.

"He told me you might show."

The statement shot by. My father would have fit into a big suitcase. How many times can you fold a human body? I wanted to take him home as a carry-on, go into the living room with the bulging luggage and show my family the life-size souvenir I got them in River City.

"He told me about you in the hospital, when he was … dying."

"Well, I guess that's better than getting the news by research."

"What?"

"Nothing," I said. I took the other wedding ring out of my pocket and slipped it next to the present one on my father's finger, the rings uniting him in a bond or two, in marriages both domestic and foreign. The bands of gold looked identical.

The widow put her hand on my arm. "Gabe? We would like you to stay."

I lay my hand over her fingers. She smiled at me. "Okay," I said. "But I'm really going to need some cake."

She snapped her fingers at her son. He responded like a *garçon* and ran for my slice. "Tell me," she said, "leading me gently by the arm to the foot of the coffin. What do you think of the body? And the suit. Be honest now. Don't worry about hurting my feelings."

"I prefer pin-stripe myself."

It turns out that everyone at the party likes music they can dance to.

The man just come out of the bar shucked Lala under the chin. "You're cute," he said. Not having an alternative, she smiled at him.

"That's enough," I intervened, stepping out of a phone booth.

"Hey man," he said, turning on me, "I could kill you."

"Sure, sure," I responded, unmoved. He glared at me and walked away.

"Thanks," Lala said.

Returning home from the encounter I sat on the bed hugging myself and darting my tongue between my lips. I felt dense with betrayal, betrayal of me. Fear hadn't come up with that guy, though he differed nothing from the rest. I had brought about possibility, proved that I couldn't even count on my cowardice for consistency. I sat for a long time. Lala flailed in the sleeping bed behind me. I'm a fanatic.

Once, my great-uncle ate a cat by accident. It was a plump cat fattened on scraps from the kitchen of its owner, an army chef. The army cook used to toss the tabby chunks of pork, ribs, even a little fish once in a while. The cat was smug.

The prisoners-of-war marched for days and nights across fields in boots with questionable soles, while the soldiers and their retinue followed in a caravan of jeeps. The prisoners watched wild boars rooting in the snow. They sat, sometimes, in bare black boughs that rattled in the wind. The ground was miles flat, criss-crossed with rivers, cancered with rooks. The frost touched everything. Old women with black handkerchiefs over their heads watched them pass from the empty windows of straw-thatched houses. My great-uncle thought there was a pride and a beauty in the impoverished and the simple that the communists had made the mistake of insulting. The soldiers gave commands and, rarely, cigarettes. Sometimes the prisoners rolled smokes in the letters they'd written on the few scraps of available paper, since there was no hope for postal delivery of any kind. My great-uncle was an artist and he drew pictures on filched napkins to keep his talent alive and then inhaled the papers away. And as the burning pencil lead entered him, mixed with tobacco, it felt like he was recycling that talent.

The cook who fed the soldiers "guarding" the motley POWs on the march owned the cat. The prisoners were given bread. The soldiers fed well. The cat had the choice bits. My great-uncle did not hate the cat. It is only me thinking about it who hates it.

They used to steal some meat on the side, usually from the animal's dish when it was momentarily left untended. When the soldiers weren't watching, the prisoners would run into the woods and gnaw upon these blackened, half-cooked pieces of flesh like the brides of wolves. They emerged with trickles of blood at the mouth and covered with frost. One day my great uncle's friend told him they had ripped off some more protein. They had to march soon so they ate quickly, scarfing the remains of some dead animal down. My great-uncle distinctly remembered it tasted like chicken.

Later that night the commanding officer rounded them up and pronounced the cook's pet missing. He wanted to know what had happened to it. My great-uncle couldn't help but begin puking. Naturally, the commanding officer found this suspicious and made him fink on his friends. The story was so funny the C.O. forgave them. After a two-year stint in a gulag my great-uncle returned to Hungary. His friends did not.

After that, the cats in his place were indivisible: one giant feline mass. They covered everything: floor, bed, dining table. The stench of cat was completely unbearable to everyone but him. He sat among them and painted pictures whenever he needed money. He spent the rest of his time shaggy with their shed hair.

Once a year, on the anniversary of the meal, he went to the graves of the friends who had killed the cat – which had gone through my great-uncle's mouth, his digestive tract and slid past his colon like a silent thief – and put the smelliest, ugliest, most wilted weeds he could find in their urns.

The cats would fuck, swoon and sing twenty-four hours ongoing. He read by the light reflected in all their watchful eyes.

In a brass bed on the third storey of the Victorian place Lala slipped a thermometer between our bodies. The wool socks on her feet prickled against my legs, the rest of her flesh at times sliding over, at times sticking to, my skin. It hadn't taken us long to fall back into her strict routine of sex, the pressing of her body against mine just another step in the elaborate game.

Almost every time we had sex now Lala introduced new techniques, forevermore repeated. We grew muscled, athletic, participated in disfigured yoga.

The thermometer?

She wanted to find out the optimal temperature for passion.

I threw Lala off me. Her body rolled off the bed and clobbered itself against the floor. I stood over her as she came to, looking up. "You're not going to make us maintain certain temperatures too," I said. "I can't live up to that." I snapped the glass thermometer between my fingers, mercury fleeing.

Walking down the antiquated winding stairway of the Victorian house I came to the kitchen, poured some white wine in the silence, added ice cubes, and drank. It took a few minutes for me to discover that maybe, just maybe, Lala had been kidding with that one.

The leg-hold trap is rusty but appears serviceable. After I test the action once, the trap does not need to repeat its offer. My sister remains bound to a hospital bed, while I remain bound elsewhere. It shall be a painful death, by way of leg-hold trap. It's fall, or summer, or winter ... in this exploded year. At any rate, it's about that time. For a painful death. I always do what clocks tell me.

In a cellar underneath Benny's workshop the rat traps are religiously emptied. Nobody knows to what extent the rats really come here, but every fugitive needs recreation. They draw straws or throw dice and the unlucky one has to spring the trap. The rest of the verminous battalion get the cheese. My dog knows their den. And I do too, naturally, for where two or three rats congregate there also am I. They are the only thing the wiener dog faces down. Perhaps the dog considers phobia of rats as just a tad too irrational. It polices the cellar, kicks occasional rat's asshole, takes their spines in its teeth and severs the connection.

I steal over to the house during noon, a fillet in my fist. I set the leg-hold trap in the cellar, baited with the prime cut of beef. Nobody will hear the wiener dog's pleas for life. Nobody will hear it call out the murderer's name. Then night will come and the rats will take to their teeth.

I smear blood from the fillet all over the cellar's threshold, then set the trap. I hide behind a crate just like any professional wiener dog hunter would.

The metal bracket bites the hind leg. The wiener dog's mouth struggles free of the fillet and howls. I emerge, two-by-four in hand. It would be simple to crack its head in half. It wags its tail, misinterpreting my presence. I wear a pin-striped suit so small it might as well be a pin-striped loincloth. I bought it for Christmas long ago. The sleeves end between my elbows and wrists. It lends itself to the execution's formality, for between me and the dog there's nothing personal. But, after reevaluation, the board falls from my indecisive grip. I'm so demure; I've always been a demure little thing. Better if the dog just starves to death, chews the leg off and bleeds a bit for me. I turn my key in the cellar door. I drive my car. An hour later the engine conks out. I'm still decelerating after the car stops. Get along little doggie. Get along.

Bill and his wife met one more time before fateful Mexico – in Los Angeles. Bill needed some second-generation reasons to hate. He wanted something to counteract the sprouting forgiveness and lethargy in him. He left his car in the lot and walked humbly over to her vehicle. Door to the front passenger seat open, she had her hand in the glove compartment, as if it was a glove itself. Bill petted the back of her neck with the shotgun barrels. "Huh?" she jumped up, hand to her chest.

"Just a joke," grumbled Bill, lowering the gun.

She screamed and Bill jumped over to muffle her with his hand. But before he could speak soothingly into her ear something crashed against his head. He fell like a lummox, whispers jutting from his mouth, shotgun clattering. A dark man stood over him. "An Indian," he hissed to me over the phone. "She was on the fucking road with an Indian!"

"So?" I said, happy to have him riled up again.

"I'm going to Mexico to kill them both!"

"Good for you, Bill."

"But, uh, Gabe, I need another gun, and they took my car, too...."

"Okay, Bill. But listen. This is the last time, okay. I don't want to hear from you again until you've gotten her."

"You're my only lifeline, Gabe!"

"This is for your own good, Bill." I disburse money for the pursuit of any old pursuits. I fund nuts and dolts at home and abroad.

Thanks to my prescience I know Bill will find his wife only if left to his own resources. If I keep accepting calls my bank account will entirely empty; Bill will end up in Mazatlan with my life savings, biding his time and growing forgetful. I'm already too sorry a fellow not to be safe as well. I look at the phone, reminiscing on all the trouble it's caused with Lala, Pauline, Frank and now Bill. I tread down to the elevator in my bathrobe, telephone balanced on my hand like a waiter's platter. I pass an old man standing in the doorway to his apartment and combing a toupee held in his hand while conversing with his neighbor, an androgyne in high-heels and pointy bra. I put my phone on a garbage can out back of the building. The phone's grown blacker – if such a thing is possible – and has a high-return curse from all the sinister dialogue patched through it. Woe to finder and keeper.

Lala always went out for the night in speed, not the narcotic but the natural equivalent. The fourth floor of the heritage home was our starting block. Lala sat on one banister of the lazily winding staircase while I took a place on the other. "Go!" Lala bawled, but she wouldn't move. Lala jumped off the banister and looked into the stairwell to watch me wind down the banister with increasing velocity. She seldom chanced a race. I usually started off hoping she was only giving me a head start. I always suffered brake failure and would, at bottom, fling off the banister into the wall, the plaster cracked in one section from all the kinetic energy my head transferred to it. Lala would run down the stairs juiced by laughter while I tried to recover. We were always drunk on something, either physical or abstract. It seemed that I was either stunned or had the wind knocked out of me. Lala squatted, lifted my arm across her shoulder and stood. We went out for the night with a fashionable sputter, like batteries dying in a radio.

In Szeged I met an uncle of mine who'd go into the shed to play a piano. "I need a lot of space around me to play in," he said. His arms got longer when he drummed those keys, joints ballooning out with power; his arms-length became a wing-span, necessitating a hangar's worth of elbow room. He cut down the wild cherry trees, built a shed, placed the piano in the middle of the floor and left the rest of the space to do its own thing. "Want to come in and listen to me rehearse?" he asked one Saturday.

His fingers hit the ivories running. They pounded, soothed and frothed over the keys. Notes spat from the top of the piano like from a crackling fire, arcing out and collecting on the floor, popping around on the parquets like water droplets in boiling oil. The notes had colors, pastels: powder blue, emerald, rose. They collected around us, around me where I sat on the floor, back to the wall, around the feet of the piano and stool. My uncle slipped in and out of Beethoven, Debussy, Liszt, weaving their pieces for piano into one all-consuming suite. The notes piled deeper and deeper, rising to cover our shoes, lapping at our and the piano's ankles while he played with increasing fervor. Soon the level of notes rose over our heads, up to the roof, jamming the ceiling fan. My uncle kept plugging away; the notes multiplied like amoebas and packed us in so tightly we couldn't move.

After he stopped we sat in the buzzing of the notes, waiting for the music to fall off. The joy of the piano filled my mind, making my brain more comfortable in its cranium. I'm still waiting for them to invent a drug that will let me feel like that, without having to do all those labor-intensive years of piano lessons and practice. I have no sense of accomplishment, only the usual five: touch, taste, hearing, sight, smell. I wouldn't recognize accomplishment from its name tag.

Afterwards my uncle told me that he had to play every day because the joy the piano produced in him was so ephemeral it didn't last longer than one full rotation of the average clock. "I top up and the level drops like a stone." If he didn't rekindle that feeling daily he'd slip into a depression more severe than Shakespeare, a depression "impossible to climb out of." Then he'd become listless, stuck, doing less and less every day until he was even too lazy to keep that part of his brain going that performed the basic functions, bellowing his lungs, keeping the heart rate, blinking. "I'd just let it all slide. You really need an obsession to get you through life."

He smashed my head against a rock while trying to scalp me, like my hair was a pelt. Minutes ago had seen me on top and everyone yelling at me to hit him. I had his arms pinned under my knees but could only go impotent. My father told me never to hit anyone in the face, ever, stemming from an incident when he'd been given a pair of brass knuckles as a child and taken them to school. Some childhood rival lost an eye in that offing. My father could have saved himself the conditioning because I doubt I would have been capable of decking anyone anyway. Nobody rescued me in the schoolyard. I'm not feeling sorry for myself, either. All I want to discuss, in this instance, are the objective facts. I couldn't hit him. Now he was lacerating the back of my head. I got him off me. It wasn't hard. What supporters I had in the schoolyard, sitting ringside, had left in disgust, with a hitch of the jeans and a harrumph. Only the neutrals and the other kid's groupies stayed. One guy, older by years, egged the kid on, maybe long after he'd wanted to quit himself. Angry and tearful, I swung blind. The contender was two years younger than me. This made him a contender. Finally, most of the viewing audience gave up on my uncontrolled swings and returned to playing soccer. Only the contender, his coach and I stayed. Finally, I stopped swinging and made to leave, but the coach told the champeen (nee contender) to keep at it. He wouldn't pursue it though. I ran, came to a railing, perched on it like a birdie and started to bawl. The girls came around me and asked what happened. I told them to leave. Where was the principal; where were the teachers? The schoolyard monitor? Absent as policemen. I cried and the girls offered sympathy. I tried to hide. I screamed at them to fuck off. They never left. So began a little secret life. The numbing polyphony of little girls doting on me. The principal finally heard me swearing, took me into his office and inserted a bar of soap into my throat. I put a bone in my closet, adding to it over the years. *Persona non grata* in the schoolyard after that. *Persona non grata* in my skin.

First you must kiss her, then fondle her breasts, run fingers over pubic bone, applying correct pressure. Then she sticks her tongue in your ear, then drops a line of kisses, thirty-six exactly, all the way down the right side of your neck and up the left, in an arc. You remove her shirt, but are forbidden to touch the bra yet. She pulls the belt out of your pants. Meanwhile your tongues touch. She slips a hand down the front of your pants. You can touch her bra now, take it off....

Naked, you slip on top of her, enter. Five minutes of this. You must stop now. She flips you over, gets on top. A couple minutes, after which she brings her legs up for you to grab the slender ankles. The muscles in her neck tense, her hands on your hips, she strong-arms herself up and down. The usual time passes. Now she lays down on your chest. Now she will call for deep kisses. Next comes side-stroke. She turns onto her right side, lifts a leg, and you, also on the side, go in from behind. She grabs your right hand and puts it into the spot (the same one) and from there you trace a route from breast to breast to smooth stomach to clitoris and back again in a revolution that only stops upon her word. She puts you in her mouth, releases it, takes it in again, exactly twenty-six times, a number falling just short of fulfillment.

Now trace with your tongue: outer labia first, the two brackets, tongue squirming in the hole, moving up to the clitoris, teasing around it, finally twiddling it directly. Her inner timer ticking off the movements. She pushes your forehead away....

She is on all fours. You have a semblance of control. In and out the pumping penis goes. She will not shudder, will not come, suppressing orgasms as incompatible with this moment in time. And out of her mouth comes always the same line of bologna: grunts, groans, whimpers. She crawls forward like a child and you follow behind on your knees, both creeping together, careful not to slip out. Her lithe body slides off the bed, you on top of her, attached like the two dogs you parted as a kid. Down across the wood floor and you're still inside. Both of you stand up, she grips the oak desk, back at a forty-five degree angle. Legs shake as you hold rigidly to a sitting position with no chair under you and she plunges in and out of your lap.

She pulls you out after a certain distance is fucked, and finally, she lays supine on the ground. You lift her legs by the ankles, going into her and into her until it ends.

This description, spoken a million times, might approach the limits of my boredom. Though as a one-shot it's kind of compelling – well, for me, anyways.

You think you have a handle on my mother, do you? Well, let me here and now destroy all illusions of character consistency.

My mother hated cats. She neither bent to pet, bothered to care about, or took notice of them – until they crossed her. That was black luck for a cat, to cross Mother.

It happened during springtime. The old rosebush outside the front steps became reduced to twigs and trunk, to bones really, by winter's dressing down. My mother had stooped like a misfit all day long above the soil, dropping seeds into finger holes, transplanting root systems, reaching into bags full of rotting starfish, salmon innards and horse shit to scatter handfuls of fertile sludge all around, building a foundation that would nurture plants. She provided for the dirt out of the life of the sea. And of course the cats came in mobs to dig up fish-heads.

Crowds of cats pranced home with fish bones bouncing between their jaws, manes coated with baby herring, salmon roe, slime. And the seeds they dug up drifted off in the wind for other, safer nooks, better protected gardens.

Our dog lay lazily beside the steps, never rising from the spot of sunlight that encircled it. This feigned nonchalance didn't cover its fear – of everything (cats being third to humans and other dogs, respectively, in its hierarchy). The dog I'd do anything to be free of. Almost anything.

Late one spring evening my mother lost control. She'd spent most of the day replanting, casting glances of almost inhumane disgust at the dog. When one murders an animal, one has an overwhelming fear that the SPCA has implanted monitoring devices and bugs in the location nearest to you. That's how I feel anyway. Mommy doesn't share many of my insecurities.

That evening she leaned over the sink when the cat came into the garden to urinate. Her face changed color. She shrank in her clothes, down to the wiry frame of a scarecrow, the way a scarecrow wears its purity of purpose. It was the last provocation. Even my father, normally iron-fisted, gave wide berth while she went for the gun cabinet, took down the key, reached for a handful of .22 bullets and the matching rifle.

All I remember is the way she walked out into her flower garden, with feline stealth of her own, so quiet the prey didn't notice, avoiding every twig that would betray her the way some people don't seem to get wet in the rain. She grabbed the cat by the scruff of the neck and disappeared into the workshop at the back of the house.

Later she told me the story, turning events around in her mouth the way a picture is turned on the wall, to get it straight. She didn't want to misrepresent the facts.

She'd let the cat go in the workshop. When it backed into a corner, she loaded the gun and fired, once. The bullet went through the cat's back, probably severing some part of the spine responsible for the motion of hindquarters. My mother had never intended to torture it, trying for a clean dispatch. And when she reached out, it crawled to her, to the executioner, still believing in the safety of the open hand.

"I had to shoot it then, you see. Once I'd done that, I had to shoot it. Kill it."

We stood in the garden. The spade stuck from the ground. I'd come out to watch her bury the cat. She was wiping sweat from her forehead with the hem of her skirt. Inside the workshop sawdust covered a pool of blood to soak it up. The sun had crawled all the way to the end of the horizon, sitting there in a corner like at the end of some corridor.

"I want you to leave me alone for a little bit," my mother said.

Our dog had been nosing around in the sawdust and came out of the workshop, a few red fibers sticking to the end of its nose. It came up to the spade, sniffed a circle around it, taking in the spoor of death. Then it retraced that same circle with a tight stream of urine, a motion circular as prayer, round as the rosary. My mother watched it all, the wrinkles on her forehead expressing not one trace of approval.

I sat in a car on a hill once, Lala beside me. We'd come back to Oxbow for the Victoria Day long weekend to see my family. A long line of cars crowded the hill end-to-end. The guy in front of me, in a dune buggy, kept letting his vehicle roll backwards. I didn't want him backing into me so I eased my car back a foot or two. Three minutes later someone knocked on the window beside my head. He stood there, blond, with the obligatory Lower Mainland mustache, quite possibly drunk, stoned and sober, all simultaneously. He asked me if I knew how to drive. Lala's and my frightened statements interfered with each other and negated all meaning. I told him the guy in front of me was rolling back and I didn't want to get hit. "That's the reason."

"It better be," he said. Five minutes later a beer bottle bounced off my car's roof. But by then I was able to drive off. This memory remains wanly-colored. Only the details, the fears, stay with me.

I've thoroughly cased myself for clues and motives explaining my cowardice, but information remains unavailable.

On the way to a cousin's house in Budapest something came over the cab driver's dashboard computer. Some Budapest cab drivers borrowed the idea of implanting electrodes into their front passenger seat from their colleagues in Prague. Flipping a switch under the steering wheel allowed them to administer a little shock to help make the fare shell out the exorbitant fee on the crooked meters, which had one setting for locals, one for foreigners and one for complete suckers. The now-imperiled cab driver had turned up the notches on his voltage transmitter too high and received a sturdy punch in the face from his American passenger. We arrived with the other battalion of cabs to the scene of the punch-up. The American had knocked the cabby's knife out of his hand and was mashing and sliding the cabby's face along the windshield. I got out of the cab and ran over. Though human violence ills and ails me I just had to see his face squished against the windshield from inside the car. My driver jumped on the American's back but the guy flipped him off. Three newly-arrived cabbies got out of their cars and the American, seeing how hopeless his odds were, took to his heels, disappearing into a small side-street between the *közért* and local bank (Budapest has a bank on every corner: a sure sign of national bankruptcy). Three cabbies gave chase with tire irons, two without. My driver had joined the lynch mob so I grabbed my things and did not pay the amount on the meter's readout. I was only two blocks south of my cousin's place.

The house she lived in was a cube of Bauhaus perfection, what was once probably the home of some wealthy fascist superman from Hungary's twenties. Now the ballroom floors were partitioned off by makeshift walls. The hallways between the various apartments were a nut-house blue; the thick white doors protecting every apartment accentuated the lunatic atmosphere. On the walk over I heard the shouts of cab drivers, running feet, tire irons dropped on the ground, a hot pursuit winding down in the lanes running between and behind these houses. I was in *Rószadomb* (hill of flowers) where the street names, like *vérhalom* (blood-heap) and *mandula* (almond), remind you of certain delicacies and past-times to which only the upper echelons had recourse during the Communist regime. Further on snaked a street called *virág árok utca* – Ditch of Flowers Street.

I knocked on my cousin's door. "Come in, come in. Help me!" I knew she and her husband, a pharmacist, had been experiencing difficulties. My family kept a running oral history on such things, but I had no idea it was this bad. For a minute I imagined running at the door shoulder-first like some nineteen-seventies teevee cop. But in the end it was easier to give the door a push. She'd left it open on purpose, so I could get in. European doors have no handle: one of those places where it's possible to lock yourself in. Not a bad idea, that.

I pushed the door open.

My cousin was bent over her balcony, the branches and leaves of a cherry tree waving in the breeze above her. I heard the noise of the cabbies clearly now. Birds roosting for the night shot up and scattered in the arc of a streetlamp. The sound of boots digging into chain link fence. Rattle of gates and rustle of bushes. My cousin held the American by the hand like a dangling man in some slapstick deck of Tarot. He tried to hook his feet over her balcony. The cabbies had not thought to look up, but then who ever thinks of looking up when they're hunting by passion instead of rationale?

I grabbed onto the American's other arm and we dragged him over the balcony's railing. My cousin was an aerobics junky, no clothes tight enough for her.

"Thanks y'all," the American said in a lazy Texas twang. He hadn't a bruise or nick on him except for a pair of bleeding knuckles resulting from the type of sandwich he'd fed the cabby.

He came from Houston. We ate in the kitchen. He mulled over the food, cabbage rolls, before throwing his taste-buds to the wind and chowing down. Here on business with a cell phone outfit, he worked nights, getting drunk afterwards in ex-pat bars shipped pre-fabricated into Budapest from Ireland piece by piece and built according to specs – where on Sundays you could order blood sausage, where they had

Celtic nights, journalists reading their poetry, Hungarian musicians taught to play Irish folk tunes, Guinness on tap, jocularity, prices just high enough to keep the locals out. He'd been stiffed with an oversize fare many times while cabbing through Budapest but he'd never before had the electric shock-treatment. He decided to show solid American reaction instead of succumbing to more Eastern European skullduggery. I was happy to see him. Good baggage to be reminded of. He made me realize that I, as a half-Canadian, was only mired in Budapest up to the knees, rather than up to the neck like my relatives. I could always bail, fly Air Canada, get off in Vancouver, find a supermarket, become relaxed in its ambient music and fluorescent love. But I also wasn't an ex-pat. I had connections in Hungary, a dual citizenship. I translated between the cowboy and my cousin.

We finished dinner and sat in her parlor drinking Tokaji Aszú, golden and syrupy. "Are we still going on that *bogrács gulyás* tomorrow?" I wanted to know. She'd organized it. I explained to the American that this involved cooking that archetypal Hungarian stew in a cauldron out in a field.

"Tomorrow?" she looked at me incredulously. "How can you think of tomorrow?" And she burst into tears. Tomorrow is rained out, canceled, excised from the plan. I reached forward and put my hand on her.

"What's wrong?" the American clucked softly; I don't know what for. Outside, the cabbies scrounged the back lanes in search of the erstwhile passenger in need of a stomping. I asked my cousin about her domestic situation: "Where's George?" Dogs rattled their chains and growled outside: one of the cabbies had met with an untimely complication. I could hear him howl as animal teeth took a chunk.

"He left to buy spinach two hours ago," she said. "No." My cousin checked her watch. "Now it's half past. Two and a half hours ago," she corrected.

"Gone for spinach?" the American asked. He'd spent too much time on cell phones, away from faces, to understand the harm this question would do if I translated it to my cousin.

Come with me and I'll show you where he is, my cousin said. She took the wine bottle by the neck and had a hit.

She led us out the front door and into the hallways. "This is a factory of adultery here," she told me, walking past the doors and tapping her finger on each. "Maria": a woman with terrible nails on her hands and feet, all painted orange. "Iluska": only nineteen, father a communist untouchable because he knows too much about those still in power. "Dora": widower, a Russian who Hungarianized her name; she lost her husband in Afghanistan.

How many changes of government had these hallways seen? I thought as she led us through the departments of betrayal. How many dissidents and suspected insurgents had been led away from here? Jackboots of different henchmen – right or left wing, communist or fascist, they all acted the same way on those midnight collection calls. They all gathered you into their arms with the same force of love, not personal love but the statistical kind, the kind that matters to institutions, to sticklers for social justice, to those who'd make the world a better place with legislation. I thought about the way marriage gets when it's made to conform to civil, moral or philosophical codes.

My cousin turned to us. "George has had them all," she said. "When I come home, sometimes, I can hear all their groans, past and present, behind every door. It's impossible to walk down the hall, to my apartment. I can only get seven or eight feet deep into the echo of the pleasure he's given and is still giving them. I have to leave and wait until the silence returns before going home, back to my husband. Sometimes I find him waiting and sometimes not."

Sometimes he went out for spinach. And this lasted hours. The American was wishing he'd stayed in the taxi cab, endured those shocks.

The first time he cheated on her she drove to the woman's house, went through the door and slapped the woman around; the other woman slapped back. The two women went silly from battle fatigue, staring at each other from their seats on the floor among the overturned bowls, broken glass, squashed vegetables and fruit. My cousin got up and left her there: mistress number one in a soon to be innumerable collection. "Why didn't you slap him instead?" I asked her. "Why should only the women suffer?"

"Because he can hit back a lot harder than she," my cousin replied – a very good point.

The American was thinking of how to extricate himself, now that the coast was clear, from these uncomfortable confidences of a stranger. I was thinking of Parisian Lala – to whom I'd never been unfaithful – and how she didn't want me around. "Are all men unfaithful?" my cousin asked. I'm faithful to the death, I thought, but didn't reply. Water dripped in the pipes of the corridor, movements behind the walls, the paint creeping up over us, all our faces coming into blue. As is usual in such situations the American had nothing to say, either. We both needed Hallmark cards to read from. I put my arm around my cousin's shoulder. The American, following my lead, put his arm around her shoulder from the opposite side.

In another two hours George would return, spinach bag in hand, with the downstairs, first-floor mistress, a neighbor's wife, coming in a few minutes after, both parties heading to separate domiciles without a goodbye kiss, the hallway humming with emptiness. George would be thinking some inglorious excuse: "The store wasn't open. I went to the one at *Moszkva Tér*, but they were out. So then I had to walk back home and get the car. That took forty-five minutes. I got stopped at a roadblock. The cops searched the whole vehicle. Then I went…." So jaded by all the cheating, he aimed only for the bare minimum of plausibility – sometimes overstepping the mark – as if strictly rationing the use of his imagination, or saving it for better days. But she wouldn't be home. Not my cousin. Not waiting for him. Everyone needs a drink: and that's where the American and I took her. Out for a good many drinks and some light different from what those halls threw back.

The last night we spent in the Victorian home I made love to Lala, the final surprise between us. On the tail-end of the nightly routine at the oak desk, myself straining above the quadruped Lala, she collapsed, did a face-plant into the desk-top, her cheek sliced open by an unsheathed fountain pen. I rolled off onto the rug. The darkness of the place tarred and feathered us. On the floor I kindly listened as Lala began to sing.

Some last-ditch effort made me rise, pick her up and ease her onto the bed. She sang a commercial jingle from God knows when, and probably expected me to sing along while I smoothed her hair with my hands and put down everything I could in the physical act of love, like cosigning an incriminating document. She stopped the song half way through, stopping when I said I loved her. Her arms circled my back, strapping me to her. The empty cradle we formed rocked.

"I love you," I said, even at the end.

"You certainly do," she conceded, speaking to her erstwhile parents or the looming world, rather than me. "You certainly do," her eyes running.

It was over. My only mistake was admitting to that before she was ready.

A few days later Lala would pay me a very formal visit, and vent some spleen; then, as usual, she'd disappear for another year, resurfacing for one more party and one more attempt at undoing the damage.

My folks haven't seen me since the night I botched the strangulation. I meet them in the park. Both wear shorts, which reminds me that bare knees come with sexual organs and other body parts. As my parents age they become less corporeal, like holograms. They die like a teevee, on the blink. Their wearing of shorts connects us through mortality. Somewhere, Jessy sits in her kitchenette rocking chair, surrounded by her bestiary, moldering away. I am the surgeon general and I've determined that existence is the leading cause of death. I've killed the dog. The rats have fed. My parents don't seem bereaved.

We're gonna have ourselves a little picnic.

Mother spreads the blanket and Benny pulls breaded, deep-fried chicken legs out of a basket. They make no mention of the dog. The sun plummets as it does in time-lapse photography. I plummet the same, but into the Greek salad.

"How are you, Gabe?" mother asks.

"I'm well," I say automatically.

"And Pauline?"

"Good."

"Gabe? Is something wrong? We haven't seen you much in a while. Last time was...."

"Unusual?" I ask, sucking my fingers.

Benny pulls out his pipe. Fragrant tobacco suffuses my face, leading me to hope it settles into my clothes, in which case I'll wear them, even in bed, until the smell fades.

"What's with the dog?" he asks.

"... I don't ..."

"You want to kill it?"

"I'm not in a position to answer that question anymore, Benny."

"If the dog were here now, would you attack it? Do you need a psychologist?" he continues to interrogate.

"Psychology? Crap. No one's motives are ever psychological."

"Well then, what are they?"

My mother tries to cut in but we're rogue moose, minus the antlers. "Genetic probably, or ethnic. Certainly illogical, absurd, unexpected. I'm as psychological as a headless chicken."

"Does something about the dog threaten you? Scare you?"

"Sure."

"Why?"

"There's no why. It just threatens and scares me. Period. If I knew why ... well, it wouldn't make any difference."

Benny whistles and the wiener dog walks out from behind a bush, slightly undernourished and a cast on its leg signed by all the family. My sister drew a big black heart on it and colored it in like a weird seed. "The dog hurt its leg," my mother puzzles. "But it's getting better."

The dog limps over, looks up at me, begging for some fried chicken.

That night I prowl the cellar. Rusty parts of the trap litter the floor, teeth marks in them. The spring is in pieces so rusty they crumble between fingers. The pin that held the spring on the trap is gone. Many animals chew off their legs to gain freedom. Our dog is the only one who ever ate the snare itself.

Hungary subjects you to strange cravings. I rarely need drugs with anything near desperation, but there was this one Hungarian day when I wouldn't have minded a little lift. Wheat fields stretched to either side of where I stood on the shoulder of a dirty road. Too many dogs had converged around me on Budapest's streets that morning when I went for milk and bread, staring knowingly from around every corner and parked car. I felt more entombed in the city than usual and hoped the wheat fields would set me straight.

The relatives sat around me in folding chairs like the last of the Mohicans. As organized by my cousin, wife of George the philandering pharmacist, we'd come out here to cook up a *bogrács gulyás*, even though she and George were too tired of their marriage to even call it quits. We cut up the onions, set out the paprika, potatoes, peppers, and beef. My cousin put herself in charge of the process, hanging the cauldron, charging us with gathering wood for the fire.

While wandering along the edge of the road with George I became severely desirous of psychoactive chemicals, in a far, far, far, off-Broadway sense. I wanted something characteristic to Eastern Europe, a drug with that Old World quaintness. But narcotics have little history here. In the outstanding old days of the communist regime there was alcohol and, for those wanting to toe a harder line, gasoline and glue, those two drugs that span cultures and nationalities, escape agents for the global village, rich and poor alike, young and old:

The Marxist dream come true –
gasoline and glue.

But I wanted something special, the stuff Lenin took before penning his rally cries, whatever made Stalin stay up late, the junk Trotsky missed most in Mexico. Lala would have approved.

I tagged along behind the pharmacist. Short and stout, with sweat soaking down the back of his suit jacket, he didn't look like a womanizer, the man no vow could stick to.

"Hey, what kind of drugs can you get a hold of?"

He bent down to gather up branches. "Why?" I picked up sticks, five or six. His arms were loaded with windfall right up to his chin. I broke the branches across my knee and piled them on until he asked me to stop. He repeated: "Why?"

"Well, I was wondering if I could score some."

"You're a sick boy, Gabe."

"Awww c'mon...."

"Forget it. Eat a good meal and live clean. Why don't you get a girlfriend?"

Back at the fire the mood was sour, everyone with old socks in their mouths. Us wood-gatherers arrived back more or less at the same time to put down our branches, and to note, yes, a crop duster had flown by in our absence and sprayed everything with insecticide. Luckily my cousin, making preparations, saw the old plane motoring along and carried the food out from under the chemical shower. The pharmacist went to clean the pot, but my cousin took it out of his hand saying: "Why don't you go back to your spinach; she probably wants you more than we do." My cousin grumbled at him while scouring the pot without water or detergent, trying to get the grime off with dry steel wool.

After my cousin hung the cauldron off its arm and lit the fire she began to prepare the ingredients. The rest of the family walked over to give the fire a hand, to help it prosper, the pharmacist leading the lot. He poked his stick in to rearrange the logs and ended up scattering the works. Everyone in the family – from the six cousins to aunts, uncles, fathers and mothers – scrambled to get the burning wood back under the cauldron. My cousin hip-checked me aside, grabbing for my stick.

"Give me that," she barked. "You're hopeless. I've never met anyone with so little manual dexterity." I felt a tirade coming on. "All the men in the family are useless," she yelled. "Get away from the fire," she shouted at her husband, whipping him in the back with the stick. Everyone in the family backed off, George a good two-lengths behind the rest.

This is the woman who noticed something amiss with the steering when driving her car one day. She put her formidable biceps into it, gripping the wheel and not letting the car drift where it willed. Upon arrival she complained to her friend: "There's something wrong with the car." She had a flat, verified by nothing more than a quick visual inspection. My cousin firmly believed in the application of brute force in overcoming whatever the universe threw at her. She knocked the logs back under the cauldron using her feet. My stick was useless. All the while her mouth emitted insults: "Fucking son of a bitch still thinks he's part of the family; he goes around screwing everyone's dog and still expects to have dinner with us; *ló fasz a segébe*." She even yelled a little at me: "Look at your father. Look at my husband, my ex-husband. Look at your grandfather. What a gallery of useless bastards. You might as well join up now."

I searched behind me for George, who'd grabbed a beer and stalked off into the field. The sun touched off the gold in every strand of wheat. I snagged myself a beer as well and joined him. "Don't for a minute think that I'm the only one screwing around," he said.

"Sure, sure, I know the story." He needn't have told me, but did.

"Okay, I did it first. She was mad. Fair enough. She had an affair in revenge." He caught them *in flagrante delicto* on a picnic spread on the balcony after returning from his own little bedroom adventure. Though a short man, he creamed the guy, tossed him off the porch into a rosebush. That was their first tit-for-tat. "It would have passed with time, I'm sure; she would have coped eventually," he explained now. "But I was young then, I was too horny to wait for our relationship to heal." And very soon – after a couple more affairs – it was too late for anything except perpetual warfare. They were set in their roles and tracks, like that mechanical rabbit greyhounds bound after at the dog races. "I'm not saying it wasn't my fault. I just want to make my situation clear to somebody."

While he spoke to me my cousin howled: "Don't talk to him! You'll be just like that gigolo." Yelling at the rest of the family: "Get him away from that son of a bitch." The rest of the family stood idly by, incapable of interfering.

The pharmacist handed me his beer. "Hold this," he said, and marched straight back to his wife. She was crouched in front of the fire holding the wooden spoon. He kicked the whole cauldron over towards her; my cousin just barely jumped out of the splash-radius of the boiling *gulyás*. Then the pharmacist stomped off down the road, in the direction phone lines ran, in the direction that crows perched on road signs turned their heads.

With the *gulyás* spilled and trampled, we had no choice but to locate a restaurant, my cousin so choked up that someone else drove her car. Her torrent of abuse had dried up. "After all these years," one aunt said to me, "she still finds new ways to deliver the same old insults." She was a poet of hard feelings, but I'd never seen her go so quiet.

The *csárda* was a brown building of wooden and mortar construction – the poles and railings on the terrace engraved with vines, leaves and grapes, in that Transylvanian high-romantic style. No raindrop could sit still on its sharply peaked roof. One of my relatives said to me: "They've kept their Hungarian heritage better in Transylvania than anywhere else." I told him I'd heard that one before.

Inside the restaurant pictures hugged the walls. My cousin voiced another stock Hungarian complaint: "If they were Western painters they would be world-renowned, but because they're Hungarian no one pays any attention to them."

We sat outside, the fallen night trying to pick itself up. The waiters pushed three tables together to accommodate us. "He'll get better," we said to my cousin, pulling every applicable phrase out of the clichébook. "He'll come around. Nothing's as bad as it seems." She sat at the table and took every toothpick out of the holder. Someone had the forethought to order jugs of wine. Soon the Gypsy string section arrived with upright bass, guitar and violin.

One of the musicians and I began talking about how the government tried to build some communal housing for the Gypsies. Within a week the project was all torn up inside. The Gypsies took anything flammable and built fires in the living room. Busted windows, shit, food, dead animals and trash everywhere inside the skeletal interiors; the place was condemned within two months. The musician and I laughed over wooden goblets of red wine. "We don't want to give up our wandering life. Why should we? For nomadic people any shelter is only a temporary shelter."

Once the other guests left, the proprietor closed the restaurant and joined our revelry. People danced. The Gypsy band, tanked now on wine, everybody's wine, jumped up on tables to play. The violinist clattered on the roof, kicking ceramic shingles off while capering around. The owner yelled at him as we howled like peasants who'd just thrown off servitude. Everyone dancing now and again. Somehow the food never stopped. I ate roast duck and left the fat shining on my chin. My cousin – now fallen into a white mood – wiped my face off with a piece of bread and gave it to the pantry dog. This party did good my old anarchic soul. Revel in chaos, or drown in the terrible preconditioned order. I needed a break from trying to set things straight all the time. Someone poured red wine on my head and I felt baptized.

The pharmacist smashed through the trellis and the wisteria growing thereupon in a turquoise Trabant. This almost did more damage to the Trabant – its body made of compressed cardboard – than the trellis. The purple sticky flowers and vines of the wisteria fell over the car. For some reason this did not drag at all on the party's velocity. The festivities expanded around the car, absorbed it. The violinist jumped off the roof onto the top of the Trabant and one of his legs punched through the roof. He pulled it out and continued to play, standing there. The upright bassist hopped over with his instrument from a nearby table and stood on the Trabant's hood, offset one level from the violinist. As he spun the bass a dislodged wisteria vine wrapped around it, twisting its way up the curvaceous instrument, getting pulled out by the roots. The pharmacist stumbled drunk out of the car to our table and began stuffing his face with bread and *marha pörkölt*. My cousin took no notice of him; he, none of her. Nobody thought it wise to wonder where the car came from.

I wandered over to the grill and saw, among the other slabs of sizzling meat, the head of a pig, cut down the middle of the forehead into two separate profiles. Both halves of the pig's face stared up at me in somber and malevolent stereo. I bent my drunkenly lolling and top-heavy head down to listen to the pig speak. I expected the two profiles to fuse together along the seam where they had been sawed apart. The wine I drank, *Egri Bikavér* – Eger's Bull's Blood – must have hallucinogenic qualities. Maybe this was the definitive Hungarian drug I'd quested after. LSD is really a type of fungus. Fungus grows on feet. Feet are used to trample the juice out of grapes. A weak chain of occurrences leading to trippy wine, but possible. Both hemispheres of the pig's face moved their lips – drawing simultaneously on the left and right side of the brain – to say: "When Hungarian's are happy nothing pulls them down." I knew what the pig meant. Us Hungarians hoard the bad times so conscientiously in order to feel like we deserve this kind of joy once in a while.

At The Oxbow Pub, the baddest bar in town (and therefore Pauline's favorite), tassels pasted over the strippers' nipples gyrate wildly. In between sets of peelers, a local band crashes through several rhythm and blues cover tunes. I feel nervous all night. The feeling begins outside the pub – Pauline and I drinking a couple of her home-brews in the backseat of my car – with an inexplicable desire to knock over the first motorcycle in a line of parked Harleys outside the front door: if only to watch the domino effect. Inside, I drink red wine because red wine lends me the bravado of a tequila drunk without the ensuing upchuck. Nobody drinks red wine at the Oxbow Pub, and so I walk with my hands behind my back. Hell's Angels lounge about.

Pauline and I dance to "Sweet Home Alabama" and she hails all bikers, knowing every single one. A short, stocky guy with a head balding in a circle perfect enough to vacuum seal his skull-cap against, picks a five dollar bill off the floor. "This yours?" he asks aggressively.

"No," I stammer; my heart moves skittishly, looking for a hiding spot somewhere in the chest cavity.

"I didn't think so," he says, really meaning: *You better not mess with me, though I'd love it if you did*. I excuse myself from Pauline and sit against the wall, watching the rednecks, keeping everyone in sight, making sure I do not bump into a single soul the way I did at that old ballroom so many hundreds of years ago.

The entry to the men's room looks like a hole in the wall. I walk in carefully and note that someone's ripped a door off one of the stalls. Inside, a gentleman of slight build sits on the toilet with pants down around the ankles. From his groin region protrudes a magnificent but embarrassingly erect weenie. He sobs with gusto and presses toilet paper to eyes. I glance around, verifying the lack of other presence in the restroom, for my heart goes out to this inappropriately aroused crybaby, and I don't want anyone testifying to my show of weakness or, worse, taking offense at my show of humanity. At the Oxbow Pub, signs of empathy lead to instant bodily harm, and other forms of free advice. "What's wrong, pal?" I ask, my voice gentle as ether.

"Boo hoo, hoo." The man moans, stops, looks up at me, then presses his face back into the wadded toilet paper to lacerate himself with another wracking sob: "Boo hoo, hoo, hoo, hoo, boo hoo." A biker walks in, beard swinging so long it nearly trails on the floor. I quickly turn to a urinal and get my dink into peeing position (though I have trouble pissing in public, especially with tough guys to either side).

"Stop crying you Goddamn faggit!" the dude in leathers yells, one hand on pecker and the other hammering at the stall's wall. The gentleman quiets his sobbing to a library whisper. "I'm telling you," the biker stares at me, "there may not be a social solution to these faggits. There may not even be a political solution. But there will always be a Final Solution." Amazing the erudition you pick up while cruising highways in V-formation, or from bartenders who keep shotguns under the mirror, or ass-busting police with their faint stink of fear.

"Leave me alone!" the gentleman howls.

"Hey, I wasn't going to touch you," the Biker admits while doing up his brass, "Keep on Truckin" belt buckle. "You might bleed on me. I'd contract some fatal disease." He clomps out in square-toed boots.

"I'm not talking to you!" the gentleman screams. "I was talking to him," and he points at me.

I retrieve my glass of wine from its hiding spot behind the strippers' costume stand, the glass covered with some kind of grease. I stand in a corner of the wall, wishing Pauline would lose her ability to force me into places like this.

She comes up. "Gabe, what's wrong with you? Come and sit over at the table with me and my friends." I look over at four men in work-boots, plaid and facial scars. Their dented knuckles turn white as they lift bottles to lips: the kind of men I have no conversation for, except such stock phrases as "Don't hit me, please!" or "It wasn't me; I never called you a homo!" or "I'm sorry, I'm sorry. Now will you let me go?" Their mustaches barely conceal quick sarcasm.

I stall for time: "You gotta see this guy in the crapper." Pauline carries her mug of beer, and walks into the men's bathroom. We clamber onto the neighboring toilet and frown down upon the erect gentleman's lack of discretion.

"What happened?" Pauline asks of him.

"My girlfriend left me for someone else."

"Aaaawwww, poor baby!" Pauline groans in pitch-perfect mockery. She dips crumpled toilet paper in the other toilet, leans over the stall and chucks it at him. It splatters in particles sticking all over his face. "Get it together!" she screams. Then Pauline takes my arm and leads me out.

"How can you be such a bitch?" I yell. "That guy's distraught!"

"How can you be so pathetic?" she asks in turn, "sitting there with a boner on, in an open toilet, crying into toilet paper? Someone should kick your ass out of here."

"What? That wasn't me!"

"I never said it was you," she shouts over the start-up squeal of Candy Floss's organ music and the howls of unbridled eros from the bar. Off to one side, someone comments on the wonderful, unique and yet superlative shape of Candy Floss's labia.

Pauline guides me towards her table like a shepherd. I fear a lot of evil in this valley of shadow. My feet want to stick to the floor in spidery ways. Again, I stall for time. "Pauline?" I ask, trying to kindle some humor. "When you come to kill me – as all my friends must, sooner or later – promise me you won't use a spike." Pauline pauses. She gazes outside the window of the pub, her face for a moment regaining that strained junkie look – a look all bony and weak – that she had before obtaining my financial assistance, and tries to make out each tree in the fog surrounding the building. "I can't promise you that," she laughs, not looking at me. Candy Floss's hips swirl and undulate to Ike and Tina's "Rolling on a River."

Pauline pulls me forward against my will. I drain my wineglass and force her to stop at the bar for more. "Just get a bottle," she commands.

"Pauline?" I ask while we wait in line. "If I asked you to mutilate me, would you?"

This time she fails to pause, though obviously still unsure whether the question sickens or amuses her. "That depends," she whispers in my ear over the sound of breaking glass, as Candy Floss leaps from stage to table. "If you asked me to mutilate your face, I probably wouldn't. But if you asked me to mutilate your genitals, I probably would."

"And my bum?"

"Only to carve a hole in it, into which I'd stick your genitals."

She pushes me towards her table. I bump into someone holding up ten bucks for Candy Floss to pluck out of his hand with the crack of her ass (a maneuver she's known far and wide for). He curls up his fist before noticing Pauline, at which point every fiber in him relaxes. "Sorry Pauline," he apologizes, turning away without another look at us.

"Hey, shouldn't he be saying 'sorry' to me?" I ask. Pauline tugs on. In the mayhem, swigging from a bottle of bitter red, I know what I've always known: that I do not want the life Pauline wants for me. I stand immobile despite her efforts to drag me down.

"Pauline, I've decided to drown the dog."

"What?" she asks.

"October thirty-first at two o'clock p.m. The dog will go down in my parents' bathtub." They're away that day. I've got a key.

Pauline licks my ear and probably stares into that dark canal a little bit, wondering where it all leads. "Maybe the energy you put into killing the dog could be channeled into sexual activity," she suggests.

"If I did that, it would become sexual aggression," I reply.

"Maybe you should just kill yourself, then," she advises.

"Too scared. I don't like pain."

Pauline snickers, then bites my earlobe and hangs on. She begins to walk, pulling me towards her table, earlobe clenched firmly between her teeth. Obviously this could never happen in the real world: therefore my life isn't entirely non-fictional.

I see Pauline's ex-boyfriend wave at me from every corner. Lala sits with a leg dangling over the back of a chair. My father entertains several women at the back tables. Pauline dangles enigmatically from my ear. And at her table I see a blond, mustachioed man beginning to turn his face in my direction. I rip myself free of Pauline and squirm between bodies alien to any deodorant apart from a hundred and twenty kilometer winds. I'm sure that if the blond at Pauline's table fully turned around, he'd have both eyes in working order, but being sure isn't enough. I need out. So, after all these years of hope, it seems red wine provides no miracle cure for cowardice either.

The treadmill I stand on runs too quickly; doors and people recede with every effort. I suddenly feel needful: to take my friends to the home I should have, introduce them to the father I should likewise have, to show my family that my plight is dandy, things run smooth, upright people cater to me, that I don't need to speak of the heartland. I want to denounce Pauline's beliefs about drinking and freedom and the lowbrow life's praiseworthy lack of strictures.

Rain drizzles gently onto alders. I search for my car but the parking lot seems a darkened maze where branches slap you in the face and side-view mirrors deliver kidney blows. I hear Pauline call my name and duck. A man swears into a payphone but then begins to listen carefully to the voice on the other end. "Gabe," Pauline calls. Amazing how little of the bar you hear out in the quiet parking lot. "Gabe," Pauline yells. I see naked Lala squatting down beside me. I wish she'd move off to a distance where I can't tell if anything's wrong with her. "Gabe!" I stand because it's better to face Pauline than squat with Lala. Beads of rain shine from Pauline's eyebrows.

"Gabe. I put acid in that home-brew I gave you," she gasps.

"That was a stupid thing to do, Pauline." My astigmatism refracts every square inch of the scene. "I can't handle it like you."

"You know I don't do drugs anymore," she replies.

"Why'd you do it to me, then?"

"I wanted to ask you something."

"What?"

Pauline pulls back her veil of hair and knots it behind her head. "Forget it," she says. "I fucked up. I thought it would make it easier for me. But this is wrong." A dog barks at us from the back seat of a car. "Some other time," she promises, staring at the animal.

I try hard to control my perceptions, try hard not to emote. "Whatever, Pauline. Whatever."

"Are you coming back inside?"

"Pauline," my reply sounds like parable, "I haven't felt my tongue in hours."

"Furthermore?" she asks, suddenly pissed off with my attitude. The birds of morning begin to chirp away the bad night of wine. Soon, blue sky will shine through the clouds, a sight that depresses me before sleep but gladdens me after it.

"Furthermore, that bar scares me," I reply.

"Like always?"

"Like always."

Pauline's gaze fumbles around, checking out my aura. "How can you be scared of an outside chance? Someone beating you up out of the blue? Especially when I'm around?"

"If there's anything I believe in, it's the upset victory."

"Gabe, you don't believe in anything."

"Oh, you're so wrong, baby," pipes my little voice, losing the baritone I put on for the benefit of the bar. The veins in my neck do the rank and file trying to suppress the shout: "I WILL TELL YOU!" Restraint kicks in and my voice turns mushy again. "I do not believe in social workers. I support police going into domestic violence with guns blazing on the fist-toting husband. I support the crackle of the electric chair, not third and fourth chances." I jump up and sit on the hood of the nearest car, which happens to be mine. "I have a theory, Pauline, that rapists should all undergo forced sex changes and be raped in turn. If I didn't believe in that, I could solve all my problems by embracing pacifism and doing the great godly Gandhi." I holler at the earth: "I BELIEVE IN AGGRESSION!" A monumental greenie horks up from my throat against the windshield. "If I believed in pacifism I could live with myself, try for peace, go down and preach, get some apostles. But I believe violence must lead justice. Firing squads for death squads. That's me," I say. The dog, a Scottish terrier, settles back on its seat. Rain obliterates my vision past two feet. "But I can't be violent. I'm too good-natured, kind-hearted, worst of all forgiving. Lala, now Lala was perfect that way...."

Pauline takes me by the elbows and stands me up against the fender, fishes the keys from my pocket and guides me into the passenger seat. "I'm sorry, Gabe. I shouldn't have done this to you. It was stupid." I don't know what Pauline means; I feel clean and sober. She closes the door gently. I slide over to the driver's side and start up the engine.

"Don't forget about my dog. It dies October thirty-first. And this time my method's foolproof," I yell out the window after her.

The night just described is October thirtieth.

My cousin lent me his Trabant, powered by a two-stroke engine even a lawn-mower doesn't deserve. Pollution-maker *extraordinaire*: I revved the engine at intersections and watched blue smoke billow up behind me. I rattled and shook and vibrated and itched within the car to the rhythm of its knocks and pings; the muffler sounded like death in the throat. I didn't know how long I'd stay alive on the crash-course streets of the capital. Lala was sampling champagne somewhere in France while I purchased Dreher beers from the local *közért*, beers that left your tongue soaked in isotope. Like most of the fruit juice around here, the main ingredient was chemical additives. The label on the bottle should have read: at least ten percent real beer!

I drove to the top of *János Hegy* and sucked on the bottles while sitting on the hood of the little car. I made sure not to inadvertently see any stars, not to look up. Stars are for wishful thinkers, not soft-nosed realists like me. I tried to find salt in the earth, but came up with a gherkin of dried dogshit.

On the way down from the mountain a police car sidled up beside me, a difficult task because I was weaving everywhere. Yes, though drunk, I could weave a very nice tight wave pattern in the Trabant, thank-you, and, not only that, but on purpose too. A seismograph couldn't draw a zigzag more regular. Most sober drivers would not be capable of this kind of car handling. The cop's face showed no emotion as they swooped up parallel and he pointed to the side of the road. I floored it and got onto the ramp leading to the Árpád bridge.

We screeched up on sidewalks, shot into tight alleys. I hoped the police were having as much fun as me. But unfortunately it ended like any good thing. I jumped out of the car, leaving it jammed on the garbage can I ran over a few blocks back. The cops stopped, opened the back door of their car, and let slip the German shepherd that came bounding towards me like something penned up and systematically starved while having my underwear shoved in its face. It bit my foot and I fell. It growled and gnawed on my ankle. I pulled my leg back and gave it a swift one in the head. Well, well, well, who would have thought I'd be able to strike back! The dog winced and released my ankle for a token yelp, then munched down again. Before I could ready boot number two, the forces of law and order beset me from both sides.

One of the policemen punted me in the ribs. "That's for kicking my dog, fucker!" What do you know, I thought, the dog chews my leg into shrapnel and he expects decorum? I wondered what the penalty for drinking drivers was in Hungary. Going motionless, I pretended not to hear the cops tell me to get up. When the cop kicked me again I even managed not to cringe or grunt, which only those versed in certain eastern pain-negating secrets – guys who get up in the morning and make their bed of nails – are capable of. For a second I was as proficient with ignoring injury as a flaming monk.

"He's passed out," one of the cops exclaimed, buying into my ruse.

"We'll see about that," replied the other. They grabbed my body and heaved it into the car.

On the ride to the station I shared the back seat with their German Shepherd. It sat over me breathing a dogfood afterburner onto my face and growling, bared teeth inches from my runny nose.

The trip went by in disorienting changes of direction. We arrived somewhere, screech of brakes and clunk of door handles. Then the two cops manhandled me again, my feet dragging on the pavement, the uppers on my shoes destroyed. I hit the cement floor like an iron-on they'd never peel off; I thought: no way these guys are going to get a urine or breathalyzer sample out of me.

I heard water splashing on concrete; then they blasted me with a jet cold as glacial run-off. I opened my eyes and, through the spray of ice-water, saw the two cops laughing, one of them holding the fire-hose. The water pressure lifted my body slightly, nudged it over on the concrete two or three feet. I only withstood one minute twenty-four seconds of the intense cold and bruising before springing to my toes as if the room had suddenly turned upside down and hurtled me skywards.

The cop turned off the firehose and glared. It was hard for me to see single.

"Take the handcuffs off him," said the older cop to the younger one, who'd been doing the hosing down. "Hand him that towel," he commanded next. I toweled down. "Put the handcuffs back on," he instructed.

I turned to the younger cop and asked, "Don't you get tired of being this guy's cum-rag?" Cop the younger kneed me in the groin and I slowly descended to the concrete like a melting figurine, the only bonus being that the drink suppressed my imminent sense of danger.

Next they lined me up in front of an old cop sitting behind a desk. He asked my name, nationality, passport number and other pertinent data. I answered insolently: "You're a cop?" He looked up, a face with no profile, a face that should have said "Made in Asia" underneath the stick-straight hair – one of those Hungarian blood-lines introduced to the gene pool by the invading Turks or Mongols of long ago. "I can't believe they let someone as old as you be a cop!" I laughed. Came another blow to the groin.

They never took any blood-alcohol reading.

I emerged out of pain into a cold and empty jail cell, the handcuffs off, wallet and passport still in pocket. I could crawl over to the latrine if I wanted. I could crawl onto the cot. I could crawl to the bars. Even in jail my world was fraught with piss-poor choices, all of which, of course, required me to crawl. But I figured on just sitting still to let the drunk peter out, become a buzz and, then, with a little luck, a thronging hangover.

"Hey! Hey! Is there anyone down there?" a voice yelled. I remained prostrate on the floor. Most people would have been screaming Canadian consulate by now, but I didn't think I had much pull with the cops. My brain drew strange blanks on everything; for instance, and thankfully, I couldn't feel my face. (Lala asked me for a wallet-sized photo once and she received a square blank of photographic paper. "Draw my picture on it," I told her, "any one of my faces you want." But I would have preferred her keeping it white.) Better blank than frank: a maxim for times like this, I thought.

"Hey?" the voice yelled from somewhere down the cell block. I lifted my head a little off the floor. I stopped considering the idea of mounting an anxiety attack.

"Yeah?" I hollered in return.

"What are you in for?" he shouted.

"Drinking and driving ... and an assortment of minor infringements." His laugh boomed down the halls. "What are you laughing at?" I screamed, letting my head down onto the concrete and getting a view of dripping pipes running across the ceiling. I continue to lay spread-eagled on my back the whole night howling.

"I'm in for the same thing," he finally replied. I wondered if this was the friend I'd dreamed of finding since I was a wee lad, a friend who looked and acted exactly like me. A friend I could stab in the back to rid myself of forever. But, no, it turned out his name was Szent-György. "Yeah, I was going to my girlfriend's place. See, my wife's working tonight so it was an excuse-free situation, but some friends dropped by for beers and it took forever to get them out. I'm speeding to her place and a ghost car pulls out in front of me. I think I've had it but some guy overtakes me on the left and the ghost car goes for him instead. A few kilometers later the sedan's pulled over. But the fucking cop has parked right in the middle of the road, totally blocking traffic, while he gives the guy the ticket. And there I sit, burning with desire."

"So what happened?"

"I leaned on the horn."

"No!?"

"Yeah." We both chuckled, our laughter bouncing back and forth down the corridors like tennis. "Yeah, I leaned on my horn. Then I rolled down my window, stuck my fist out, and told the cop to move his fucking ass."

Amazing the heedlessness booze builds in you.

"Better to be foolhardy than scared," he said, but I didn't reply to this. We then began telling each other jokes, shooting down the hours as they passed by.

In the morning the cops came to my cell. "Well, boy, how are you feeling?" I brushed the seepage out of the corner of my eyes and tried to trigger those nerve impulses that normally lead to a smile, but those same impulses now made only for a pain in my stomach. I wondered if I tried triggering the nerves that normally lead to a pain in my stomach, whether a smile might form. The ache in my head required so much space that all the ear-wax squeezed out my ears.

"What are you doing?" I asked. They opened the door and stepped into the cell, inspected each other, then me. For the first time since landing into the jail I moved off the floor to sit on the cot. "Just don't hurt me," I whimpered. Both cops laughed and hooked their thumbs into their belts. "Please?" I groveled, now attuned to the real situation.

"We don't know what we're going to do," the older cop said. I lifted up my hands and pressed them against either ear to hold up my head, balanced the elbows on my knees to hold up my hands, pushed my feet against the floor to hold up my knees. The earth did the rest. I was the usual cardhouse. Someone whispered, "Forty thousand forints." I looked up at the cops and one of them was dragging on a cigarette while the other picked his teeth. I went back to searching the ground. "Forty thousand forints," spoke the nearly subliminal whisper again. I glanced at the cops. One of them was drinking water from the tap while the other ate a chocolate bar. I rested my gaze on the ground. "Forty thousand forints." Looked up again. One of them stood by my window with index fingers in his mouth, whistling to someone in the yard, while the other had pulled out a small toothbrush and was brushing his teeth in the sink below the mirror. Down. "Forty thousand forints." Up.

"Stop it!" I yelled, trying to rise and hitting my head on the top bunk. Colors flowed across my eyes. Forty thousand forints, forty thousand forints, forty thousand forints. A hundred million little whispers.

Looking over, one of the cops was gargling and the other slipping his false teeth in and out while holding the tip of his tongue extended and pinched between the fingers of his other hand. “Okay, okay, okay,” I shouted, reaching into my wallet and handing over all the money. They were not allowed to talk of bribes, so they invented telepathy. Nothing like capitalism to bring out the best in human creativity and conniving. If ever there was a reason for evolution it would be in the interests of a cold quick turnover.

On the outside a small man approached me. The moment of opening his mouth I recognized the voice from the guy down the cell block. “How much did you pay?” he asked. I told him forty thousand. “Man, you got ripped off!” No matter how long I hounded him he wouldn’t let on the reasonable price.

I returned to my great-aunt’s, broke, beaten and dejected. I picked up the phone and dialed. “I’d like the next flight back to Canada.”

I walked straight out of the heritage home that night Lala and I finally made regular love. At home, I listened to Baroque music through the dark in hopes it would scrub me clean, and trashed unnecessary items from my bookshelves.

I found a scrapbook of photographs of my father’s second family, presented to me at the River City airport by the other wife. I thumb through the pages, the old black and whites centered two-by-two on each page, pictures of my father with a different son, all smiles beside my mother’s alter-ego. In some photos a lake slops around in the background, or a picnic cloth flutters, or alpine meadows blow back and forth – too much motion for a photograph to properly convey, but try not to let the continuity errors faze you. My father seems genuinely happy, relaxed, blending in as he does with the landscape.

We stood in the tiny wood-panel waiting room. Macy and her son Bob stood beside me, waiting for the plane to arrive. Bob missed his father; in other words, he kept examining the likeness between my face and the one on the man they'd buried that morning (Bob and I both helped to shovel the dirt on, a not altogether unpleasant job; I even got the once-in-a-lifetime chivalric opportunity to offer my hanky to my bawling half-brother). Macy struck me as the gifted type who never missed anything gone for good.

"Gabe, I wish you'd come back to visit now and again," Macy said, "never mind what your father would have preferred." She kept opening and snapping shut her large black purse. The rings on her finger attracted me the way baubles attract a crow.

"Look, Macy. You've been kind. But this isn't my place." At this news, Bob relieved himself of the longest sigh I've ever heard. Snap, snap, snap, snap – Macy's purse opened and closed. I knew Bob would put nicer flowers on my father's grave, and more frequently, than I ever could. "I've got to go back to Oxbow. I'd like to spare my family anything more to do with this place."

Macy gently pinched my cheek. "I like to think of us all as one giant family, Gabe."

The twin-engine buzzed down on the runway like an old beater without a tailpipe. It skidded along a little and then taxied over to the passenger waiting area. "I've never felt like I was in a family," I said to her, "and I see no reason to start feeling that way now. Too much to defend in a family," I stated, glancing at the backs of Bob's large veiny hands. Macy reached into the purse and extended the small photo album forward.

"Think about us, at least," she requested. And this simple request finally dropped me into her arms. Macy held me and Bob forced me to accept his handkerchief, which canceled out my slight emotional lead on him.

I weighed the album on my hand. "Hey, Macy, do you think I could have the purse, too?" She flexed her toes in their black patent leather shoes, thinking. She gave me the purse. I ran up to the airplane with it dangling from my shoulder, the book of photographs stuffed inside. The red of my eyes and the sunset complemented each other. I mentally urged the engines ever higher. We circled River City twice. My last memory of Macy and Bob is a memory of dots.

That night in Victoria I dumped the album in the garbage and wished my father *bon voyage*. He looked so human in the photographs that I found it impossible not to understand the total lack of answers plaguing his life.

Lala walked over to Trixy's, the Unknown Roommate's and my place from the heritage house with a scroll seven feet long trailing in the wind. She finished reading the 123rd question off her handwritten list. She interrogated me: "If you wanted to break up, why did you, last night, while having sex, tell me you loved me?"

Under such grueling pressure I answered: "Because that's how I felt at the time." I glanced at the questionnaire and pointed to the word "four," which should have said, "for." "You misspelled that one," I said with a certain amount of insensitivity. Then she freaked. I don't remember what came first, claws, eye-teeth or fists. She directed all the damage she could muster exclusively at my face.

"I can't replace your mother," I sobbed. "I could understand you wanting a father-figure from me. After all, I've got a dink at least. But your mother, never!"

Lala began to hit me faster and faster. A few minutes more pummeling and we'd finally be finished with this crazy little thing called love.

Some of her dialogue went like this: "Why did you break up with me? Why? Why?" The diatribe unfolded like a bad nursery rhyme, or baby-talk – goo-goo, ga-ga, things of that nature. Luckily there weren't gas ovens around or she'd have wrapped her head in tinfoil, plopped it onto a cookie-sheet, inserted it into the hissing box, and turned the dial to "bake." I talk with candor now, but you can imagine my behavior at the time. "You want to be free? What about the shit I've gone through? You want to be wild? Why don't you just fuck me right now, then, huh? Come on! Come on! I won't ever let you forget me!" I wondered, while failing at fending her off, whether she was still following the questionnaire or if we were acting out a supplementary clause to the document. I finally managed get out from underneath.

"I'm leaving," I tried to say, in a nauseous little voice. I knew leaving my own home in a huff was pathetic, but nothing mattered.

"No, don't leave, please," Lala pleaded.

I fingered the laces of my shoes. "Well, it is my house after all."

"Please don't leave." I stayed, pinching my thighs through my pockets.

At seven thirty-five, the Unknown Roommate returned. I sat with Lala on the couch and contributed to a three-way conversation while blood dripped off my cheek into my collar. The Unknown Roommate averted her eyes twenty-seven and a half times and finally just left the room wordlessly.

No longer deigning towards dialogue ourselves, Lala and I walked out together, goose-stepping shoulder to shoulder. On the sidewalk we turned about-face and parted in opposite directions – no words and no nothing.

I swung from the rim of the world, legs kicking in space. The day went black like a dissatisfied photograph. Needing to staunch the blood I tamped my face into my shirtsleeve. Our penultimate argument and Lala's reprisals had anesthetized me. Tombstones instead of dogtags hung around my neck. I toiled under Jupiter's pull. So I walked part of the night, as I had to do, down to the sea.

A deck of smokes kept me going. Lala had done me violence for her own benefit, enfeebled me. A physical harm is just a physical harm. A smile is just a smile. But this memory Lala left: now there's an iron lung I'll never be free of. Long as I want to live. Perhaps it was then that I decided on a replacement for myself, the way the old man did with the goat. Or maybe I still contemplated suicide.

I went past a twenty-four hour corner store where two boys sat on the steps outside in stark light, bicycles at their feet and a box of potato chips between them. They even had chip-dip (sour cream and onion, by the colours on the container) and called to me, perhaps an invitation to dine. But there was a necessity to get beside the sea. I let them keep the dip all to themselves. Blood dried on my sleeve. I needed stitches.

I gave up on the moon showing by the salty water that night. Some drunk lady with a veil of matted hair washed her hands in the saline near me and then walked in shoes with broken heels. Morning came and the sky had changed to blue. I began to see past my hand. A ship outfitted with many white sails stayed level with the horizon despite the steep waves. Shiver me timbers, I felt marooned. And I didn't have the panache to re-enact the Ophelia scene.

Now I hankered after a ham and eggs place. In the greasy spoon's restroom I looked into the mirror at eyes bruised purple and almost swollen shut, at cheeks and forehead with centimeters-long scratches in them. My scalp was missing patches of hair. So much for the repairable exterior. The interior damage was more thoroughgoing though, with a warrantee to last.

This neo-end with Lala, and Victoria's December, had left me emotionally penniless. I went back to Oxbow for consolation and cross-dressing in Pauline's trailer. I would return to Victoria for one last miserable attempt at education and, almost a year to the day, one final party with Lala.

The kid under the extended roof of an Eastern European marquee was me: like an image under Alcatraz in the encyclopedia. Films no longer played there.

The kid in the cheetah costume, soggy tail in hand, eye-shadow thick as cable dribbling down his cheeks, was yours truly. Wet hair draped my forehead, black spots like suns in the yellow velvet of the costume, a white paper bag, with empty bottom disintegrating, held in my hand. The costume, so old and soiled, looked stitched together from dirt. The marquee's bulbs trafficked rainbows fugitive as watercolors on a lake's surface. The rain had peculiar silver light, like hooks floating underwater. I looked over my shoulder.

Across the street, near a telephone booth, a lanky man leaned over, rag in hand, to clean something off his patent leather boots. He greased his black hair back with rain. An unnaturally long shirttail came untucked, and flapped, from between his suspenders, far behind him with whip-cracks. As a man in the rain he was unconcerned about the weather. As a man he was sharply tailored. I could not see his goatee. He wasn't a great man, but had mystery, with a style made to stand only for an instant. The poseur told no single story, was full of scuzzy, sleazy, downtrodden plot lines about underground company, the kind who ran at the sight of police. In short, he gave good image, albeit an image torn at the elbows.

The rain spliced everything together. Posters went to pieces. Strips of newspaper waddled in the wind like men in flippers.

There is no Halloween in Hungary, but I insisted and my parents got me a costume. You'll find out one way or another, they said, and after half a dozen houses I learned that Halloween won't be forced.

You can't hold a private Halloween. It's public or nothing.

The claw-foot bathtub sits in a niche under a skylight, with its cracks, bulbous faucets and the baritone groan it emits when flesh slides against it. You could drown in the watery depths of my mother's bathtub, deep as a shallow lagoon, long as the body. A late afternoon comes by the date of October thirty-first. Nobody celebrates Halloween in Oxbow; children get egged or stoned; apples contain razor blades; chocolate bars teem with poison; everyone washes their hands after handing out candies.

Pauline sits on the counter-top around my sink. Toothpaste and soap drippings stain the seat of her jeans. Her unusually greasy hair hangs in front of her face like on a tawdry doll. She flaunts sanity, buttons on her shirt missing down to the navel, the fly on her jeans busted, mud-caked sneakers. Wardrobe provided by charity boutiques.

I wear shorts, T-shirt with cigarette burns. I wish I were a lounge act, or a *mâitre d'* in a Ramada hotel. There must be careers other than dog-catcher for one of my aptitudes.

The bathtub's water radiates cold and depth. The wiener dog sits hostage in my arms, whining softly. I look one last time at Pauline, lift the dog above my head and plunge it down. Both my hands hold it under. The dog's ass rises above the thrashing. The tail slaps around, whipping my face. My lips stretch into a concise grin. Behind gritted teeth my tongue flails like the tail. I'm in the white water of the bathtub. Moisture races up my clothes. Soft claws on the back leg of the dog scrape my jeans.

Pauline lights a cigarette.

The wiener dog's face hides under the foam. I'd spend dollars to know what its fleas are thinking.

Pauline says, just in time: "Can't kill reality with any kind of scheme."

With a massive grunt I heave the lifeless dog out of the tub. Water splashes and sprays. I plunk the dog down on its back. I try hard to remember the training course. Short stacked breaths shall be required, like for a newborn. I spread my lips over the dog's muzzle – deep-throat it Swedish-style – and blow air back into its lungs. I concentrate very hard on remembering the times it's licked its balls, or shoved its snout up another dog's bung-hole. I recall details from all the times it's eaten feces – a coprophiliac's catalogue. I shove oxygen forward with small compressions of my lungs. The dog's entire muzzle stuffs my mouth, the nose squishes against my tonsils, hairs between my teeth: a most unsanitary act of absolution.

The dog hacks into my throat. I suck my mouth off its muzzle; guy-wires of saliva attach our orifices. The dogs splutters, turns onto its side, exhales water, gets up, shakes itself.

Turning around, there's an engagement ring in a velvet case before my face. Pauline holds it and smiles, down on one knee.

"Here's what I did with the money," she confesses, fingering hair out of my eyes. "Want to get married?" I stutter until speechless. She slips the ring onto my finger. "It looks pretty classy" – a wink and smile.

For once, the bell saves my ass. With Pauline ardently kneeling on the wet bathroom floor, my dog and I gazing aghast at the size of the rock on the ring (both of us thinking maybe I should accept just for that: diamonds being, after all, a girl's best friend), the phone tinkles. This grants me a temporary reprieve from a rash decision. So I jump to it.

The operator asks about a person-to-person call from a Mr. Forty-Four Magnum Bill.

"Bill, how'd you get my parents' number?"

"Directory assistance, Gabe."

"What are you doing calling me here!" Pauline tugs at my elbow, badgering me to hang up and choose. I clasp my hand over the mouthpiece and say, "It's important," before getting back to my ex-coworker: "What was that, Bill?"

"I said your phone's disconnected!"

"Oh yeah ... I forgot. What's shaking?" The engagement ring glints off the hand I use to answer the telephone. Pauline looks uncertainly around the kitchen.

The theft of car and shotgun was a petty setback but it made Bill hell-bent. He got my last cheque in the mail and purchased another used car and illegal shotgun. The chase resumed straight into the folds of Mexico.

Pauline yells: "Gabe, put down the Goddamn phone, or I'm outta here!"

Bill pauses: "Is there someone else there?"

"Look, this is long distance, Pauline." Then I speak into the phone: "It's okay Bill. Go on."

"I can't believe this," shouts Pauline, stomping around the kitchen. "I cannot believe you are going to do this to me!" The wet wiener dog rolls on the little patch of carpet where it habitually sleeps, rubbing its own scent into itself. I keep my eyes on the friend in the kitchen and an ear to the friend calling from the bottom of the continent. I divide between them.

Bill went to Mexico city, sorted through poverty and corruption, but didn't find a dime spent by his wife. Deprived of her red pumps – which disappeared along with the last car and unregistered firearm –

Bill had no psychic touchstones. He made Mazatlan pimps turn out their wallets, drunks tell the truth. Bill only investigated the underbelly. In the end he turned up one pump of the pair from a fruit vendor. The vendor told how it had been hurled from a car screaming past at two hundred kilometers an hour the day before.

Bill touched the shoe and experienced a secular Pentecost.

He got into the car and closed his eyes, letting the markers and milestones in his head be his automatic pilot. When he lifted his lids again he was in some scruffy village surrounded by cacti. He got out of the car at the first hotel, loaded the shotgun and, concealing it under a four foot round sombrero bought on the way through Tijuana, walked in and went up to the concierge to get his wife's room number.

"What's your name?" the concierge asked.

"Forty Goddamn Four Magnum fucking Bill. What's it to you?" he bellowed.

The concierge adroitly said a message had been left. Bill demanded it. The note read briefly. "Love ya to come up and see us on yer way through town. Room 405." Signed Lily and Otto. So Otto is that Indian's name, thought Bill. Bill filed the note in a wastepaper basket, licked his fingertips, smoothed down his eyebrows, and walked through the lobby, four foot sombrero in hand, up the stairs.

Pauline rummages in the kitchen drawers. She pulls out an enormous butcher knife, and weighs it carefully in her hand, muttering: "You're going to answer me. One way or another, you're going to answer." I trap the receiver between shoulder and head and grab the phonebook to shield me from whatever monkey-business she devises. Pauline glares at me while skimming a thumb along the edge of the heavy blade.

Bill found 405 no problem. The door seemed to have stepped open a crack. He pushed it and looked through the room at Lily and Otto seated between margaritas on the balcony. Doffing the sombrero he raised the shotgun to shoulder height and walked to them. Both targets acted like casual vacationers.

"Well, hello there, Bill," Lily smiled. "Thought you might pop by for a bit of breky."

"Why don't you have a seat, Bud?" said Otto, pulling a chair away from the table.

Bill squared him up in the sights. "Don't 'Bud' me, shithead."

"Aw, Bill, lighten up and have a drink. Plenty of time to kill us later. Don't be such a salami bitch." (Apparently his wife – from the same northern Italian village – had problems with that phrase as well).

Another big hoodwink, thought Bill. He was parched though. He hemmed and hawed and sat down and finally took a sip out of something with an umbrella in it. Fruity.

Butcher knife held above head, Pauline prowls past me. She saws the telephone cord back and forth across the dull blade. A race begins between Bill finishing his allegory and Pauline cutting off our one line of communication. Normally, I'd reproach her for this behavior, but she looks like someone used to manhandling frozen carcasses.

"So what the Hell happened after that?" I quickly ask Bill.

"I don't know. Next it was dark and I was on a bed, naked. She was giving me a hand job. Hell of a good hand job, too. Otto was rubbing some kind of oil over my body. All of us nude!"

"And...?"

"Well, you're a grown boy, Gabe. I won't go into it. But shit, things got out of hand! Steamin'! Let's just say I was saved by hedonism."

"You mean...?"

"God bless her tender heart, Gabe. She had it planned from the start. Knew I was dying at the mill and Oxbow, like she was. She wanted to juice up our marriage."

"And Otto?"

"Love the man, Gabe. Never thought I'd say it. He's the son I never had, and, by Jesus, every man should have a son like that."

"Goddamn, this knife is dull," swears Pauline. She wraps the untouched cord a few times around the knife and hefts the blade on high, balancing herself before bringing it down against the tiled floor and severing me from Mexico.

My voice goes frantic: "Bill. What the Hell happened to you? What kind of fairy tale are you giving me?"

"Don't know, Gabe. But Mexico is a beautiful place, Gabe. I think we're going to stay, Gabe. Your savings go forever here, Gabe. I love my wife, Gabe. I know what life's all about now, Gabe. Never postpone things, Gabe. Why, just yesterday, Gabe...." With the sound of metal on stone, and a burst of sparks, Pauline cracks a floor tile right in half, chopping the cord itself into tiny lengths. The line dies just as my head finally differentiates between its needs and wants.

"I'd like an answer, Gabe," Pauline extends the blunt front of the knife straight out before herself, like a hatchet thrower taking aim.

I pull engagement ring from finger, feeling sick about passing up on something that cost me so much money. "Sorry for the anticlimax...." I begin but Pauline interrupts me.

"I know, Gabe," she sighs, putting the butcher knife down on the table. "Even if you were inclined to accept my proposal you'd still force yourself not to. I know, I know. But I just don't understand."

I pull Pauline over to the mirror and have her run her fingers through the hairs on my head. "Our marriage, Pauline," I say, "would be a spell of errors and heartbreak. Look at my head carefully. Do you see the easily numbered hairs still attached to my pate? In a few years they'll all traitor on me and leave. Can you see a beautiful woman like yourself married to a bald insecure man?" Pauline nods her head just to contradict me one last time. "Well I can, too. I can read the future, Pauline. You'll love me for a while. Maybe. Then you'll get bored. Better looking guys will come along. You'll have affairs, maybe even divorce me. What can a bald middle-aged man start after a divorce?" I drop the ring down the front of her pants. "Then I'll have nothing except," and I impart a major groan, "my pessimism. That's why I can't marry you. Keep your ring." I open the phonebook, lick my index finger and begin to rifle through the list of names, all this in order to give some visible indicator of my mental and emotional state. "You see, Pauline, I have to choose someone from my level of ugliness, like K. Bearden, or, or, uh, Tom Bondwell, or Maxine Charney. I brought Lala down and I refuse to take anyone else down again." Closing the cover on the book, I notice it reads Oxbow Telephone Directory 1988.

So few folk move to or from or within Oxbow that phonebooks rarely need updating. It must still list Lala's father's old number....

"Why is letting me bring you up not an option?" asks Pauline, feeling for the wedding ring amid luxuriant pubic hair.

The room realizes something and she stops. The wiener dog freezes. Pauline's voice just spoke.

And then – and this is no doubt the most infuriating part – I go back to not listening. I run my finger down the list in the directory, looking for Lala's name.

Lalalalalalalalalalalalalala: my mantra, my loony-tune.

And so, because I despise long good-byes, we'll just stop abruptly, thank you very much. We'll box up my lessons gleaned from Giovanni, Forty-Four Magnum Bill, from Jessy and Pauline, lessons learned and filed, lessons to take out and inspect from time to time like trophies. An optimist might call my collecting of sound advice "the pursuit of excellence"; except that pursuit suggests progression, and, in Gabe's case, progress means more comfort with guilt over love, ideals, history.

Awwwwww, do you feel ripped off?

Get used to it.

What end did you expect anyhow? A five star wedding between Pauline and me? Lala turning up mentally stable enough for two?

Or maybe you wanted conclusions on the condition of daughters and sons of immigrants. Here it comes: I belong to no country; I belong to two; I belong to one and then the other. Sometimes this makes me sad, sometimes glad. Chose one or none or all three. Don't ask me how the other kids feel.

Perhaps you wanted a summation on Giovanni's, the goat's and my interchangeability? How should I know? We were stoned, for Christ's sake. And the wisdom of Jessy? Knowing something's wrong doesn't enable you to change it.

My father managed to maintain two lives. The thought of all the answers I requested from him horrifies me now. I may at times seem inhumane but I don't wish anyone the pain of devising explanations or, worse, the agony of watching those explanations implode under life's endless succession of contradictions. Syntax may have activated his bigamy, but it never expressed it. You think you've unmasked a motive? You think you're peddling more than mystery? Hey, it's your dime.

But please use it to call another, for I've no longer a telephone. Yes, it's difficult being disconnected, and still more difficult attempting to locate Lala's number. But, as Bill proves, it's therapeutic having something to find. And if I snap instead? So much the better. I'm trying for Lala anyhow.